Praise for
Patricia Sprinkle's Mysteries

Who Left That Body in the Rain?

"Forming a triumvirate with Anne George and Margaret Maron, Sprinkle adds her powerful voice to the literature of mysteries featuring Southern women. . . . Highly recommended." —Linda Hutton, *Mystery Time*

"Who Left That Body in the Rain? charms, mystifies, and delights. As Southern as Sunday fried chicken and sweet tea. Patricia Sprinkle's Hopemore is as captivating—and as filled with big hearts and big heartaches—as Jan Karon's Mitford. Come for one visit and you'll always return." —Carolyn Hart

"An heirloom quilt. Each piece of patchwork is unique and with its own history, yet they are deftly stitched together with threads of family love and loyalty, simmering passion, deception and wickedness, but always with optimism imbued with down-home Southern traditions. A novel to be savored while sitting on a creaky swing on the front porch, a pitcher of lemonade nearby, a dog slumbering in the sunlight." —Joan Hess

"Captures true Southern customs and personalities, small-town politics and mores perfectly." —*Romantic Times*

"Authentic and convincing. This series is a winner." —Tamar Myers

continued . . .

Thoroughly Southern Mysteries

WHO INVITED THE DEAD MAN?

WHO LEFT THAT BODY IN THE RAIN?

WHO LET THAT KILLER IN THE HOUSE?

WHO LET THAT KILLER IN THE HOUSE?

⤜ A THOROUGHLY SOUTHERN MYSTERY ⤛

Patricia Sprinkle

A SIGNET BOOK

SIGNET
Published by New American Library, a division of
Penguin Group (USA) Inc., 375 Hudson Street,
New York, New York 10014, U.S.A.
Penguin Books Ltd, 80 Strand,
London WC2R ORL, England
Penguin Books Australia Ltd, 250 Camberwell Road,
Camberwell, Victoria 3124, Australia
Penguin Books Canada Ltd, 10 Alcorn Avenue,
Toronto, Ontario, Canada M4V 3B2
Penguin Books (N.Z.) Ltd, Cnr Rosedale and Airborne Roads,
Albany, Auckland 1310, New Zealand

Penguin Books Ltd, Registered Offices:
80 Strand, London WC2R ORL, England

First published by Signet, an imprint of New American Library,
a division of Penguin Group (USA) Inc.

First Printing, October 2003
10 9 8 7 6 5 4 3 2 1

Thanks to . . .

Judge Mildred Ann Palmer, magistrate from Burke County, Georgia, remains my inspiration for the character of MacLaren Yarbrough and continues to give technical help when I need it. I thank her and her delightful family—who know, I hope, that MacLaren's family in no way resembles theirs.

Judge Curt St. Germaine, chief magistrate of Burke County, patiently answered questions about various aspects of the Georgia judicial system as it relates to the work of magistrates. Eddie Slay, coordinator of the Cobb County, GA, CASA program, explained procedures involving juvenile offenders.

Emöke Sprinkle provided information about hospital psychiatric wards and introduced me to Dr. Greg Brack, associate professor of counseling and psychological services at Georgia State University and a trauma specialist, and Dr. Michele Hill, a conflict resolution specialist. Drs. Brack and Hill helped me understand the psychological dynamics of various characters in this book. They also spoke of the characters as real people and discussed them as such—a rare and precious gift for any author. And they steered me to *Trauma and Recovery* by Judith Herman, which provided further insights into not only the trauma of several characters but also possible outcomes for their lives.

Since I knew nothing about girls' fast-pitch softball when I began, I am very grateful to Jaime Caroti, who played the sport both locally and in national games, and to Leonard Hill, a fast-pitch softball coach, who helped me understand the game.

High-school chemistry teacher Dwight Jinright researched several methods of killing yourself in a high-school chemistry lab. Thanks, Dwight. I hope you forget all you learned.

I also thank my agent, Nancy Yost, for finding a home for the book, and I especially thank my editor, Ellen Edwards, for helping me shape it into what it was meant to be.

CAST OF CHARACTERS

MacLaren Yarbrough: amateur sleuth, Georgia magistrate, co-owner of Yarbrough's Feed, Seed and Nursery

Joe Riddley Yarbrough: MacLaren's husband, a former magistrate, co-owner of Yarbrough Seed and Nursery

Ridd: the Yarbroughs' elder son, high-school math teacher and part-time farmer

Martha: Ridd's wife, an emergency-room supervisor
Cricket (4) and **Bethany** (16): their children

Clarinda Williams: the Yarbroughs' longtime cook
Ronnie Hayes Clarinda's grandson, just graduated from the University of Georgia

DeWayne Evans: high-school science teacher, coach of the Honeybees fast-pitch softball team

Yasheika Evans: DeWayne's younger sister, just graduated from Howard University

Sara Meg Stanton: widowed owner of Children's World, a clothing/toy shop

Garnet (18) and **Hollis** (16): her children

Buddy Tanner: Sara Meg's younger brother and a local CPA

Smitty Smith (17): young skinhead, leader of a gang of hoodlums

Tyrone (Terrible Ty) Noland (17): member of Smitty's gang who likes Hollis

Willie (Wet Willie) Keller (16): another gang member

Art Franklin (18): poet, student at community college, waiter at Myrtle's, likes Garnet

Charlie Muggins: police chief
Isaac James: assistant police chief

❧ 1 ❧

An empty locker room shouldn't have anybody in it—not even a dead body.

My son Ridd pushed open the door and called, but he got no answer, of course.

To make sure, he pushed the door wider and put his head inside. "Anybody he—?"

He cut off midword, gave a lurch, and clutched the door for support. "Oh, God, no!" He clung to that doorframe and his knees buckled.

I will never know how I covered the distance between us in time, but I caught him before he slid to the floor. Holding him tight around the waist, I peered past him into the dimness.

That was the morning we found the body.

This story didn't begin then, of course. I'm not sure that even the United Daughters of the Confederacy could trace its genealogy with reliable accuracy, but for me, it began the first Saturday in June, the day Hollis Stanton socked a softball the center fielder couldn't catch. Nobody had an inkling that day that evil, like contained poison gas, was fixing to be released, that it would ooze across town in an invisible cloud that, by the end of the month, would leave one person dead and another clinging reluctantly to life.

We were all there. How did we miss what was going on? How did I?

When Hollis hit her ball, two hundred people in the high-school bleachers gasped in surprise. Hollis was a great little catcher, but she was a dreadful batter.

Brandi Wethers left second base and flew toward home. We leaped to our feet and cheered as she crossed the plate a gnat's second before the ball reached the catcher. We kept cheering as Hollis rounded first base, and when she slid in safe at second, hair streaming behind her like a banner of pure copper, everybody was jumping up and down. Her uncle Buddy, four rows below us, waved his arms and screamed like a wild man.

Beside me, my cook, Clarinda, grunted in disgust. "Even that didn't get Garnet's nose out of her book." Sure enough, Hollis's older sister was a solitary island of calm, head bent over her book, thick auburn hair spread across her shoulders like a mantle. Anybody could tell that Garnet Stanton thought fast-pitch softball an enormous waste of time.

I didn't have time to waste on Garnet. I was watching a family in front of us: two fat little boys, a pudgy father whose belly strained his yellow T-shirt, and a plump blond mother in black spandex pants and a tight pink top with two tiny straps and far more beneath it than it was designed to hold. The way they had screamed and carried on while Brandi was running, I figured they were her family. It wasn't so easy to figure whether their combined bulk, jumping in unison, would get all our names in next week's *Hopemore Statesman* under the headline "Bleachers Collapse, Killing Dozens."

As they finally sat down, Clarinda leaned over and muttered, "I personally wouldn't wear that pink top without a bra." I elbowed her. Clarinda has a carrying voice. She also has far too much bosom to wear any top without a bra.

Clarinda had come with Joe Riddley and me to watch the Hopemore Honeybees, our recreation department's summer season, senior girls' fast-pitch softball team, play the county championship game. Our store—Yarbrough's Feed, Seed and Nursery—was team sponsor and both our older son, Ridd, and Clarinda's grandson, Ronnie, were assistant coaches. The real reason Clarinda and I were there, though, and why Joe Riddley had taken the unprecedented step of shutting down the store for this game, was because Ridd's daughter, Bethany, was the team's star pitcher. All three of us were a bit biased where Bethany was concerned.

It was a glorious day for a ball game. At the edge of the field, mimosas waved small pink pom-poms. Up near the school, a huge old magnolia spread blossoms as creamy and wide as dinner plates while fat blue hydrangeas nodded approval. The sky was deep blue, dotted with dollops of whipped-cream clouds, and new-mown hay and honeysuckle scented the breeze. It looked like half of Hopemore—county seat of Hope County, located in that wedge of Georgia between I-16 and I-20—had come out to watch the Honeybees play what we all expected to be their final game.

Summer sports in Hopemore had never produced a winning team. We'd been amazed that the Honeybees had gotten this far—largely due to the coaching of high-school chemistry teacher DeWayne Evans and his sister, Yasheika. Now, at the bottom of the last inning, the team was two runs behind, had two outs, and had reached the bottom of their batting lineup. Beside Joe Riddley on the bench, Bethany's little brother, Cricket, squirmed. His mother, Martha, gave him an encouraging hug, but she looked anxious. I saw several Honeybees eyeing the other team's coach. The winning coach would choose three or four players from each county team to play on an all-county team at district play-offs the last week in June. I'm sure every Honeybee wondered if she would get picked.

As the next batter sauntered toward the plate, adjusting her helmet over a long brown ponytail, I heard groans.

"Do it, baby!" Clarinda called.

"Send in a pinch hitter!" Brandi's mother yelled. Her husband and sons took up the cry. Others followed, stamping their feet so the bleachers throbbed. "Pinch hitter! Pinch hitter!"

If I'd had a sword, that woman's frizzy yellow head would have rolled, county magistrate though I am. That wasn't just

any old ballplayer she was razzing—it was my oldest grand-
child. Sure, she might bat to fielders' mitts like her balls contained a homing device, but she had a great windmill pitch.
She didn't deserve to be insulted by adults who ought to know
better.

Bethany trudged toward the plate like somebody heading
for the guillotine.

I saw her daddy give her an encouraging slap on the back
and heard him say, "Come on, Yarbrough, hit a homer." I
wished he sounded a little more convinced that she could.

Bethany and Hollis had played ball together since they
were little, but it was Yasheika's after-practice work and De-
Wayne's good coaching that had turned them into a catcher
and pitcher the *Statesman* had started calling DeWayne's
Deadly Duo. Unfortunately, no amount of coaching had ever
made them good hitters. That's why they batted last.

"Come on, baby. You can do it!" Clarinda yelled again.

Martha, an emergency-room supervisor who daily faced
gory scenes without flinching, covered her eyes. "I can't
watch. Tell me when it's over."

Joe Riddley cupped his mouth and begged at the top of his
lungs, "Hit one for Pop!"

I was considering disowning the lot of them, when I realized I was clenching my fists and whispering, "Please, God,
please, God, please, God," as if the Almighty had nothing better to do that afternoon than make sure my granddaughter hit
a ball.

Bethany flickered a quick, nervous smile in our direction,
then gave Coach Evans a pleading look like she wanted to lay
down her bat.

Cricket bounced on the front of his bleacher seat, ready to
fly down and help his big sister. "Hit it, Beth'ny," he roared
into a sudden silence. "Hit it, for a change!"

Bethany visibly cringed.

"Time out!" Coach Evans left his position behind third
base and went to home plate. He was dark as semisweet
chocolate, his face a shadow in the afternoon sun. I couldn't

see his expression as he spoke into Bethany's ear, but she listened gravely, then nodded and lifted her chin. As he stepped away, Yasheika left her first-base coaching spot and trotted to the plate.

Yasheika was much closer to the ages of the players, a tall, slender young woman with coffee-and-milk skin. She'd graduated from Howard University in early May, then came to Hopemore to help her brother coach because, as Bethany and Hollis told us at least weekly, she used to pitch for a fast-pitch team that had won the national championship.

Whatever Yasheika said made Bethany laugh. As the coach trotted back to first, Bethany took a few practice swings with what looked like a whole lot more determination.

Poised on the balls of her feet, she waited for the pitch. She didn't swing when the first ball crossed the plate, but the umpire called, "Strike one!"

I glared in his direction. "Anybody could see that ball was low."

Joe Riddley reached across Clarinda and laid a big hand on my arm. "Take it easy, Little Bit. It's not over yet." His eyes didn't leave the game.

"You tell her, Judge," joked a man behind us. Joe Riddley was no longer a county magistrate, but he had served thirty years before he retired the previous fall, so folks were still apt to give him the title. I'd been a magistrate myself for nearly nine months, but a lot of folks were still apt to call me Mac or Miss MacLaren.

Another ball flew from the pitcher's mound. "Swing, dammit!" yelled Brandi's dad.

Bethany swung.

She hit it so hard, I thought her bat had cracked. The ball rose in a perfect arc above the diamond, eluded the left fielder's mitt, and dropped with deceptive humility behind the back fence. Nobody made a sound. Even Bethany stood, mouth open, gaping at that fence.

We all soared at that moment, but like the ball, we would soon fall back to earth.

❧ 2 ❧

Cricket broke the spell. "Run, dummy! Run!"

Bethany took off with a spurt of dirt.

She and Hollis pounded around the bases, across home plate, and into a jumping, squealing, hugging mass of teammates. I was jumping up and down so hard, I felt like I might fly. Even Garnet noticed something was going on. She stood and dutifully clapped, but when she saw Hollis break away from the mass and fling her arms around DeWayne Evans's neck, and saw DeWayne squeeze Hollis back, Garnet sat down abruptly and opened her book. Buddy bent to speak in her ear, but she shook her head and kept reading.

The rest of us yelled ourselves hoarse. Brandi's mama jumped up and down so hard her whole front jiggled. Cricket was fascinated. Martha quickly gave him a box of juice to distract him. I wished I had a juice box for Joe Riddley.

The crowd sat down again just in time to see the next batter—usually our best—hit a fly ball straight to the pitcher's mitt. The Honeybees merged into an ecstatic swarm and somebody started a chant: "We're county champs! We're county champs!" The other team's parents trickled down their half of the bleachers in a disappointed stream.

Cricket swallowed the last of his juice and heaved an enormous sigh. "Poor Uncle Walker is sure gonna be sorry he missed this game."

Poor Uncle Walker—our younger son—had sold so much insurance last year, he'd won a month's, all-expenses-paid vacation for his whole family at a Hawaiian resort. "Yeah," Clarinda agreed, "he's prob'ly cryin' his eyes out right this minute."

Joe Riddley peered at me around Clarinda. "You sure look smug, Little Bit."

"You look pretty smug yourself." We beamed at each other, happy as worms after rain.

"Ronnie's plumb slaphappy." Clarinda peered down at her grandson, a brand-new accounting graduate from the University of Georgia and the third assistant coach. He was slapping every shoulder in sight.

Ronnie had grown into a tall young man, good-looking in a skeletal kind of way, but to me he'd always be the thin five-year-old with huge, bewildered eyes who stood in my kitchen a week after his daddy shot his mama—Clarinda's daughter, Janey. I had told Clarinda to bring Ronnie on down to work with her. Our house felt empty without children.

Ridd, home from grad school that summer, had been enchanted by the child. Every morning he took Ronnie out on his tractor to the fields. By August, Ronnie was bragging, "Ridd's taught me to drive as good as him!"

When Bethany was born a year later, Clarinda kept her after Martha went back to work. To hear Ronnie tell it back then, he raised that baby. I'll never forget the day he came in the store—skinny, eight years old, and the color of fudge icing—carrying a squirming, pink, two-year-old Bethany, and startled a tourist by assuring her, "This here's my baby."

He had missed very few of her ball games through the years, and he was delighted when DeWayne asked him to help coach that season. As we watched, Bethany left the others and flung her arms around him.

Hollis, meanwhile, was squinting toward the stands. When she found Buddy—who was still whooping and hollering—she raised one fist and pumped air. He raised both fists over his head and yelled down, "What-a-go, girl! What-a-go!"

Nobody would have guessed to look at them that Hollis and Buddy were related. Her eyes were bright blue, his hazel. Her lively copper hair was flecked with gold, green, and purple, his was walnut brown. Hollis's body was sturdy, square, and strong; Buddy had the lean physique of an avid tennis player. As he nimbly started down the stands toward the field, I saw a lot of single women and a few married ones giving him the eye. At thirty, Buddy was one of Hopemore's most eligible bachelors—if he'd had time to date. Martha must have been thinking the same thing, because she said indulgently, "Lots of women are gonna be glad when Hollis and Garnet are grown and Buddy gets free time again."

For six years—ever since Fred Stanton had died and left Buddy's sister a young widow—Buddy had helped her raise the two girls. She had used Fred's life-insurance money to open a small store, and because she couldn't get away in the afternoons and Buddy was a self-employed CPA, he was the one who left his office to drive the girls to after-school activities. I couldn't remember him ever missing one of Garnet's piano recitals or Hollis's games.

He was certainly a lot more interested in this particular game than her sister was. The whole time he'd been jumping up and down and hollering, Garnet had kept on reading.

Down on the field, DeWayne, Ridd, and Ronnie were pounding each other's backs like kids. Although Ridd was forty, DeWayne twenty-eight, and Ronnie scarcely twenty-two, the three of them were great friends. They often played a round of golf or drove down to Dublin for a NASCAR race. Ridd, who taught math at the high school, had led the campaign for DeWayne to coach the team after our former (and spectacularly unvictorious) coach retired. Ronnie, who used to pitch for Hopemore High, seconded his choice. In DeWayne's favor, at a previous school he had coached a high-school fast-pitch team to state finals. But Coach Evans was black and single while the Honeybees were young, female, and predominantly white. We're making progress in Middle Georgia, but we still have a ways to go.

"Let's go join the party," Joe Riddley told Cricket. He swung him onto his shoulders and headed for the field. I watched anxiously to be sure they got there safely. Joe Riddley had been shot in the head ten months before* and hadn't been walking without a cane very long. He was getting more confident in his abilities every day, but it was taking me a little longer to accept that he was almost back to normal.

Cricket wasn't worried. He snatched his granddaddy's cap from his head and waved it, with no fear of falling whatsoever.

Brandi's daddy and brothers also headed to the field, leaving her mother surrounded by a mess of candy wrappers and soft-drink cans. She said to Martha, "That child sure looks like you." He did. Both were plump, with round faces, soft brown hair, and light brown eyes.

Martha grinned. "It's only fair, considering how much Bethany looks like her daddy. Mac and Clarinda, do you all know Shana Wethers, Brandi's mother?"

We all extended sticky palms. I said, "Weren't those girls terrific?"

"They sure were. I nearly had a heart attack while Brandi was running her bases." I couldn't place her accent, but it wasn't Southern.

While Martha and Shana rehashed some of the plays, Clarinda and I gathered up our little bit of litter. Down on the field, Yasheika joined the other coaches. Ronnie shifted so he was around the circle from her. Those two were as tall and as slim as two swords and about as friendly. Seemed like they couldn't be on the same patch of earth without clashing. Bethany said they got along fine on the ball field, but I suspected that was because both respected DeWayne. Any time they weren't coaching, they were saying mean and

*But Why Shoot the Magistrate?

hateful things to each other. Clarinda muttered so only I could hear, "That girl may know softball, but she don't know men from nothin'. Men need time alone together, without some baby sister all the time hangin' round."

"She's not just a baby sister, she's a coach," I reminded her.

"Whatever she is, Ronnie can't stand her. Says she's all the time pushing herself in where she's not wanted." She bent and picked up the small cooler she'd brought. "Well, I gotta be gettin' home. We got a dinner after church tomorrow, and I still have to do my cooking." She made her way down the bleachers and stopped by the fence to call to Ridd and Bethany.

I thought fondly that nobody could see those two and Joe Riddley without knowing they were related. They had the same long legs, lanky frame, and way of walking like their joints were connected by rubber bands. They even had the same tinge of cinnamon under the skin from Joe Riddley's Cherokee grandmother. The primary difference between them was hair. Joe Riddley's was coarse, almost black, and straight. Bethany's was softer and a slightly lighter brown, while Ridd, like my daddy, had lost most of his before he was thirty.

I saw another patch of scalp down there, so when Martha stopped talking to Shana and began to gather up her stuff, I asked softly, "Is Buddy losing his hair?"

Martha gave a gurgle of laughter. "Hollis says he is. She claims he mousses it, to make it look fuller."

"She ought to be ashamed to tell other people. Not many handsome bachelor uncles spend afternoons and weekends carting nieces around."

"And until she started driving, that niece needed a lot of carting." I'd heard that criticism from Martha before. She and Ridd didn't permit Bethany more than two activities a semester, but Hollis played several sports, sang in both the school chorus and the church youth choir, and was in the school drama group. "She's teaching swimming and lifeguarding at the city pool and taking voice lessons this summer." Martha made voice lessons sound like the very last straw.

"It's something to do besides hang around the house," I pointed out. "That big old place could seem real empty with Sara Meg at work and Garnet's nose always in a book." Sara Meg and the girls lived in the house Sara Meg and Buddy had grown up in, an enormous Victorian.

Poor Sara Meg. That house and its furniture were about all she had from her ancestors, although the Tanners had been right prosperous for several generations. Josiah Tanner founded a general store in 1845 that evolved into Tanners' Clothing. For more than a century, three generations of Tanners dressed Hope County and places beyond. Unfortunately, Sara Meg's daddy, Walter, inherited neither his daddy's business sense nor his excellent taste in clothing. Once the interstate was built, folks preferred to drive to Augusta to shop. Walter went bankrupt the year before he died and would have lost the house, too, if his lawyer hadn't urged him earlier to put it in the children's names. Walter, an impractical, self-centered man, decided to give it to Sara Meg, with the stipulation that he could live there all his life and she'd take care of him. To his son he left "the rest of my estate"—which turned out to be nothing.

After Walter died, Sara Meg came home from college and went to work at a construction company to support herself and eight-year-old Buddy. When she met Fred and they fell in love, he treated Buddy like his own kid brother. After they married, he insisted they have the house appraised and pay a sum each month into the bank to buy what he and Sara Meg both called "Buddy's half of the house." That fairness was what put Buddy through college—including the year he wasted in architecture before he decided to become a CPA. Now, since Fred's death, Hollis was real blunt about the fact that, "If it weren't for Uncle Buddy, we couldn't belong to the country club, Garnet couldn't take piano, and I couldn't play sports."

Down on the field, Buddy grabbed Hollis in a bear hug and swung her around and around.

Brandi's mother propped her fists on her hips. "That young man is far too old for Hollis. What are her parents thinking? They are *never* around."

I spoke sharper than I intended, because I was a tad annoyed at how she jumped to conclusions without getting the facts. "That's her uncle Buddy. Her mother can't afford to leave work on Saturdays."

"That's the busiest day of the week at Children's World," Martha added.

Shana shaded her eyes against the sun. "Is that where she works? I haven't been in. We just moved here in March, from Chicago."

Maybe she didn't mean to sound like the move hadn't been her idea and she thought Hopemore had tacky little stores, but I felt another spurt of indignation. Granted, Hopemore isn't as big as Chicago—we have about thirteen thousand people in what our Chamber of Commerce calls "Greater Hopemore." But we've got some fine people here with reason to be proud of their family businesses. Sara Meg Stanton was one of them. She started that store with nothing but Fred's life-insurance money and was making a go of it by sheer hard work. "She owns the business," I informed Shana, "and it's a great store."

Martha picked up a candy wrapper Cricket had dropped. "*Southern Living* said last year that Sara Meg has one of the best collections of hand-painted children's furniture and smocked children's clothing in the South. She paints the furniture and smocks the clothes herself."

"She's a great painter," I bragged. "She studied three years at the Savannah College of Art and Design."

Shana primped up her mouth. "That's nice, but children need their parents around. She could at least shut down for her daughter's games—or hire more help." She bent to retrieve a shirt one of her boys had left under the seat and started stuffing it into a canvas carryall.

I opened my mouth to tell her how hard it is to get and pay good help in a store with a small profit margin, but Martha touched my arm in warning. As an emergency-room nurse, she's had a lot of training in anger management and keeping things calm. "Sara Meg would love to be here," she assured Shana, "but she can't afford to close the shop or hire help. There's a rumor that a big superstore is going to be built just outside of town, and—"

"Those old boll weevils!" I muttered to myself.

Shana stopped stuffing the shirt into her carryall. "What do you mean by that?"

"Boll weevils are bugs that suck the heart out of cotton and leave it dead. They plagued the South years ago. Now, superstores are doing the same thing to little towns across the country."

She propped one hand on her hip, her face as pink as her shirt. "My husband was sent here to build that store. It will eventually provide a hundred jobs in Hope County."

My mama didn't raise me to be rude to strangers, but this woman had pushed my button once too often. "Not at the management level, it won't. It may employ a lot of people at minimum wage or a little above, but business owners and managers will lose their jobs, local stores will go under, and all the profits will leave the county. Stockholders in California and Michigan may smile, but folks in Hopemore won't. Our whole downtown will dry up into antique stores, thrift shops, and cell-phone offices."

"It's the wave of the future, sweetie. Get used to it." Shana hefted her cooler and smacked it down on the bleacher like she'd rather whack me on the head.

I felt like she already had. For weeks we'd been hearing a rumor about the superstore, but nobody had confirmed it until now. Martha's worried eyes met mine. A superstore would not only put Sara Meg out of business, it would hurt the nursery side of Yarbrough's. We could offer better-quality plants and advice, but we could never match their prices. Joe Riddley and I had no mortgage and both our kids were grown and married, so we could support ourselves selling fertilizer, seed, and animal feed, but we'd have to let people go. The thought made me ill.

Maybe Shana noticed how quiet we'd gotten, because she offered us a sop. "The new store won't be carrying hand-painted furniture and hand-smocked dresses." She wadded candy wrappers and set them beside ten drink cans and three water bottles on the bleacher.

I heaved a sigh from my toes. "Sara Meg can't support two girls and put them through college on painted furniture and smocking. Most of her business is school clothes, birthday party presents, and toys." My throat clogged with tears. "She'll never survive."

The woman shrugged—which she shouldn't do, dressed that way—and said tartly, "My mother used to say God shows how much He loves us by giving us burdens to make us stronger."

That raised even Martha's hackles. "Then Sara Meg ought to be the strongest woman in Georgia. Her mother died when she was fourteen and her brother two. She raised him until she went to art school. Her senior year there, their daddy died leaving them without a penny. She quit school without complaint and came home to work in order support herself and Buddy."

"Well, she's done all right for herself. She lives in one of the biggest houses in town. I asked about it when we were looking for a place—it would have been perfect for us. But the Realtor said she wouldn't consider selling."

"Of course not!" I wanted to shake her until her eyeballs rolled. "Sara Meg's great-great-granddaddy built that house, and besides, it's paid for."

"She could sell it for a bundle and buy a smaller place. Then she could hire help and come to her daughter's games. Support is so important to a child at this age. And where's Hollis's father? He's never around." The woman's blue eyes were wide and hot, framed by sticky lashes. If she didn't already know her mascara had run down one cheek, I wasn't going to tell her.

"Hollis's daddy is dead," I snapped.

"He was a fireman," Martha explained, "and got killed in a fire. Her uncle Buddy's been the only daddy Hollis has had for the last six years."

At least Shana had the grace to look ashamed. "I'm sorry. I didn't know. Well, I gotta be going." As she picked up her cooler to leave, she suggested, "Maybe Ms. Stanton can get a job in the new store." She clomped down the bleachers, leaving her trash.

When she was out of earshot, I told Martha, "She's got a mighty peculiar notion of God."

Martha laughed, sat down, and stretched her short legs onto the bench Shana had left. "As if God needs to bring trouble on us, the way we're so willing to bring it on ourselves. And what we don't bring on ourselves, other folks are generally happy to provide."

I watched two clouds drift together to cover the sun. "Fred Stanton was killed because our fire equipment was substandard and the county commission had refused to authorize money to replace it."

Martha laid a plump hand over mine. "As that group of folks you and Pop took to the next meeting so eloquently pointed out."

The clouds were almost together now. Only a sliver of sun remained. "I just wish we'd spoken up earlier."

"Do you ever wonder, Mac, how many awful things happen around us because we don't get involved? It's a sobering thought." She gave a puff of dismay. "Speaking of which, Shana forgot her bag."

I would have let that bag rot right there, but Martha picked it up and headed down the bleachers. I sat watching the sun come back from behind the clouds and remembered how glad most folks were when Sara Meg married Fred. Of course, there were a few who thought a Tanner ought to marry only a doctor, a lawyer, or a businessman, but most were tickled that she'd found that big gentle fireman with a face full of freckles and hair like a penny. With her splendid auburn hair, they made a striking couple. When the girls came along, everybody loved to see the Stantons, hair blazing in two shades of red, sharing ice cream downtown or walking down the aisle at church. For fourteen years they seemed a storybook family—until Fred was killed.

The amazing thing was, all the while that trouble followed her up one year and down another, Sara Meg kept smiling. She had a drop-dead gorgeous smile with white, even teeth and a brave happy look in her dark eyes that made the whole town love her. Only Joe Riddley said there was something not quite natural about Sara Meg and her smile. "She doesn't let things touch her," he claimed. "Walks around with her eyes half-closed and doesn't see a thing except what she wants to see." Sara Meg had seen so much trouble, it seemed to me she had a right to shut out as much as she could.

Speaking of trouble, who was that handsome blond man Bethany was all twined around down on the field? I asked as soon as Martha panted back up the bleachers, still carrying the bag and gasping, "I couldn't catch her. But I saw Buddy and told him to meet us at Myrtle's."

"That's good. But who is that boy with Bethany?"

Martha heaved a disgusted mother's sigh. "Ridd calls him her latest mistake. His name is Todd Wylie. He's nineteen, and he lives over in Louisville. They met at some party, and he's been hanging around her for nearly a month. We think he's too old for her, and too fast, but every time we say a word against him, she gets all stony-faced."

I could have said a few words against him myself. He was kissing my granddaughter down on the ball field in front of God and everybody, and she didn't seem to mind a bit.

Martha sighed again. "I've been wondering whether I ought to ask Hollis to caution Bethany a bit."

"Honey, I'm not sure right now Bethany would hear a word anybody said."

Martha looked down to where Buddy was shaking Garnet's elbow to tell her it was time to leave. Garnet shut her book with obvious reluctance and rose to follow him. "Sometimes I wish Bethany were more like Garnet—interested in nothing except books and music."

I personally was glad Bethany was Bethany. She was a whole lot more alive than Garnet, who would look better if she'd stop hunching her shoulders and would wear something besides a shapeless maroon shirt and long black skirt. I couldn't understand how a woman with Sara Meg's artistic taste could let a daughter go around looking like she bought her wardrobe from passing bag ladies. Of course, Garnet was a musician. Maybe that's what made her so peculiar.

"I guess Garnet still takes piano lessons?" I asked Martha.

"Oh, yes. Buddy drives her to Augusta every Friday afternoon."

"Why doesn't she drive herself?"

"Hollis says they won't let her drive. Right after she got her license, she had a little fender bender and lost her confidence, so Sara Meg said she should wait a while and Buddy canceled her insurance." Martha peered down at Bethany and Hollis, who were finally heading toward the locker room. "Those two have enough confidence for four. Has Bethany told you of their plan to drive from here to California as soon as they can convince their mothers to lend them a car?" We shared a laugh at the incredible assurance of high-school seniors, but our laughs were bittersweet. Those girls might jump up and down like preschoolers right now, but who knew to what distant places and dangers they'd be heading for in little more than a year?

That reminded me of something I'd wanted to ask. "Why is Garnet still around? Wasn't she accepted at a New York conservatory?"

Martha made a face. "Yeah. But also according to Hollis, it was Garnet's piano teacher who helped her apply. Sara

Meg felt she was too young to go to New York City, so she talked Garnet into deferring her admission and doing her first two years at Hope Community College."

"I'm sorry to hear that. I think a child develops wings by practicing flying."

"I agree. However, nobody asked us."

I hadn't noticed Brandi's mother returning until she demanded, "Who is that girl? She looks way too young for him." She was watching Buddy help Garnet down the bleachers.

Martha handed her the bag. "That's Hollis's big sister. Isn't she gorgeous?"

The woman flared her nostrils. "Pretty is as pretty does, my mother always said. She scarcely paid the game any attention. You wonder why she came."

I much preferred Hollis, friendly as a Labrador puppy and open as a sunflower, with flyaway curls, freckles, and honest blue eyes. Garnet was as distant as the far horizon. But I wasn't going to let a newcomer disparage a local child. Especially since Garnet was undeniably gorgeous. Her hair was the same rich red as her mother's, and she also had Sara Meg's clear white skin, perfect teeth, deep brown eyes, and delicate black brows. The only difference between them was that Sara Meg was tall and thin, while Garnet was curved and petite under those baggy clothes. It would be hard to find a prettier eighteen-year-old.

I stood and gave Shana Wethers what my boys always called "Mama's Killer Glare." "My mama used to say, 'Pretty is pretty, no matter *what* it does.' And you'll need to take that trash with you. We clean our own bleachers in Hopemore. Are you ready to go, Martha?" I picked up my pocketbook and headed down the bleachers. "I'll wait for you by the gate." I'd had all of Shana I could take for one day.

"I doubt if Shana's going to buy her bedding plants from you," Martha warned as she joined me.

"We'll survive. She probably doesn't know how to grow anything, anyway, except deadly nightshade."

$\approx 3 \approx$

Just as we got to our car, I got a call on my cell phone from a deputy wanting me down at the jail for a hearing. Putting him off for an hour delayed us a bit, so Myrtle's parking lot was crowded by the time Joe Riddley pulled in under the big sign: COOKING AS GOOD AS MAMA USED TO DO.

I grabbed his arm. "Don't say it again," I warned.

"But it's true, Little Bit. She ought to take down that sign. It's false advertising. She cooks like a Yankee now. The food just doesn't taste the same at all."

After Myrtle's husband had bypass surgery, she started broiling her meat and simmering her vegetables without bacon grease. "Okay. You're right and you've said it. But we came for pie, remember, and she's still got the best pie in town."

Myrtle also still had the chrome tables and chairs with green plastic seats that were in the place when she bought it, back when Ridd was in high school. The old tan linoleum was pitted with holes. I'd been warning Myrtle for years that her floor was a disaster waiting to happen, but she kept saying she just didn't have the money to remodel. She never would, so long as she kept driving expensive cars and taking a fancy cruise each year.

The place was nearly full, mostly families of Honeybees. Slade Rutherford, editor of the weekly *Hopemore States-man,* occupied one booth with his camera handy. A town like

Hopemore relies on city papers for world and state news. What we expect the *Statesman* to give us is the straight story on local affairs, especially anything our local grapevine has distorted, and stories about people we know—the more pictures, the better. Slade was an excellent editor for a small-town paper. He had an instinct for news people wanted to read.

Ridd and Martha had claimed a big round table in the middle of the room, and Buddy and Garnet were with them. Cricket and Garnet were both coloring place mats, but I suspected that Cricket would spend as much time instructing Garnet about her mat as he did coloring his own.

Close up, Garnet looked more like a ghost than a live person. It wasn't that she was pale—not with that hair and those dark brown eyes—but she gave the impression that she existed on a remote and different plane. Maybe that's what made us adults so determined to draw her into our conversation. We wanted to connect her to earth.

Martha began by telling the rest of us, "Garnet helped me with the four-year-olds at Bible school last week, and the kids adored her. I really appreciated your help, Garnet."

Garnet looked up and said in a voice we could scarcely hear, "I enjoyed it. The kids were fun." She made it sound like as much fun as going for a mammogram.

As she bent back to her coloring, I noticed an unusual pendant she wore, a dainty silver spiral wound around a tiger's eye. "What a lovely necklace!" I figured any girl likes to be complimented on her jewelry.

Hollis would have devoted half an hour to telling who gave it to her, when, and for what. Garnet just said, "Thanks," and shoved it down her shirt. She twisted a few strands of hair with her left hand while she colored with her right.

Myrtle arrived to serve iced tea. "You all want to wait to order until your star players arrive? I heard it was a great game." We assured her it was fantastic.

As she left, Ridd said, "It is entirely due to DeWayne that those girls have come so far. He's an amazing coach."

Garnet surprised me. She looked up and volunteered, "He's a good teacher, too."

"You had him for chemistry?" Ridd is a farmer at heart—every year he grows corn and cotton on thirty acres adjoining our homeplace and grows a big vegetable garden and flowers that Joe Riddley calls "Yarbrough's Best Advertisement"—but he also teaches high-school math nine months of the year.

Garnet bent back to her crayons, her face a rosy pink. "Yessir."

Buddy frowned. "Was DeWayne Evans the teacher you worked for your senior year?"

"Yeah." Garnet tugged her hair so hard, it went straight and taut. That must have hurt, but her eyes stayed on her work. "I was his lab assistant."

"You didn't tell me he was—uh—" He didn't need to finish. We all knew what he meant. Buddy had a scary experience with a black man as a little boy, and he'd had a nasty racist streak in his nature ever since. It always jarred me like a crack in a nice vase.

Joe Riddley stepped in to change the subject. "What are you reading, Garnet? Must be fascinating to hold your attention during the game."

She leaned down and held up a psychology textbook. "Summer classes start Monday. I wanted to get a head start."

"She finished last year with a 4.0," Buddy bragged.

Garnet shoved the book under the table and didn't indicate by a blink that she cared.

"I'm talking to a psych class next Wednesday," Martha informed us all. "How about that? Martha Yarbrough, college professor. They wanted me later in the semester, but this was the only time I could come." Martha works extra shifts in the summer while folks are on vacation. She also knows a lot about different types of trauma. None of us were surprised she'd been invited to lecture. We were surprised it had taken them so long to ask her. She took a long drink of tea, then added, "You have a gift for working with children, Garnet. Do you know that? You could be a great teacher. Or maybe a children's counselor."

That finally spooked the ghost. "Oh, no, ma'am, I couldn't. I just couldn't." She stood abruptly. "Excuse me. I need to wash my hands." She hurried to the ladies' room.

"I need to go, too," Cricket announced. When Joe Riddley rose to take him, though, he frowned. "I like the wimmen's room better."

"Not this time, honey," his mother told him. When they'd gone, she warned, "You'd better watch out, Buddy. Cricket's got his eye on Garnet."

Buddy chuckled. "That's the kind of suitor I approve."

He and Ridd started rehashing the game again. I leaned toward Martha's ear and said softly, "Garnet worries me. Do you reckon she could still be grieving Fred?"

I hadn't spoken softly enough. Buddy had heard. "She always was a daddy's girl," he said across the table. "Skipped everywhere beside him, holding his hand, talking a blue streak."

Now that he mentioned it, I remembered that, but I had to drag the picture from behind Garnet's present shadow. She'd been all knees and elbows then, her hair pulled back in pigtails, and she never met a stranger. If she knew you, she greeted you by name. If she didn't, she asked your name. As hard as it was to believe, Hollis was the shy one in those days—a freckled cherub with copper curls, hiding behind her big sister and letting her do the talking for both.

Martha rested her elbows on the table with a serious face. "She's changed a lot, Buddy. Do you think Sara Meg has noticed? She's so busy and all—"

Buddy reached for the pitcher and poured himself some tea. I hoped he wasn't upset with Martha for being concerned. He sounded defensive when he said, "Sara Meg's had to depend on her a lot."

Martha chuckled. "To hear Hollis tell it, *she's* the one

who does all the work while Garnet sits around reading. She says Garnet gives orders like she was her mother, not her sister."

Buddy chuckled. "Good old Hollis the Martyr. She doesn't kill herself around the house, believe me. Garnet does most of what gets done, plus goes to school full-time."

"She doesn't work?" I asked, surprised. A lot of teenagers in town had jobs to help out, and it seemed to me if anybody needed help, it was Sara Meg.

Buddy squeezed some lemon in his tea. "She teaches piano students on Saturday mornings. And she's talked about getting another job, but Sara Meg and I want her to concentrate on her studies while she's in college."

"Does she still play tennis?" Ridd asked. I'd forgotten that Garnet used to be real good at tennis, back when Fred was alive. She used to play in tournaments all over the state.

Buddy shook his head. "She hasn't played competitively in years, but we play at the country club a couple of times a week. She beats me sometimes, too." None of us had noticed Garnet arrive until she slid into her seat. She didn't say a word, but she gave him a look that made him admit ruefully, "Okay, she always beats me. But I taught her everything she knows."

Cricket climbed back up on his chair. "I taught her to color."

Garnet's smile flickered. "I do that best," she assured him softly. She set her pocketbook on the table and reached for the crayons. Buddy moved her purse to the floor. He was one of the most persnickety men I knew about keeping things tidy. I often thought the reason he hadn't married yet was that he hadn't found a woman who was neat enough.

Hollis and Bethany arrived just then, glowing with excitement. They'd changed out of their uniforms into jeans. Hollis had on a soft yellow shirt that made her hair look like autumn leaves, while Bethany wore pink, which matched her cheeks. They looked as cute as they used to back in third grade, when they'd announced they were "real best friends forever."

I was glad to see that Todd Wylie wasn't with them. Hollis had driven them in her mother's car, an almost-new silver SUV. I wondered where Sara Meg had found money for that car with all the other demands she had on her checkbook, but I had learned long ago that how other people spend their money is not my business.

As usual, Hollis came in talking a mile a minute. "Were we, like, great, or what?" she called from the door, addressing the room at large and pumping her fists in the air.

All over the room, tables of Honeybees' families burst into applause. Then a husky voice shouted from the large, round corner booth, "Good hit, Hollis. You were great."

That's when the afternoon started falling apart.

❧ 4 ❧

Hollis must have heard, but she took a chair without looking that way, still talking. I turned in my seat to see if I was right about that voice, and sure enough, it belonged to Tyrone Noland, a tall, beefy teenager whose mother had raised him alone after her husband left. She didn't deserve a son who dyed his blond hair black and wore baggy jeans slung low to show his boxers. She didn't deserve a son who hung out with Smitty Smith, either.

Smitty Smith—his legal name—was born to a mother short on imagination and shorter on morals. Under her influence and neglect, Smitty had grown into a strutting banty rooster who headed the gang of young thugs currently filling Myrtle's corner booth. They were a tougher, grungier crowd than previous rough elements at Hopemore High. Their clothes, hair, and nails would make you think Hope County had no running water. Their bodies were mutilated with piercings and tattoos. Whenever I see kids like that, one part of me wants to isolate them from other kids so they can't do any harm. Another part wants to feed them, pay them attention, and see if I can't kindle a spark of promise that I hope is still buried in there somewhere. They were all sweet babies once. When infants turn into these kids by sixteen or seventeen, society has failed them in some dreadful ways.

That doesn't mean those boys made me feel soft and cuddly. Most were regulars in juvenile court, and I dreaded the day they turned eighteen and started appearing before me. Smitty himself was mean enough to curdle milk. He shaved his head except for one long strand of greasy bleached hair that dangled from his crown. His face was long and cruel, with eyes the color of cold dishwater. Silver earrings bristled from his ears, nostrils, eyebrows, and lower lip. His sleeveless black T-shirt displayed dragon tattoos on bulging biceps. Beneath black cutoff jeans, he wore lace-up shoes strong enough to maim anybody he chose to kick.

He was, at most, five feet nine, but he had the other boys so cowed, they'd look a judge in the eye and swear Smitty was with them when a deputy knew he'd been committing theft or bodily assault. Witnesses who agreed with the deputies changed their minds with frightening regularity. So far, nobody had been able to put Smitty away, but not for lack of trying.

Smitty was not a young man whom parents wanted noticing their daughters. No wonder Buddy tensed when Smitty called, "Hey, Hollis? Terrible Ty was speaking to you."

Cricket looked up and giggled. "Terrible Ty?" He giggled again, but Garnet quickly distracted him. I appreciated that. I didn't want Smitty's eye on my grandson.

Hollis didn't need Smitty's eye on her, either, but she handled it well. She just kept talking, pretending she hadn't heard.

Beside me, Bethany muttered, "Me-mama, can't you put Smitty in jail for life?"

"I would if I could, honey. Magistrates don't deal with juveniles."

Smitty called louder. "Tyrone said, 'Good game, Hollis.' You got gum in your ears?" He added something else softly. From the way the others snickered, I knew it was vulgar.

Hollis looked over her shoulder and smiled in her usual friendly way. "Thanks, Tyrone. I didn't know you were at the game."

"Tyrone's always there for you, baby," Smitty replied. "Snap your fingers and he'll come."

Hollis gave him what Bethany called a princess smile. They both practiced it in mirrors. "Why don't you hold your breath 'til I do, Smitty? You'd look so good in blue."

One boy sniggered.

"Hush your mouth, bitch," Smitty snarled, "or I'll hush it for you."

Buddy shoved back his chair and started that way. Ridd jumped up to follow him. Joe Riddley followed Ridd. That's when I got real worried, because since Joe Riddley got shot, his temper has been a bit unpredictable.

"Ignore them!" Hollis called, her freckles standing out like polka dots.

Myrtle hurried that way, flapping both hands. "Don't make trouble. Please, no trouble."

The place had grown real quiet. Slade's camera was cocked and ready. Looked as though we'd get our names in the paper after all: "Massacre at Myrtle's."

Buddy reached for Smitty's arm, but Ridd grabbed his hand in midair. "You don't want him accusing you of assault."

Joe Riddley bent toward Smitty and said in his usual mild voice, "Boys, we don't want trouble here. Why don't you all clear out?"

Smitty flared his nostrils. "Buzz off, old man. We got as much right to be here as the rest of these—"

Before his mouth got as filthy as his fingernails, Ridd pushed his daddy aside and rested his palms on the table. "Look, Smitty." He bent to look into those cold gray eyes. "I know you're supposed to be in summer school next week, but if you'd rather spend time in court instead, I can arrange that." He pulled his cell phone from his pocket. "One call, and it's a done deal. I'll charge you with hassling a young woman and threatening an elderly man, and we've got witnesses."

Smitty narrowed his eyes. "I didn't threaten that old man.

I got witnesses, too." He looked around at the others. They nodded like he was jerking their strings.

Ridd's voice was still pleasant. "Even so, you'll miss summer school while you're going to court. You miss a single day of summer school, and you don't get credit. You'll have to repeat that class and graduate late. Is that what you want?"

Smitty didn't blink, but a twitch in one cheek showed he was thinking it over.

Ridd pressed his advantage. "You can either clear out, or sit here and leave our table alone. It's your decision."

Smitty sat so long without moving, I figured we'd all be dead and buried before he made up his mind. Finally he muttered something I didn't hear. Ridd stood up straight. "All right. But you bother us one more time, and I make that call." He took Joe Riddley's elbow and led him back across the restaurant. Buddy threw Smitty a glare as he followed Ridd.

Joe Riddley took his seat and considered Ridd for a very long minute. Finally he nodded. "Good work, boy. Just fine. But the next time you call me an elderly man, you better be prepared for some serious arm wrestling."

Ridd laughed. "I was afraid you'd give me a hiding then and there."

I decided it was time to change the subject. "What's that you've got around your neck, Bethany? I haven't seen it before."

She held out a silver softball charm on a dainty chain. "Coach Evans gave them to us. Every member of the team got one."

"Don't you just adore him?" Hollis looked around the table to take a vote. "He's the best coach in the state—and the best looking, too. I just lo-o-ve him."

Everybody at that table knew she was baiting Buddy and could have predicted what would happen. He turned so red, the tops of his ears looked sunburned. "You can't go around talking like that. People might get the wrong idea. I know how you mean it, but—"

Garnet glared at her sister and clenched her fist so tight, her crayon broke.

Even Hollis could tell she'd gone too far. She fingered her own charm. "Mine's still got the tag on it. Buddy, could I borrow your knife?" Nobody could have asked in a sweeter tone of voice.

"Of course." He reached into his pocket and handed over a Swiss Army Knife. "I keep telling you girls to always carry one of these." He kept it so sharp, it cut the plastic in one slice. Before Hollis could say anything else outrageous, our waiter, Art Franklin, arrived.

I knew Art only by reputation. He was an artistic boy in a football town, with a mother who had been a cheerleader in Ridd's class. Ridd claimed that her life stopped when the last game was over. She married the summer after graduation and had Art five months later. Her husband abandoned them both when the local meat-packing company went out of business a year after that, and from what I'd heard, she'd consoled herself since then with various married men. She was openly contemptuous of a son who preferred drama and poetry to sports. I'd seen Art in supporting roles in a few high-school plays and had read a couple of incomprehensible, gloomy poems he'd published in the *Statesman*, but mostly he drooped around town in a black trench coat, looking down his nose at us unpoetic types.

I vaguely remembered Art as a gangly little boy with long bones, dark curls that flopped in his eyes, and big teeth. Now he was a lanky youth who tried to hide the curls by skinning his hair back in a ponytail.

"Ah—are you ready to order, or do you need a menu?" He spoke directly to Garnet. As he waited for her answer, he swiped at a tendril that curled on a forehead dotted with pimples. His lips looked very red and wet, probably because he licked them so often. Maybe one day he'd be handsome, when his face cleared up and he filled out some. Right now he was mostly bones and big gray eyes.

She looked up, then down again. "Just a scoop of vanilla ice cream, I guess."

"We got some fresh pecan pie. You want a piece with the ice cream? It's warm."

She shook her head. "I don't like nuts."

I don't think she meant it as an insult, but he flushed to the roots of his hair. "Okay, one ice cream coming up." He had turned toward the kitchen before he remembered to ask, "Oh, you all want something, too?"

As he loped away with our orders, Hollis jeered, "He's got a crush on Garnet."

Garnet glowered. "Don't be silly."

"What's a crush?" Cricket demanded.

"He likes her," Hollis explained. "He can't even look at her without stuttering and turning red. He writes her poems, too."

Garnet pressed back in her chair like she'd been physically attacked. "How do you know?"

"You left your backpack on the table."

"Stay out of my stuff!"

Buddy looked like a thundercloud ready to burst. "Stop deviling her, Hollis."

Hollis tossed her hair, setting it swinging on her shoulders. "Poor Art. It won't do him any good, anyway. Garnet's not interested in anything except piano and studying."

"It wouldn't do you any harm to study," Garnet snapped. "You'll be lucky to get out of high school."

"Stop it. Both of you." Buddy frowned, unconsciously arranging his silverware precisely. The girls hushed, but glared at each other. I felt real distressed, like I'd just cut into a lovely cantaloupe and discovered it was rotten in the middle.

Joe Riddley turned to Bethany. "How'd you learn to bat like that, sugar pie?"

"We've been practicing in the afternoons," Ridd answered for her.

"You did great." Martha beamed.

Bethany's smile showed she knew they were all pretending nothing was happening. "I hope Hollis and I get picked for the county team." She fingered her little charm again.

"What did Coach Evans say before you went to bat?" Martha wondered.

"He told me everybody gets a few chances in life to make a difference for other people, and we don't only get points for succeeding—we get points for how hard we try—so he said for me to just do my best, for the whole team."

"What did Yasheika say?" I wanted to know. "She sure had you grinning."

Bethany smiled again at the memory. "She said if I pretended the ball was Brandi's daddy's head, who but me would know?" We laughed, but I remembered how he sneered just before she swung and how hard she'd hit that ball.

Although Hollis was now chattering normally across the table, I was still bothered by their fuss. "Do they fight like that a lot?" I asked Martha, too soft for anybody else to hear.

"Don't get upset—it's nothing," she whispered. "But I wish Hollis wouldn't tease her."

Bethany leaned over me and hissed, "You always take Garnet's side, but she's mean as the dickens when nobody else is around, to Hollis and their mother both. Some of the things she says to them would make you cry." Bethany did, in fact, look close to tears.

I put my hand over hers and whispered, "Your mother doesn't think Garnet ever got over her daddy's death."

Bethany shook her head and whispered back, "But she seemed fine right after it happened. Sad, but—you know—like always. It was later that she got so mean and went into her shell."

That's exactly how Garnet looked—like a princess in a shell. All I knew to say was, "Death affects people differently, sweetheart. I'm grateful you've never had to learn that firsthand." I was also grateful that Art arrived just then with our desserts.

I was taking my first bite of chocolate pie with three-inch meringue when DeWayne and Yasheika Evans arrived. Ronnie was with them, and anybody could see he and Yasheika each wished the other gone. When Hollis and Bethany jumped up and threw their arms around DeWayne's neck, Ronnie and Yasheika moved in opposite directions.

"We did it! We did it!" the girls squealed. A flash went off.

As they turned to hug Yasheika, other teammates ran to join them.

DeWayne looked around the restaurant and said so everybody could hear, "That was the best game I can remember, and I've seen a few. You've got some fine ballplayers here. Don't ever forget this day." He led us in another round of applause for the team.

His sister nudged him. "Stop showing off and find us a table."

Bethany grabbed Yasheika's hand and Hollis grabbed DeWayne's, and they started pulling them our way. "Come join us."

Bethany called over her shoulder to Ronnie, "You come, too."

Yasheika curled her lip like she'd rather sit at any table except where Ronnie was, but DeWayne was already taking a vacant chair and Ridd was dragging up more. Myrtle came bustling over to get their order.

Joe Riddley asked DeWayne, "Have you met Buddy Tanner, Hollis's uncle?"

DeWayne hesitated, then stuck out his hand. "Hi, Buddy. You got two mighty fine nieces." He beamed across at Garnet, who had looked up and was giving him a quiet smile. "Garnet was the best lab assistant I've ever had. If she weren't set on music, she'd make a good chemist. You taking chemistry in college?" he asked her.

She nodded, her eyes happier than I'd seen them all day. "I had it last year, but my prof wasn't as good as you."

His big laugh rumbled through the restaurant. "We can't all be great, now, can we?" To my astonishment, she laughed. She could use some practice, but it had a pleasant sound.

As Hollis narrowed her eyes at Garnet, Bethany asked quickly, "Did you all know Yasheika's going to Yale Law School in the fall?"

"Whoa!" Ridd exclaimed. "I'm impressed."

"Next thing we know you'll be running for president," I teased.

Yasheika shook her head. "All I want to do is get one innocent man out of jail."

Ronnie gave a little puff of disgust. In the privacy of our kitchen he'd used words like "bossy," "pushy," and even "uppity" to describe DeWayne's little sister. It was easy to see he didn't think she had a chicken's chance in a foxhole of getting anybody out of jail.

Joe Riddley clapped him on the back. "Speaking of degrees, Ronnie just got his, too. In accounting."

Buddy looked up. "You lookin' for a job? I got a man leavin' next week." Buddy's racism excepted people he knew. When Ronnie nodded, he said, "Come by Monday at one. We'll talk."

When Myrtle set DeWayne's pie before him, we heard a scuffle of shoes and the corner booth emptied. As they approached our table, Tyrone said gruffly, "Like I said, Hollis, good game." His plump face was pink and flustered.

Smitty looked deliberately from Coach Evans to Yasheika to Ronnie, but he waited until he was past us before he muttered, "Didn't use to let trash into decent eating places."

"Folks had more sense back then," agreed a kid whose grandmother wasn't born when the Civil Rights Act was passed. How did a person get so tough in so few years?

Joe Riddley called after them, "The judge here would love to drive any of you down to the jail who'd like a ride."

Smitty swaggered out the door without a word, looking like he owned a sizeable chunk of the world and had his eye on the rest. Tyrone, however, stuffed his hands into the pockets of a big khaki jacket he wore winter and summer and gave our table an embarrassed look over one shoulder. Maybe he was remembering how Ridd used to stay after school to help him with geometry, or how Joe Riddley let him sweep our office and storeroom to earn spending money back when he was in elementary school.

Tyrone had been an insecure, fat little boy, but he'd been sweet and honest. I wondered how far you'd have to dig to find that child again. Certainly past the dyed black hair parted in the middle and hanging below his round chin. Past the rings of cheap beads worn close to his thick neck and past the silver rings on almost every finger. The only thing I could find in his favor right then was that he hadn't gone as far as a piercing or a visible tattoo. Yet.

I also noticed that he stopped by the register and handed Myrtle a bill, unlike his pals.

"I don't know what to say," I apologized to DeWayne, "except that anybody can see they are pure white trash."

DeWayne shook his head. "Don't pay them any mind. They're little kids trying to act big."

"Not Smitty," Ridd disagreed. "He's dangerous."

"Smitty, yeah. He's one you gotta watch."

"Mean as a snake, and no more sense," I contributed. "I wish he'd get on his horse and ride out of town."

None of us suspected that one of the people at Myrtle's that day was going to ride out of town real soon. Not on a horse, but in a hearse. And it wouldn't be Smitty Smith.

⋨5⋩

A deluge descended Monday about three o'clock, accompanied by lightning that scissored across the sky and thunder like somebody rolling barrels down a bowling alley. Joe Riddley was at our nursery on the edge of town, unloading sod. I was alone in the office with the scarlet macaw we inherited after a dead man turned up at Joe Riddley's last birthday party.* The bird was christened Joe by his former owner, who'd been put out with Joe Riddley for sending him to jail, but we'd recently decided to prevent confusion by renaming him. Cricket chose Rainbow, for the cascade of blue, yellow, purple, white, and red feathers down his back. We'd shortened it to Bo, and I put up with the danged thing because Joe Riddley doted on him. Besides, the bird had been real helpful in making Joe Riddley walk again. Bo slept in our barn and came to work with Joe Riddley every day. He'd been left with me that afternoon because Joe Riddley had a couple of errands to run before he went to the nursery, and Bo was unreliable in nice offices. He tended to leave calling cards on people's carpets.

Bo hated storms. As the rain thundered on our store's tin roof, he paced the curtain rod and muttered, "Not to worry. Not to worry." After a particularly loud crack of thunder, he flew off his perch near the window and marched up and

*Who Invited the Dead Man?

down the floor at my feet, examining cracks for crumbs and bugs that might be hiding there.

I turned off both computers and made sure there was oil in the antique lamp on top of my desk, then sat enjoying the light and music show.

Joe Riddley and I share the same office at the back of our store that his parents and grandparents did. We use their oak rolltop desks, desk chairs, and filing cabinets, but have added computers, a fax machine, and other technology over the years. I also replaced the shade they had on the tall, thin window with a colorful valance and nice oak blinds, but we'd never felt a need to put a rug over the uneven old floorboards or plaster over the beaded board walls. It was real homey anytime and particularly cozy that afternoon.

Bo squawked his disagreement as wind whipped the crepe myrtles beside our parking lot into a crazy dance. When we heard a crash that probably meant another brittle pine had gone to meet its Maker, he flew to my shoulder and hung on tight. Fire engines wailed in the distance. I hoped nobody's house had been hit.

Then our lights went out. I heard a yelp of dismay from the windowless storeroom next door and Bo squawked, "Back off! Give me space!"

"It's just Bethany," I told him. She was working for us full-time that summer and taking inventory in our storeroom that afternoon. I didn't want her breaking her neck, so I lit my lamp and went out like Florence Nightingale to rescue her.

The rest of the staff bumbled toward the light like moths, so I took them all back to my office and brought out a tin of cookies from my bottom drawer. Somebody went for Cokes from the machine, and we had a party. We couldn't talk much, though, the rain was so loud. Bo subsided to a series of low mutters on top of my desk.

We all jumped when my phone rang. "Little Bit?" Joe Riddley's voice was accompanied by crackles and spits from the storm.

I paused for a bright flash of lightning and kettledrums of thunder, then demanded, "Are you sure it's safe to be calling right now? I don't want us to end our lives at opposite ends of a telephone wire."

"I'm not going to talk long. Lightning took out a transformer, and they won't get it fixed for hours. Go on and send folks home. You go, too."

"How's the sod?"

"Sodden. Be careful driving, now. I'll see you at the house. And leave Bo—I'll swing by and get him when the rain stops. You know he hates to get wet."

Who doesn't? As the staff gathered up the umbrellas they'd all thought to bring, I remembered mine was in the backseat of my car. "Grab a big plastic garbage bag for each of us," I ordered Bethany, "and I'll run you home."

We cut holes for our faces and dashed through the downpour at such a pace, I collapsed into my car panting. We sat there dripping all over my upholstery like drowned possums while rain drummed on the roof and the sky flashed bright, dark, bright, dark.

Bethany looked worried. "Could we swing by the pool to see if Hollis is there? She bikes to work, and she'll get soaked riding home."

"She's a lifeguard," I pointed out. "She doesn't mind getting wet, and she's got a mother and an uncle to pick her up." However, since I'm her grandmother and not her mother, I added, "We can swing by, if it will make you feel better."

It took a while. A big pine was down in the road, so we had to make a several-block detour. When we arrived, the pool and its building were dark and empty. I edged away from the curb. "I'm sure they closed before the lightning even got close. Hollis is probably a lot drier than you are right now."

"Could we drive by her house? She's real scared of lightning." Bethany spoke through chattering teeth.

"I can't imagine Hollis being scared of anything, and

she's got Garnet and her mother home by now. Besides, you're soaked."

"But—" She must have realized she'd gotten to the edge of her grandmother's indulgence, because she subsided. "Okay." She fiddled with her stringy wet ponytail. "I'll call her later. After Todd calls."

"Who's Todd?" I asked in my "grandmother-doesn't-know-anything" voice.

She turned so pink the car temperature went up five degrees. "Oh, just a boy I've been seeing. A man, actually. He was at the game Saturday—a real cute blond man?"

She was obviously waiting for me to say I'd seen him, so I did. And since Martha and Ridd had tried talking sense into Bethany without results, I decided to try another tack. "Pop and I would love to meet him, honey. Why don't you bring him down for a swim and dessert some evening?"

"Maybe . . ." The way that doubtful word hung between us, I knew she wasn't real sure how we'd like Todd.

"We won't bother you or anything," I assured her. "You all can swim and then come in for cake and ice cream. Just let me know when."

"Thanks, Me-mama." She jumped out and ran through the rain.

To tell this story properly, I need at this point to do something a judge generally doesn't: I need to rely on hearsay evidence, report what other people did and said when I was not present. However, all of this comes from reliable witnesses, so I can say with integrity that I am certain this is what happened on the afternoon of the storm.

Tyrone, Smitty, and a few friends hung out at Tyrone's because his mother was working. Once the power went out and they couldn't play video games, they passed their time plotting mischief.

Martha, Cricket, and Bethany decided to finger paint by candlelight. Cricket painted a big red heart and flowers and told his mother, "This is for Garnet."

Ronnie dropped by DeWayne's to tell him about the new job, but only Yasheika was at home, so he left to fetch Clarinda from our place. Clarinda, like Hollis, is nervous of lightning.

Ridd and DeWayne were on the golf course, and—being men—waited until the bottom fell out before they called off the match. Both were soaked when Ridd dropped DeWayne off. DeWayne invited him in for coffee, but Ridd felt he ought to get home and into dry clothes. DeWayne and Yasheika made coffee on his gas stove and lit candles. With nothing else to do, they talked.

Sara Meg had few customers that afternoon, so she spent most of it getting ready for a summer sale. She didn't even notice the storm until water streamed from the gutter outside her plate-glass window. Since she'd left her umbrella at home and had parked nearly a block away, she decided to stay and keep marking down prices as long as her flashlight batteries held out.

Hollis got off work before the storm arrived, because the pool manager shut down at the first flickers of lightning. She biked the mile home, praying she wouldn't be struck before she got there. As she rounded the corner near their house, she saw a car she recognized pull out of their drive and head in the other direction. She stared, puzzled. Garnet usually practiced the piano all afternoon.

When she got inside, she heard the shower running. She ran upstairs and stuck her nose in the bathroom door. "You better get out. It's lightning."

Behind the curtain of the old claw-foot tub, Garnet shrieked in surprise. "When did you get home?"

"I just did. Get out of the tub. You could get killed." Hollis had a mental file of stories about people who had been killed by lightning in their cars, on the street, and in bathtubs.

"Then get out of here. I'm ready to dry." Garnet was as modest as a Puritan—wore long sleeves, long skirts, and never let anybody, even her sister, see her naked.

Hollis backed out of the bathroom and went to her room to play music to drown out the storm. When she discovered that Garnet had taken several of her CDs without asking, she stomped down to Garnet's room to retrieve them. At the door, she stopped, astonished. Garnet's bed, usually as pristine as a nun's, was rumpled and bedraggled.

Hollis didn't understand. She refused to believe what common sense told her could be true, but ripples of doubt chased fear up her spine. Hollis generally challenged what she did not believe, so she pounded down the hall, flung open the bathroom door, and demanded, "What's going on here? Your bed's a mess. And why are you taking a shower at this time of day? You even washed your hair. You just washed it this morning."

Garnet clutched the towel around her. Her hair hung down her back like long red tails. "I was taking a nap and it got all messy." She turned around so Hollis couldn't see her face, but Hollis got one glimpse in the mirror. It was enough.

She stared at Garnet's naked back, as lovely as the rest of her, and shock went through her like an electric jolt. "I saw the car drive away," she said in a menacing voice.

Garnet shrugged. "So?" After a little pause, she added, "Maybe somebody rang the bell while the water was running and I didn't hear. Now get out of here, you hear me?"

"Garnet?" Hollis grabbed her shoulder. "You aren't"— she stopped; Hollis had always believed that saying bad things could make them come true—"in some kind of trouble?" she finished lamely.

Garnet jerked away. "Of course not. So don't you go worrying Mama."

Worrying their mother was something both girls tried to avoid. Uncle Buddy was like a broken record sometimes, warning them that their mother already had enough on her shoulders, just paying bills.

Hollis clumped downstairs and headed to the refrigerator for yogurt and carrot sticks. She settled herself at the table and tried not to picture Garnet—the very idea made her shiver. Not Garnet! In many ways Hollis was still young for her age. At that moment, she refused to grow up. Then thunder clattered overhead and lightning flashed outside the window, so close she felt she could reach out and touch it. Hollis cringed, laid her head down on the table, covered it with both arms, and moaned.

She heard Garnet start drying her hair. The pleasant hum of the dryer drew her back upstairs. She wished Garnet would talk to her. How long had it been since they really talked? She thought wistfully of how they used to sit and sing along with the radio when they were little. Before Daddy died. Before Garnet went so far away.

Sadly, Hollis returned to her own room. The big old house was always dim. Now it grew steadily gloomier as dark clouds came down around it. She turned on the lights and music and wondered if Bethany could come over. She reached for the phone, then remembered you could get killed talking on a telephone if it were hit by lightning.

Trapped with her fears, Hollis jumped at another flash outside her window. She hurried to close the blinds, turned up her music to drown out the thunder, and started polishing her nails.

With one enormous crash, both lights and music disappeared. Hollis trembled in the darkness, waving her hands to dry her nails and watching in terror the flashes around the edges of the blinds. Sara Meg had bought cheap, precut blinds, and these old windows weren't standard widths. Which finger of fire would hit the roof, burn down the house, strike her dead?

When she could stand it no longer, she felt her way down the wide hall toward Garnet. She didn't see the lightning outside the hall window because her eyes were squeezed shut. Heart pounding, she fumbled for Garnet's doorknob.

The door was locked.

That was so unexpected, she opened her eyes and stood very still. That's when, behind the door, she heard Garnet sobbing.

Hollis stood for what seemed a very long time, feeling like she'd stepped to the edge of a bluff and it had slid out from under her.

Hesitantly, she knocked. "Garnet, are you okay?"

Garnet's voice was muffled. "I—I stubbed my toe on the leg of my bed. It really hurts. But I'll be okay."

"Can I come in?" Lightning flashed again in the window at the end of the hall and Hollis panicked. She cried out like she was six, not sixteen, "Please, Garnie! Lemme in!"

The door clicked and swung open. Garnet held out her arms like she used to when they were small. "Oh, honey, don't be scared." She stroked Hollis's hair and murmured over and over, "I'll take care of you. It's gonna be all right. It's gonna be all right."

Hollis felt her sister's warmth up and down her body. She had no idea how long they stood there, pressed against each another, mingling their tears.

❧ 6 ❧

If I'd had any sense Wednesday, I'd have stayed in bed.

The day started all right, with breakfast on our screened side porch. My pink climbing roses were mostly finished, but the scent of the few remaining ones made for a mighty pleasant meal. I was picking up my pocketbook to leave for work when Clarinda arrived. She's worked for us for over forty years, so I can judge her mood by the way she comes through the door. That morning I took one look and asked, "Who ate your candy?"

Clarinda huffed, to show that working for anybody so insensitive was real hard on her. She thumped her pocketbook on the kitchen closet shelf and tied on her apron before she announced, "You gotta talk some sense into that girl."

"What girl?" I checked the mirror on the closet door. I like to look nice when I go out.

Clarinda propped fists on her sizeable hips. "That Yasheika. Ronnie says he never gets to see DeWayne anymore. They were supposed to go fishing this comin' Friday night, but now DeWayne says he can't go because they're having practice and then he's takin' Yasheika to Augusta for dinner to celebrate her birthday. He invited Ronnie, but Ronnie said he won't eat with that adder—that's what he calls her because he says she's so puffed up with herself. Not that he says that to DeWayne, of course."

"Of course not." I fluffed my hair. "Ronnie's got some sense."

Clarinda huffed. "He's got a lot of sense. But he's all the time moping around the house these days, on account of that girl interferin' with his fun."

"She'll be leaving in a little while."

Clarinda huffed again. "However long she stays is too long. Ronnie says she is one french fry short of a Happy Meal—all the time talking about getting her daddy out of jail."

I turned, surprised. "I didn't know their daddy was in jail. For what?"

"I don't know, but Yasheika swears he's innocent and she means to prove it."

"Everybody in jail is innocent, to hear their family talk." If I sounded disgusted, I was. "I got hauled out of bed at three this morning to go down to the jail for a bond hearing. Man broke into a dry cleaner's and stole a whole lot of clothes. Last night, his mama was down there crying and carrying on, claiming he's a good boy and it's all his wife's fault, because she spends too much money. Speaking of money, did Ronnie go see Buddy about a job? I forgot to ask."

"I noticed. But yeah, Buddy offered him a job. Ronnie's supposed to start tomorrow. But that ain't gonna solve my problem. I got to live with Ronnie, and I hate to see him mopin' around. You got to do something. Talk to her. Tell her to find herself some girlfriends, that menfolks need some time without women around. You'll know what to say."

"It's none of my business," I pointed out. "Yours, either, if we come right down to it." The look Clarinda gave me was exactly the look I suspect Mary gave Jesus after he told her the empty wine barrels at that Cana wedding weren't his business. It had the same effect, too. I knew good and well that before the day was out, I'd have called Yasheika on some pretext or other and tried to tactfully suggest that men need some time together without women around.

First, though, I wanted to arrange some new rosebushes and bedding plants on the sidewalk in front of our store. Hopemore has wide, old-fashioned sidewalks, and colorful plants make our place real pretty.

I finished, stepped back to admire my work, and ran smack into somebody. I staggered like a drunk and fell against a big, soft chest. Two large arms steadied me. "Sorry," said a gruff voice above me. Morning breath overpowered the scent of roses.

I turned and saw I was in the arms of Tyrone Noland. He turned bright red and dropped his arms at once. I stepped away and patted my hair. "Thanks for catching me. I need one of those beeper things for when I'm backing up."

"It's okay." He looked half-asleep. His teeth were yellow and dirty. His dyed hair hung limp beside his face. His black pants were wrinkled and slung low on his hips, and his black T-shirt and khaki jacket looked like they'd been used for dog bedding.

"How've you been keeping yourself?" I took a step back so I could breathe fresher air.

"Not real good." He looked at the ground and shuffled one thick shoe.

I found the way his socks drooped over the high tops of the shoes a bit endearing. Walker's socks used to droop just like that. "Looks like you could use some sleep."

"Yes, ma'am. I'm headed home to bed. Been playin' video games with friends all night." The way he'd said "friends" was boastful, like he wanted to make sure I knew he had some.

On impulse, I said, "I'm not real crazy about that crowd you're running with these days."

He shrugged. "They're all right."

"They're trouble, and you know it. Don't you let them get you into trouble."

"No, ma'am. I won't." He picked up one foot to amble

on, then put it down again. "Judge, do you think Hollis—"
His voice cracked on her name. He cleared his throat and
started over. "Do you think the girls on the team ought to be
hugging and kissing Mr. Evans?" His eyes were very blue
against his black hair. "You think it means anything, like—
you know?"

I did know, and I didn't think so. "It was just because
they won the game. It's okay, Tyrone," I said firmly. Un-
convinced, he slouched down the street. I went to the office
to justify my existence to Clarinda by calling Yasheika.

In the way things happen, the phone rang before I dialed.
"This is Yasheika Evans. Could I come by and talk to you
for a minute?" Her voice was breathy, with a pleasant rasp.

I couldn't help picturing an adder speaking with just that
voice, but I banished the image and said, "Sure, honey, that
would be great. Anytime this morning is all right. I'll be
right here."

She got there so fast, I suspected she'd called from her
cell phone in our parking lot. She tapped at the plate-glass
window in our office door and came in looking dainty and
pretty in a yellow sundress and yellow and turquoise san-
dals. Not adder-ish at all.

"Have a seat." I waved her to the wing chair by the window.

She got right down to business. "I hate to bother you, but
I don't know who else to ask. I need to find some records
from a trial that happened in this county twenty years ago.
Gerrick Lawton was accused of murder."

I sure was glad a deputy interrupted us right then with a
warrant to be signed. I didn't know what to say—not because I didn't remember, but because I did. Right that
minute, Gerrick Lawton was serving a life sentence for
killing a ten-year-old girl in the Confederate Memorial
Cemetery behind her house.

The Lawtons were another old family in Hope County,
their lives intertwined with that of the Tanners for many
generations. The difference between them was that the Tan-

ners' ancestors came to Georgia with Oglethorpe as convicts, but later generations had managed to erase that from their memories and prosper. The Lawtons came to Georgia as slaves, and even after emancipation, they never rose above being sharecroppers and domestics. Each generation lived in small unpainted shacks with newspaper stuffed in cracks to keep out the cold. Gerrick's granddaddy farmed Buddy's granddaddy's land. Gerrick's mother was the Tanners' maid, until Walter died and Sara Meg couldn't afford to keep her.

Gerrick had been the first in his family to get a job with decent wages. He had worked as a butcher at the Colders' meat-packing plant, and he and his family lived in a small brick house on the edge of town. The Colders lived next door to the Tanners, and on Saturdays, Gerrick mowed the Colders' yard and trimmed their bushes. He'd always seemed fond of Anne—even brought his little boy, who was a year or so younger, to play with Anne and Buddy. That week, though, Gerrick had had an argument with Anne's father over a raise he'd been promised. The prosecution claimed he killed Anne out of spite. Hopemore was horrified. He'd have gotten the death penalty if the evidence hadn't been mostly circumstantial. Even the prosecution's best witness hadn't actually seen him do it.

I thought about that with one part of my mind while I read and signed a warrant with the other. After the deputy left, I asked, "Why do you want to know?" I was afraid I knew.

Sure enough, Yasheika gave me a stare both proud and defiant. "He's my daddy, and I don't think he killed anybody. But I need to read up on the case. I didn't know it happened here until Monday. Now that I do, I want to find out what I can while I'm down here."

"What do you know already?"

"Not much. It happened before I was two. Growing up, I didn't even know Daddy was alive. Mama moved us up to Washington, where her sister lives. When I was real little, I asked where our daddy was, and DeWayne said not to bother Mama, that Daddy died. He started trembling when he said it, which made me think it must have been gory. I was real into gory back then, so I begged him to tell me how it happened. To shut me up, he promised he'd tell me when I turned twenty-one. I think he figured that by then I'd forget."

"But you didn't."

"I found out before, right after DeWayne got his job down here. He went to visit Daddy, and he called Mama afterwards. I heard Mama fussing at somebody on the phone, saying she didn't want to expose 'her' to prison, and 'she' didn't know 'him' anyway. I could tell she was talking about me, so I picked up the phone in another room and heard DeWayne saying that Daddy wanted to see me real bad. When I heard that, I jumped right in and made them tell me where Daddy was. Then I said I was going to see him whether Mama liked it or not. Turns out she'd been visiting him two or three times a year—she just never told us. We went together during my next school break."

"Have you seen him since?"

"Several times. He swears he never killed that little girl, and I believe him. DeWayne and Mama do, too—sort of. They say Daddy isn't the kind of man to kill anybody, and he knew and liked that child. But it's different for them. They aren't the kind to push, like Daddy and me. Daddy has already tried everything he knows to do without money or a law degree, so it's up to me. I need to find something to persuade a judge to reopen the case."

Was I ever that young and confident?

"There was an eyewitness," I reminded her. "The girl's best friend had gone home to get them a picnic lunch, and when he got back, he saw your daddy bending over Anne with a bloody rock in his hand. Your daddy jumped up and ran. Later that day, Gerrick tried to leave town. The prosecution convinced a jury those were admissions of guilt."

"Daddy says she was dead when he got there, that he

took a shortcut through the cemetery on his way home for dinner, and when he saw her on the ground, he thought she'd gotten hurt. The rock was lying on her head. He was moving it to see how bad she was hurt when the boy found him. The kid started screaming, 'You killed her, you killed her!' and Daddy says he was scared to death he'd be accused of the murder, because he'd had an argument the day before with her daddy. That's why he ran. I don't excuse that, Judge, but being scared isn't the same as committing murder. I don't think his lawyer did a good enough job defending him."

I had to admire her conviction, and she was right about the lawyer. Gerrick got assigned a fellow right out of law school, who got such a stomachful during that case that he quit law and went to work in his daddy's real-estate office. But I sat through the trial, and the old judge who ran it made sure it was run to the letter of the law. Yasheika's chances of getting a new trial on the grounds of a poor trial were about as good as my chances of getting Joe Riddley to coordinate his clothes without my assistance.

I didn't say that, of course. I said, "I never suspected DeWayne Evans was Gerrick Lawton's son. He used to be called Little Gerrick back then."

"DeWayne's his second name. I guess he started using it when we got to Washington. Mama took back her maiden name and legally changed ours to match. She said since Daddy was in jail for life, they both thought that was the right thing to do."

"Why on earth did DeWayne come here to teach? Does he want to reopen the case, too?"

Yasheika gave a short, unfunny laugh. "Not DeWayne. You wouldn't know it to look at him, but he's real fragile inside. What happened to Daddy hurt him worse than anybody will ever know. Growing up, he had bad dreams all the time. Even now, if he thinks about what happened he starts to shake. He missed a whole year of school right after it happened, because he was so scared of police and strangers. He still has bad dreams about the police stopping our car and taking Daddy away, or about kids pointing at him and laughing. Trust me, he would never go looking for trouble. He's not at all in favor of my 'stirring around in this pot,' as he puts it. He hadn't even told me until Monday that Hopemore was where it happened."

She paused, then seemed to remember my first question. "I asked him why he came here to teach. He said it was a good job, and he figured it was time to forget the past and get on with his life. But you know what I think?"

She'd make a good lawyer. She went right on without waiting for my answer.

"I think he hoped coming back would get rid of his dreams. It hasn't though—I heard him hollering and crying in his sleep last Friday night. He was nervous about the game, and that always makes him dream." She paused. When she spoke again, her voice was bitter and sad. "The way DeWayne talked on Monday during that storm, you'd think we were the happiest and most respected family in Hopemore. While we were sitting around in candlelight waiting for the lights to come back on, he started going on about the good times our family had down here. He told me about a swimming hole where he used to swim, about his school, about his teachers—he really liked his third-grade teacher. Said she's dead now, but it was because of her he became a teacher. When the storm stopped, he drove me over to see the house where we lived. There's a big tree in the yard, and he said Daddy built us a sandbox under it and we used to play out there for hours."

"You had a good family," I agreed. "Your mama and daddy both had good jobs, and they loved you children. Kept you looking nice, too. And your mother worked at the school cafeteria so she could be home for DeWayne in the afternoons."

Yasheika's voice grew wistful. "I wish I could remember being a family. The only thing I remember that I think might have happened here is sitting on the floor across from a baby who had a red ball. I wanted that ball and was reaching out to grab it when he leaned over and just gave it to me with the happiest smile. I can still see that baby's smile, clear as anything." She looked toward the window. "I wonder if that happened here in Hopemore."

I wasn't going to win points with my answer, but I gave it anyway. "If it did, I know who the baby was. Clarinda's daughter Janey kept you while your mother was at work because you and Ronnie were almost the same age. She brought you down to our house a few times when she came to see her mother."

Astonishment spread across her face like sunrise, then crumpled into disgust. "Ronnie? That smiling baby was *Ronnie*?" She made a face like she'd seen something particularly nasty. "He hasn't changed much, has he? Still the kind of guy who'd give up his ball without a fight." She bit her lower lip and gave me a disgusted grin. "But you know something funny? The first time I met him, I said to DeWayne, 'I don't much like him, but I like his smile.' "

"He's not smiling much lately." I tried to make it sound like a joke. "You're taking up so much of DeWayne's time, Ronnie's feeling a bit left out."

She shrugged. "DeWayne can do whatever he wants to. I don't have him tied to my belt. Besides, I'm gonna be real busy for a while, looking up all this stuff. If Ronnie and DeWayne want to go places, that's fine by me."

The chubby little doll in diapers, with colorful barrettes on ten tiny braids, had turned into a sophisticated young woman who still knew what she wanted and aimed to get it. I remembered something Janey used to say: "Elda's baby is no trouble. She and Ronnie get along real good." Janey was wrong. Elda's baby might be a peck of trouble, both for Ronnie and for Hopemore.

Something Yasheika had said a couple of times finally got my attention. "Why did DeWayne tell you about Hopemore on Monday?"

"I don't know. Maybe because it was raining and we didn't have anything else to do."

"Did he know Buddy gave Ronnie a job?"

Puzzled, she nodded. "Yeah, Ronnie came by to tell him, and I passed the message when DeWayne got home. DeWayne said it was time to forgive and forget. When I asked him what he meant, that's when he told me that it was right here that Daddy was accused of murder."

"But he didn't say anything about Buddy?"

Her brows drew together in a frown. "What's he got to do with it?"

I wanted to bite off my tongue and spit it a mile, but Yasheika sat there looking like she'd dig the truth out of me with those strong young fingers. "Buddy's the one who found your daddy with the rock."

"Buddy Tanner?" Her voice rose on the last word. "Hollis's uncle? It was him who put Daddy in jail? How come DeWayne didn't tell me that?"

"He had better sense. I wish I had. I'm real sorry."

She stood abruptly. "You don't need to be sorry. I'm glad I know. But Ronnie ought to have more pride than to take a job from a white man who'd put an innocent black man in jail." She turned at the door and pointed to my filing cabinets. "I'd like to stand Mr. Buddy Tanner up against that wall and shoot him."

Not knowing what to say, I said the first thing that came to mind. "Buddy was only ten, remember, and Anne was his best friend. He had to tell what he saw. But it was real hard on him. Buddy's had a lot of bad dreams, too."

"Maybe so, but he's got a good job, his family, and he can come and go when he pleases. He took all that away from Daddy. I aim to get it back." She jerked open the door. "So if you could tell me where to find those records . . ."

She thanked me politely for the information and left. Afterwards, I sat there with summer sunlight streaming into my office, but all I saw was the darkness that had covered our town twenty years before.

⟨7⟩

Hopemore seldom knew so grim a time. Sara Meg and Fred were on their honeymoon but hurried home as soon as Fred's mother—who had come up from Swainsboro to stay with Buddy—called them. She was one of the prosecution witnesses at the trial. She testified that Buddy and Anne spent the morning playing—as they often did—in the Confederate Memorial Cemetery that backed up to many big houses on Oglethorpe. At noon, he came to ask for a picnic, and she gave him banana sandwiches, cookies, and a thermos of lemonade. She figured he was home around half an hour while she fixed the lunch. Not more than three or four minutes after he left with the food, he ran back, hysterical.

Sara Meg told me later that Buddy woke up screaming every night for months. She had to sleep in the extra bed in his room. He'd become terrified of black men, too, even those he knew. After all, he had known and liked Gerrick all his life. Sara Meg tried to keep him from having to testify, but except for Fred's mother and somebody who overheard Gerrick's argument with Anne's daddy, Buddy was the only witness the prosecutor had.

Buddy looked little and lost in the witness chair, legs dangling, but he told exactly what he had seen. He hadn't tried to add anything and he hadn't cried until he left the chair. Then he buried his face in Sara Meg's lap and sobbed.

Sitting in my office twenty years later, tears stung my

eyes as I thought of the children whose lives were shattered that day: Anne, Buddy, DeWayne, and Yasheika. As I reached for a tissue to blow my nose, Bethany peered through my window and opened the door a crack. "You all right?"

"Yeah, but you've got to start knocking, honey. You're an employee now."

"Sorry. But can I use your phone? I'm meeting Hollis for lunch, and I don't know where."

"Be my guest."

I needed to make up payroll, so I wasn't paying much attention until she said into the phone, "What about?" She stopped. "Why can't you tell me?" She listened again. "Look, you've been acting weird since Monday. You could at least talk to me." She waited. "But why? Did I do something?" Silence. "I don't think this is any way to treat a friend." She slammed down the phone and slumped into her grandfather's big leather desk chair like she planned to stay awhile.

"Problems?" I swivelled my chair to face hers. She sighed, fiddled with a strand of hair, and crossed and uncrossed her feet. "Stop fidgeting and tell me what's the matter," I demanded.

"Hollis. She's going to talk to Coach Evans and can't meet me for lunch. It's too late to call Todd to come eat with me."

"I'd invite you home with us, but Clarinda said she was making pork chops, and there wouldn't be enough. Why don't you run home for lunch?"

"Nobody's there. Daddy's plowing, Mama's talking to some old college class, and Cricket went to day care." She pouted a minute, then asked, "Do you reckon Hollis got on the team and I didn't? And she doesn't want to tell me?" Her eyes pleaded for reassurance.

"I hope not, honey, but that's up to Coach Evans. He's got to pick girls from all the county teams, remember."

"Yeah, but . . ." I read in her face what she didn't want to say. She and Hollis had done everything together since they were eight. They used to fight and make up on a regular basis, but lately they'd been as close as bread and peanut butter. "She's been acting weird all week."

"Did you have a fuss?"

"No. Everything was all right Sunday. Then Monday— remember I wanted to go see her because she's scared of lightning, and you wouldn't take me?"

"I told you to call her." I refused to bear the guilt for whatever was the matter.

"I tried, but she didn't answer until late. Then she sounded funny, and said she couldn't talk." Bethany sniffed. "She didn't go to work yesterday, either. I went by the pool on my way home, and they said she'd called in sick. I went by her house, but she wouldn't let me in. Said she'd call me, but she didn't." Bethany's eyes flashed with indignation. "Now she says she can't meet me for lunch, like we always do on Wednesday, because she has to talk to Coach Evans. I may never speak to her again." She flounced back to work, swinging her ponytail.

I wish I could report that the day got better, but it didn't. I got home at dinnertime to find our riding mower sitting smack in the middle of the yard with the yard half-mowed and a note from Clarinda on the kitchen table: *Yasheika came by and yelled at Ronnie. He got so mad he tore out after her, leaving the mower where it is. I've gone to be sure he's okay. Your dinner's in the oven.*

The pork chops were so dry that I gave them to Lulu, our three-legged beagle, and carried sandwich makings out to the porch. As Joe Riddley and I ate, I admired the bed of coral and pink Gerbera daisies I'd planted out by the old well and watched scarlet cardinals at the bird feeder. A rabbit we called Peter Yarbrough explored our dandelions. Lulu would have liked to join him, but Joe Riddley warned her if she didn't stop begging, she'd have to go inside. She settled herself at our feet and snoozed. Bo marched silently around his own place mat, pecking up seeds and bites of vegetable.

At first, I didn't notice Joe Riddley wasn't talking much. I was going back over the conversations I'd had that morning, thinking of things I wished I'd said.

Only when Joe Riddley grunted did I realize he'd been worrying something around in his mind and had failed to come up with a single way to keep from telling me bad news. I reached for a handful of grape tomatoes. "You might as well spit it out and get it over with."

He spread mayonnaise on his bread with the care Michelangelo devoted to the Sistine Chapel. Only when each swirl was perfect did he finally say, "I ran into Hubert this morning."

"That shouldn't have ruined your day." Until Hubert Spence had moved to town the previous winter, he'd been our nearest neighbor, across a watermelon patch and a pasture with a cattle pond. We lived half a mile down a gravel road, and Hubert's was the only other house on the road, except for the Pickens place up near the highway. Joe Riddley and Hubert never agreed on religion, politics, or whether Georgia or Georgia Tech was the better school, but they were friends. "What did he say?"

Joe Riddley slapped three pieces of ham on his sandwich. "He said that the superstore that folks have been talking about is really coming. They're bringing in bulldozers tomorrow. Hubert's worried sick they'll close him down."

I stared. I'd been so busy Saturday celebrating the Honeybees' victory, I'd plumb forgotten to tell him what Brandi's mother had said. Joe Riddley knew I was shocked, but misunderstood why. He laid his hand on mine. "We'll be all right, honey. They won't carry cotton seed. And their roses won't be as nice as ours. Don't worry. We'll be fine."

"Hubert may be fine, too. They won't carry big appliances. But we'll both have to let people go. And what about folks like Sara Meg?"

He took a big gulp of tea as though he were washing a bitter taste out of his mouth. "As a boy, I heard about tidal

waves and lay awake for a lot of nights wondering how it
felt to see something huge coming right at you and know
you couldn't get out of its way. Now I know." He set his
glass down with a thump. "I don't mind telling you, Little
Bit, I'm worried about this town."

We should have *all* been worried. But the new superstore
was a speck on the windshield of the wreck heading our
way.

When DeWayne Evans made an unprecedented visit to
my office late that afternoon, I figured somebody must have
added a bit to my JUDGE YARBROUGH sign: PALMS READ AND
PROBLEMS SOLVED. He filled my door with his sturdy body
and wide shoulders. Seeing him with a bare head, wearing
khaki slacks, a yellow shirt, and loafers, took some getting
used to. I usually saw him on the ball field in his coach's
white and red uniform and cap.

"I hate to barge in on you like this, Judge, but I've got a
little problem. I understand you've been talking to
Yasheika." My wing chair creaked as he lowered himself
into it.

I swivelled my desk chair to face him. "And I've got a
bone to pick with you. She said you're Little Gerrick Lawton, and you never told me."

"You remember me?" The man's face lit up just like the
child's had when he was unexpectedly pleased.

"Of course I remember. I used to give you suckers when
your mama came in to buy hen bran and tomato plants. You
liked red ones." Now that I knew to look, I could see the re-
semblance. That stocky little boy had grown into a man with
the same big round head, high forehead, friendly eyes that
met yours with a trace of shyness, and the same wide mouth
that curved easily into a bashful smile.

"I didn't think I should tell anybody, since I didn't mention it in my job interview."

"Why didn't you?"

He looked down at his hands, which he was rubbing back

and forth with a swishing sound. A college ring gleamed on one thick finger. "This was the first chance I'd had since college to teach in my subject, and I didn't want to mess up. My previous school valued me more as a coach than a chemist. I figured most of the kids I went to school with would have moved away, and frankly, it didn't occur to me that grown-ups would remember me." The sweet, self-effacing little boy had become a sweet, self-effacing man.

He leaned forward, clasped his hands together between his knees, and examined them like he'd never noticed them before. The shiny toes of his loafers swivelled back and forth, pendulums marking passing time. "But that's not what I came to talk about." He came to a dead stop.

"Is it about Yasheika, or Hollis?"

He looked up, startled. "Hollis?"

"She told Bethany she was going over to see you at lunchtime."

He shifted his feet uneasily and rubbed his palms together again. "Yeah, Hollis came in for a little chat. Did she tell Bethany what it was about?"

"No." I hesitated, then added, "Bethany's scared you've picked Hollis for the team and didn't pick her."

That made him laugh. "I wouldn't do that. And I wouldn't go into a championship game without my Deadly Duo. Don't tell Bethany—I'll start calling the girls tonight after I talk to one more coach down at the south end of the county—but she and Hollis are definitely on the team. We'll be practicing every day, starting Friday. We need all the work we can get in."

"They're going to be thrilled." I hoped that was true. Surely this spat, whatever it was, would soon blow over.

I was so busy wondering whether we'd close the store again for the district championship game, I didn't understand what DeWayne meant when he said, "It's about Ronnie." Seeing my blank look, he added, "What I came to talk to you about. Apparently you told my baby sister this morning that it was Buddy Tanner who—who identified our daddy at his trial—" His left hand started to tremble. He pinioned it with his right.

I jumped in to defend myself. "I didn't know she didn't know."

"Oh, I'm not blaming you. She'd have found out as soon as she started poking around the records. She doesn't blame you, either. But she went down and jumped all over poor Ronnie, saying he ought not have taken a job with Buddy, after what he'd done."

"I doubt if Ronnie even knew," I pointed out. "He was an infant when it happened, just like Yasheika. The Colders shut down the meat-packing plant and moved to Mississippi right after that, and Buddy had such nightmares that folks didn't bring up the subject any more than they had to. I doubt if Ronnie ever heard Anne Colder's name, growing up."

Now both DeWayne's hands and arms were shaking. He clutched the arms of my wing chair like it was about to take off with him in it, but kept talking like I couldn't see. "That's what I figured." He shook his head. "Yasheika has gone off the deep end about this. She's convinced there's a way to prove Daddy innocent and she's the one who's gonna find it. She also thinks Ronnie is a traitor to the whole African American population by accepting a job from Buddy."

"Never seemed to me like she cared whether he agreed with her or not."

Laughing again stilled his tremors some. "You got that right. Those two are like cats and dogs. I won't let them be in the same room if I can help it. Pick, pick, pick, that's all they ever do. Or at least Yasheika picks at him. She's the dog. He's like a cat, stalking away with his nose in the air. I've told him and told him she'd respect him more if he'd give as good as he gets."

"He won't fight," I told him. "He grew up with a daddy who beat his mother and saw him kill her when he was five—"

"He never!"

"He certainly did. Ronnie was right there in the living room when Buck shot Janey. The miracle was that Buck ran out of the house and didn't kill the child. Ronnie had a bad temper, too, when he was little, but we've all worked to help him keep it under control. He won't fight now, especially with a woman. He's too scared of how it might end."

"I can understand that." DeWayne was trembling again, so fiercely that the whole chair shook. He spoke through tight lips. "Kids shouldn't have to go through things like that."

"Kids shouldn't be in cars when their daddies are arrested." I leaned over and put both hands on his. "Have you ever gotten counseling for this?"

His forehead was beaded with sweat and he spoke in gasps. "Twice. In college and again before I moved down here. Nothing seems to help. I keep seeing the police stop our car and haul Daddy out. I never saw him again until I went to visit him in prison when I was in college, but I see that in all my nightmares. I also see kids at school, staring, pointing, whispering, laughing behind my back." He shuddered. "Some would tag me and run, like they had done something real brave. Others sang a little jingle they made up." He sang in the falsetto *nyah-nyah* tune of children, " 'Gerrick's daddy killed a girl. Now he's gonna fry-y.' "

"Oh, honey!" I didn't know what else to say. I wanted to gather him up and hold him like he was still eight years old, but he was at least twice my size. All I could do was keep my hands on his until they grew calm.

He tried to smile, but it looked like rictus. "It'll pass in a minute. But now you know why I didn't want Hopemore to know who I am. I couldn't stand going through all that again."

I wished I could tell him that we were a well-mannered town, that not one soul would stare, point him out, or whisper behind his back if they learned who he was. Unfortunately, it wasn't true. I could list several people who'd have a field day if they knew the Honeybees' coach and high-school chemistry teacher was Gerrick Lawton's son. I decided the best thing I could do was take the conversation back a bit. "Do you think if Yasheika knew about Ronnie's past, it might help her understand him better?"

"It might. Is Ronnie's daddy still in jail?"

I hated to answer that question. "Ronnie's daddy was executed."

Seeing his face, I decided it was time to lighten up a bit. "You'd think, growing up around Joe Riddley, Ronnie would have learned that a man and woman can fight without him hitting or shooting her. Joe Riddley can be an ornery old coot."

DeWayne rewarded me with a faint smile, so I added, "Of course, Ronnie doesn't have to fight for most things he wants. He's so sweet, folks just give it to him."

"Not Yasheika." DeWayne's tremors subsided again, and he stood to go. "Ronnie will never get along with her unless he stands up to her. She'd eat him alive and despise him for letting her. It's a shame, because they're both fine people except when they're together. It's like they're magnets with the same pole." He stood. "I wonder if Ronnie would benefit from assertiveness training." Then his rueful chuckle rolled between us. "Of course, I took a course in that once, and it didn't do me a speck of good. But maybe Ronnie learns better than I do. I've already told him to go ahead and work for Buddy. It's a fine opportunity, no matter what Yasheika thinks."

I couldn't help but be curious about one thing. "Have you told Buddy who you are? You used to play together, didn't you?"

He turned at the door. "All the time. Daddy would take me over on Saturdays when he cut the Colders' grass, and Buddy, Anne, and I played in the cemetery. We used to climb on the gravestones, and Buddy made up all sorts of games." A shadow darkened his face, and another tremor passed over his whole body. I appreciated the courage it took for him to stand there and say, "I'd have been there that day, except I had a cold and Mama kept me home. If I'd gone—" Now he was shaking so hard he had to hold on to Joe Riddley's desk. "I'm sorry, Judge. I'll be all right in a minute. This never happens except when I start thinking about all that mess."

"Sit down." I shoved Joe Riddley's desk chair his way. When he'd lowered himself into it, I asked, "You don't believe your daddy killed her, do you?"

He shook his head. "Daddy loved children. He'd never have hurt Anne. I think he was trying to help her, like he said, when Buddy found him. It was somebody else who killed her—somebody who found her in the time Buddy was gone. I'm sure of it." Beads of sweat broke out on his forehead again. He pulled a handkerchief from his pocket and wiped them away. "You see how it is. Any time I start thinking about that day or talking about what happened, it all rolls over me again. I feel like I'm drowning or something." He stared at his hands, willing them to grow still.

"I don't want to prolong your suffering, but tell me one thing. Do you have anybody in mind who could have killed Anne?" As far as I knew, nobody had ever talked to Little Gerrick about that day.

"Not anybody in particular, but tramps were all the time hanging out around there. Freight trains still stopped in town back then, remember? Men would climb off and stay a few days, hang out in the cemetery." He was growing calmer again.

"Why didn't I know that? Did other people?"

"I don't know. The fellas were real quiet and stayed back in the bushes if folks were around, but we kids saw them when we were playing. Sometimes one would be asleep with his foot sticking out from a bush, or we'd leave a sandwich on a tombstone and watch until a hand crept out to grab it. They didn't bother us and we didn't bother them, but I always figured one of them might have been a little crazy, so he killed Anne, then caught the next train out." He exhaled a long, sad breath. "I'm not a fighter like Yasheika, so I've never tried to do anything to help Daddy except go see him pretty regular."

"How is he?"

He lifted his big shoulders in a shrug. "Mad, frustrated, hopeless. I wish Yasheika could get him out—Mama's never cared for any other man. But I don't think we'll ever learn the truth about what happened that day. Who could trace a tramp after all this time?" He stood again and headed back to the door. "And to answer your earlier question, no, I haven't told Buddy who I am. I—I hadn't really seen him until last Saturday. He generally drops Hollis off for practice and doesn't hang around. . . ."

He stopped. We both knew that wasn't the real reason he hadn't said anything, even at the table last Saturday. When he, Anne, and Buddy played together as children, it hadn't mattered that two were white and one was black, or that one's daddy owned the meat-packing plant where the other's daddy worked. They had not yet crossed the divide where such things begin to define us. I couldn't fault De-Wayne for wanting to meet Buddy as the chemistry teacher instead of as the yardman's son.

A worry wrinkle appeared between his eyes, though. "You think maybe I ought to tell him and warn him that Yasheika plans to stir around in the case?"

"He might like to know ahead of time if it's all going to be raked up again. Buddy's had some bad dreams, too."

He heaved a sigh from the soles of his loafers. "Some days it *all* seems like a bad dream. But I'll talk to him." He added, to himself, "Maybe I can sound him out about this Hollis thing."

"What Hollis thing?" Bethany stood in the doorway brandishing my new *Statesman*.

Before I could remind her again that employees knock— and that nobody reads my paper before me—DeWayne said, "Just something she came over to talk about today."

Bethany lifted her chin, sending her hair swinging from

side to side. "I'm glad she's talking to somebody. But look! Look!" She thrust the paper at him and pointed to the front page.

A broad grin creased his face. "Well, just look at that. We're famous."

She turned pages. "And there's two pictures with the story on the sports page. Look!"

While he browsed, Bethany asked, "May I borrow your car for a minute, Me-mama, to run over to the paper office for some more copies?"

"As long as you leave my paper where I can read it." I couldn't help sounding snippy. It was, after all, my paper.

DeWayne handed it to me with a happy laugh. "We even made the society page. Here, Judge. I'll go get a paper of my own."

"Give me your phone number before you go," I told him. "I want you and Yasheika to come over some evening for supper and a swim."

He took a card from his wallet. "This will reach me almost anytime. We don't have a phone, just cell phones." Seeing my surprise, he grinned. "That's what a lot of folks do in cities these days."

I stuck the card in my pocketbook and decided that was a real sensible plan. Why attach a phone to a house instead of to the person who used it? I thought for a second about canceling our phone and getting Joe Riddley a cell phone, but changed my mind. The way he lost his keys since he'd gotten shot, that would never work.

Once DeWayne and Bethany had gone, I enjoyed the *Statesman* almost as much as Bethany had, particularly references to her pitching ability in the sports section and the big picture on the front page under a one-inch heading: "We Won!" It was the shot Slade took of Bethany and Hollis hugging DeWayne at Myrtle's front door. The three of them looked happier than Christmas.

Slade had written an editorial about DeWayne, too. He'd interviewed the high-school principal, several students, and two other girls on the team and wrote glowingly about De-Wayne's contributions to the community. His column concluded, "Coach Evans has been in Hopemore for two years, but he is making a major impact on this community through lives he touches—those of his students and the girls on his team."

I called the paper to say I was real pleased with the stories and to put in my order for an eight-by-ten print of the picture. And I vowed that not by one word or facial expression would I let anybody know that DeWayne Evans was Little Gerrick Lawton unless he chose to reveal that himself.

Not until the next morning would we learn that not everybody in Hopemore was happy with that week's *Statesman*.

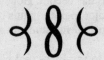

Bethany ran straight into my office Thursday morning and didn't give me time to fuss. "The school's a mess! Somebody's painted stuff all over it."

I flapped a hand at her. "Calm down. It happens almost every year. Some kid with too much time on his hands filches spray paint from his daddy's workshop and decorates the door. The principal will make him take it off and work around the place for a while. I'm surprised it happened so early in the summer, though."

Bethany heaved the sigh of a teen dealing with an ignorant adult. "This isn't like usual, Me-mama. It's awful. I won't tell you what they wrote—I don't even want to think things like that—but I hope Daddy can catch Coach Evans before he sees it."

I got a funny feeling somewhere under my belt. "What kind of things are they, honey?"

"Nasty." She wrinkled her nose. "Not true, of course, but some people may believe them."

I reached for my pocketbook. "Let's go over there. I want to see."

Hope County has two lovely new regional high schools, but Hopemore High, which serves the town, has merely added wings over the years to the old redbrick building Joe Riddley and I attended. Almost everybody in the crowd on the sidewalk had graduated from that school. We all stared

in dismay at the front of the building, which was now decorated with red, white, and blue designs—a horrible parody
of patriotism. The artwork ranged from nasty racial epithets
to Confederate flags and swastikas. Right over the front
door was a huge caricature of DeWayne Evans with a message beneath: *Coach Evans ♥ White Girls*. An arrow pointed
from the heart to the word "touches," written at an angle.

Anger swelled up in me until I felt I could burst. Bethany
sniffed and dabbed her eyes with a soggy tissue. As I handed
her a fresh one, I noticed other Honeybees sidling our way,
equally teary and outraged. They greeted us in bursts of indignation.

"It's not true."

"Of course not."

"Coach Evans is the kindest, sweetest coach in the world.
He'd never . . ."

"How could anybody be so awful?"

My own question was: How could anybody have drawn
that caricature without getting caught? It must have taken
time, and we had police cars patrolling the town all night.

I turned Bethany away. "I hadn't imagined it was this
bad, or I wouldn't have brought you."

Far back in the crowd somebody muttered, "No smoke
without fire."

Her head shot up, lashes damp and spiky. "That's a lie.
Anybody knows it who knows Coach Evans at all."

To forestall a shouting match, I asked loudly, "How will
they ever get the paint off?"

Other voices joined the chorus. "Have to paint the whole
danged building."

"That'll cost a pretty penny."

"And once you paint brick, you have to keep painting it."

An approaching siren wailed a coda to our tune.

I hadn't noticed Brandi's mother until she spoke. "They
could paint the front. In Chicago, a lot of houses have fancy
bricks on the front and ordinary ones on the sides and back."
Everybody in the crowd turned to glare. Apparently Shana

hadn't learned that the fastest way to unite a southern crowd is to tell us a better way things are done up North.

Miffed at our lack of enthusiasm, she climbed into a red Volkswagen parked at the curb. As she drove away, the siren deafened us and a shiny new cruiser slid into her space.

Two weeks ago the *Statesman* had carried a feature about Police Chief Charlie Muggins's new car. I doubted he'd get much call for most of the equipment he'd ordered, and as far as I knew, this was the first time he'd been able to use that fancy siren. He climbed out and swaggered my way. "Well, Judge," he said with that leer that passes for a smile, "what have you been up to now?"

Charlie Muggins is one of my least favorite people, and the feeling is mutual. Thumbs in his belt, he looked me over like he suspected I was concealing spray paint in my pocketbook.

"This is dreadful," I told him. "Do you have any idea who did it?"

He took off his cap and smoothed back his yellow hair for any camera that might be pointed his way. "Give me a minute. I just got here." He sashayed off.

Bethany and I stayed a few minutes longer to watch officers look for clues, but nobody seemed to be finding any. "We need to get back, honey," I finally told her.

"Could we go by Hollis's on the way? She's not here."

Hollis's house was not on our way. Our store is on West Oglethorpe, a block from the courthouse square.The Tanner Harem, as it is still called, is on East Oglethorpe, in the last of a string of lovely Victorian homes plus three antebellums General Sherman missed in his torchlight procession through town. Furthermore, it takes a while to drive those blocks in nice weather, because Oglethorpe is part of a federal highway and gawking tourists drive slow to admire those houses. Joe Riddley says we could speed up traffic through town by creating an alternative historical route with markers at a number of sites: *General Sherman Burned Here.*

Still, I turned my car, as Bethany and I had both known I would.

Few families these days are rich enough to afford the paint, lumber, and roofing shingles those big houses soak up, so most are law offices, antique stores, or realty companies. A few are subdivided into apartments. As I pulled into Sara Meg's gravel drive and parked under one of the big oaks in her front yard, I saw that her house needed painting again. "You go in. I'll wait in the car," I told Bethany. While waiting, I sighed over former perennial beds, now a mass of weeds, and over scraggy camellias and azaleas near the porch. Overgrown ivy snaked up the hydrangeas near the steps and was working its way up one column. Even if Sara Meg didn't have time to work in her yard, she could fill the concrete urns flanking her front steps with mounds of colorful impatiens. It might lift her spirits. But with the supestore coming, how long could she even afford to keep the house?

Hollis came to the door in shorts, holding car keys. Bethany poured out the story and Hollis sagged against the doorjamb, her head shaking from side to side in disbelief. Bethany threw me an anxious look. I let down my window. "Why don't you take today off and go to the pool with Hollis?" I called.

I didn't feel much like working, either. To make myself feel worse, I drove by the lot outside the city limits where bulldozers were leveling an enormous field. The new superstore would sit all by itself, surrounded by cotton and corn, but I knew that cotton and corn would soon be replaced by pizza parlors and video stores. I suspected Smitty and his boys had painted the school. Who else in town was mean, or arrogant enough to think they'd never get caught? But it occurred to me that Smitty and his band of young thugs were junior versions of the educated older thugs who are taking over the world field by field. Was it Teddy Roosevelt who said if you take a boy who steals rides on boxcars and give him an education, he'll steal railroad companies?

Back at my desk, when I found myself writing the same

check a second time, I reached for the phone. "Hey, Martha. Did you hear about that awful thing over at the high school?"

"Ridd called. It makes you sick, doesn't it?"

"Makes me want to go eat chocolate pie. I heard that chocolate releases chemicals in our brain that cheer us up. You and Cricket got time to meet me at Myrtle's?"

Martha's chuckle warmed me all over. "Sure. Another study has shown that in times of stress, women should spend time with other women and children. That releases some chemicals, too. And if you walk over, the exercise will reduce *you.*"

I reached for my pocketbook. "Hooray for science, if all it takes to make me feel better today is a pretty walk, good company, and chocolate pie."

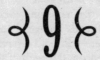

Myrtle's had a thriving breakfast crowd of widowers and men whose breakfast clause in their marriage contract expired when they retired. By the time I arrived, however, only two booths were occupied. The customer at a back booth was hidden by a newspaper. Smitty's gang filled the corner booth, their heads in a huddle, squirming and sniggering like boys half their age.

Myrtle was sitting at a corner table having herself a cup of coffee, a half-full pot beside her.

"Get ready for a rush," I warned her. "Did you hear what happened over at the school?" Whenever trouble strikes Hopemore, folks naturally gravitate to Myrtle's.

She hadn't heard, so I sat down across from her and filled her in. "Somebody painted up the school real bad last night. Nasty things I won't repeat—"

A shout of laughter made us both turn toward the corner booth. "Ignore them," Myrtle begged in a low voice. "If that Smitty gets riled, he can be mean as a copperhead."

"So can I," I assured her, "but I won't today. I'm going to take the next booth, though, to see if I can hear what they're talking about. I wouldn't be surprised if they painted the school."

"You want your usual?"

"Not yet. Martha and Cricket are joining me in a few minutes."

She nodded. "Two chocolate pies and a chocolate ice cream with a place mat and crayons. I'll bring it when they get here." Myrtle knows her regulars.

When Smitty saw me moseying their way, he made a chopping signal. His friends lounged back like young collegiates enjoying summer vacation. I'd have ignored them, but a spiral of smoke rose from the back of their circle, so I detoured in their direction. "No smoking in here."

Smitty's chin might sprout only a few yellow hairs, but his eyes were insolent and older than mine. "We ain't smoking."

"*We* may not be, but one of you certainly is." My eyes roved around the table and stopped at Willie Keller, known as Wet Willie because his eyes were always red and watery. Willie had the biggest ears I'd ever seen on a child, but he seldom heard a thing unless you said it twice. "Willie? Willie! Put out that cigarette. Do you hear me? I said, put out that cigarette."

"I ain't got—" He got that far before he glanced up and met my eye.

I saw his right shoulder tense. "Don't you drop it on the floor. Put it out in your glass. Now! In the glass!" I didn't raise two sons for nothing. Reluctantly his grubby hand crept from beneath the table. A lit cigarette sizzled as it hit the ice, then sputtered out.

Smitty slid out of the booth and jerked his head. "We got places to go and people to annoy. Let's head out." The others scrambled to follow, displaying the combined intelligence and manners of cows spying an open gate.

Only Tyrone muttered, as he passed, "Hey, Judge." He turned slightly away, but I'd seen what he was trying to hide: a smear of blue paint on his jacket. He saw that I'd seen it and gave me an anxious look over one shoulder as he followed Smitty as fast as a big kid can scurry.

Halfway to the door, Smitty turned. "What's that you were saying, Judge? Somebody painted the school? Imagine that. Must be real purty." He drawled the word like a television cowboy. "Come on, fellas. We oughtta take a stroll and have a look." He sauntered past the cash register and out the door like his daddy owned the place. Nobody paid. Myrtle didn't mention it.

"Thanks, Judge, for clearing out the vermin," Buddy Tanner said, lowering the *Wall Street Journal.*

"Glad to do it. Wish we could make it permanent. Did Ronnie start work today?"

"He sure did. I vacated the premises to let him learn the ropes from the guy he's replacing." Buddy gave me a genial nod and returned to his paper. I would have asked him to join Martha and me, but he didn't look like he wanted company.

Smitty or one of his friends had left a green spiral notebook on the seat of the booth. I leaned over and used a paper napkin to flip the pages. It contained a number of caricatures of teachers at school, all done in purple ink. I recognized Ridd, his bald head elongated and his hair in tufts like a mad scientist's, writing elaborate formulas all over a blackboard. Another showed Hollis sliding into second base, hair streaming behind her. With only a few lines, the artist had caught every expression of her body.

Then I froze. After Hollis, the next two pages were covered with pictures of DeWayne: a king with a crown, a chemist blown up by his own explosion, a lecher leering at a white girl. The rest of the notebook—five sheets—was empty.

I pulled out my cell phone and punched in the number for Assistant Police Chief Isaac James. Isaac would have been police chief of Hopemore if life were fair and our enlightened city fathers had been willing several years before to promote a competent local black man instead of importing an incompetent white one. Joe Riddley and I like and respect Ike, and the feeling seems to be mutual. When I explained what I'd found and where, he was instantly alert. "Leave it in place, and don't let Myrtle sit anybody else in that booth. I'm on my way."

"I'll be in the next booth," I promised. "Oh, and Ike—Tyrone Noland's jacket has blue paint on it. You might try to find him before he gets rid of it. He left Myrtle's a minute ago."

"Thanks, Judge. We'll pick him up."

I slid into the next booth along the side wall. I couldn't see the notebook—it was on the part of the bench with its back to me—but I could keep an eye on the booth and the front door.

A few more people straggled in. When Myrtle got in speaking distance, I motioned her over and said, "Don't sit anybody in that corner booth. Isaac James is coming to get the green notebook that's there, and he'll want you to tell him who was sitting there when it was left."

She scowled. "I don't want trouble with those boys. They'll slash my tires, break my windows—who knows what else?"

"You mustn't let them terrorize you," I reproached her.

She hefted her coffeepot. "In case you hadn't noticed, Judge, they already have."

Cricket spoke from under her elbow. "What's terrorize?"

"Scare you," I explained briefly as she moved away. "You want the outside or the inside?"

"Outside." He climbed up beside me and heaved an enormous sigh as he settled himself on the bench. "It's sure hot out there. Can I go swim in your pool?"

I took my cue from Martha, who was shaking her head. "Not today, honey. Oh, look, there's Garnet." Cricket brightened.

Art Franklin was ushering her in, his eyes almost as bright as Cricket's. Garnet's looked anxious. Furtive, even. She wore a drab brown skirt with a long-sleeved cream top and had a book bag slung over one shoulder, so I figured she was going to or coming from class.

"Have a seat anywhere. I'll bring you a Coke," we heard Art say, "but I have to clock in and put on my apron." He hurried toward the kitchen door.

"Garnet, come sit with us," Cricket called.

She turned in our direction, but I heard the rustle of Buddy's paper behind me. "Garnet?"

She froze as solid as Myrtle's fresh fish.

"Come here." His voice was stern. Garnet headed his way with dragging feet. I heard him say in a low voice, "Hollis said *she* was driving you to class and picking you up."

I could hear only snatches without looking over my shoulder. " . . . first week . . . out early . . . drove me back." Finally, clearly, "I was going to call Hollis, to tell her not to come."

"Sit down." He laid down his paper. "I'll wait for you to drink your Coke, then take you home." I heard her slide into the booth.

Cricket had knelt on our bench to watch all that. Now he turned around and plopped down, lower lip a shelf of disappointment. "I wanted her to sit with me."

"She's busy right now," I consoled him.

Art bustled out the kitchen door, carrying our order plus a large Coke on a tray. When he saw where Garnet was sitting, he snatched up a coffeepot and headed for their table. My back was to them, of course, but Martha filled me in. "He's filling Buddy's cup like he's offering a libation to the gods," she said softly.

"Maybe he is. You think it'll work?"

"Apparently not. Buddy's still frowning. He's going to have to realize pretty soon that those girls are growing up."

Art hurried from their table to ours. After I'd thanked him for our pie, I added, "I don't know if Myrtle has told you yet, but don't let anybody sit in that corner booth until a policeman comes to get the notebook that's there."

He stepped toward the booth and glanced down. "Okay." He hurried away.

As if my thoughts had conjured them, Smitty, Tyrone, and Willie sauntered through the door. Smitty looked our way, then led the other two toward the entrance to the bathroom hall, using a route that didn't come anywhere near us or the corner booth.

"Watch them," I ordered Martha. "Tell me if they start this way."

A few seconds later, she reported, "Smitty's come back out

and is lounging in the archway leading to the rest rooms. The other two haven't made an appearance."

Cricket bent over his place mat and began to adorn his dogs and cats with fierce horns, big black eyes, and long marks from their paws. When I asked what the marks were, he muttered, "Swords, o' course. To kill the bad guys." Martha gave me a wry smile. Grown-ups who think children don't know at least the mood of what is going on are only fooling themselves.

Myrtle and Art moved back and forth, refilling cups and setting down plates. We didn't discuss the school at our table, but everybody else did. At each table, Myrtle performed her usual service of keeping everybody up with what the rest were saying.

"They found the ladder under the bleachers."

"Paint cans were in the Dumpster, but nobody has said if they have fingerprints on 'em."

"There's a company in Augusta that thinks the paint will come off if they steam clean it within twenty-four hours."

Martha and I motioned her to silence whenever she came near our booth, pointing to Little Big Ears. While we ate our pie and talked about their family's plans for a week at the beach in July, I kept wondering what was keeping Ike.

I hadn't heard Buddy and Garnet exchange a single word since she sat down. "Are Buddy and Garnet talking?" I asked Martha softly.

Before she could answer, Cricket climbed onto his knees to peer over the bench. He leaned close to my ear and murmured, "He's reading his paper and she's reading a book and drinking her Coke." He returned to his station, practically hanging over the booth, while his ice cream melted. In a few more minutes he reported, "Now he's getting up and going to the bathroom. Hey, Garnet!" He waved.

"Turn around, sit down, and eat," Martha ordered.

I signaled Art to refill my cup and made a face when I sipped it. "Tepid," I grumbled.

Martha wasn't paying me any attention. A worry pucker

had appeared between her eyes. "Forget your manners, Mac, and turn around. Cricket, sit down and finish your ice cream."

When Martha used that voice, everybody obeys. I turned and saw Smitty standing beside Garnet, arms akimbo and pelvis tilted forward. "What you reading?" he crooned.

When Garnet didn't look up, he bent closer and asked again. This time he sprinkled the question with profanity. Martha slid from her bench. "Let's go to the bathroom, Cricket. You've got ice cream on your face."

He obediently slid out and followed her. He said, "Hello, Garnet," as they passed her. Garnet waved but didn't speak. Her eyes were glued to her book.

Smitty slapped both palms on the end of Garnet's table and bent right over her ear. "Cat took your tongue when he left you alone?" He reached out and jerked her hair lightly. She lifted one shoulder and moved slightly toward the wall. Smitty sat down on the end of her bench. She cringed and moved farther away.

When Smitty started to put one arm around her shoulders, Art dashed over, carrying his coffeepot. "Leave her alone!"

Smitty looked up and sneered. "Says who?"

"Says me." Poor Art looked stringy and weak beside Smitty's biceps.

"Says *who?*" asked Smitty again.

"Ignore him," Garnet begged, without looking up. "He'll go away."

Smitty leaned over close. "I'm never going very far. I'll be real close to you all the time." He reached over and stroked her cheek with the back of one forefinger.

Art lifted his pot and poured coffee all over Smitty's lap. Smitty yelped and swore. Then he jumped up and struck Art in one catlike move.

Art toppled backwards, taking one of Myrtle's tables with him. "No!" cried Garnet, sliding across the booth. But she couldn't get out. Smitty blocked her path, waiting for Art to rise. Women gasped. Men hesitated, maybe wondering if breaking this up was worth getting themselves hurt over. Garnet sat frozen, pale as skim milk and eyes wide. Art climbed awkwardly to his feet. Smitty continued to swear, brushing the soaked front of his jeans.

Art clenched his fists and Smitty crouched again, ready to spring. I flew out of my booth and hurried their way. "Stop it, right this minute!" I commanded. "Both of you. Get out of here, Smitty. You know better than to brawl in a public place. Art, go back to the kitchen."

"He burned me!" Smitty put one hand over his crotch. "You saw it, Judge. He poured boiling hot coffee all over me. I ought to sue."

"He—" Art began. His face was scarlet with fury or embarrassment.

They were both still talking at full voice when Buddy spoke behind me. "What's going on?" I was sure glad he'd arrived. Garnet sat in their booth, shaking, looking at the floor like she hoped a hole would appear in the tatty linoleum and swallow her up.

"These two were wrangling, but it's over. Go on, Smitty, get out. You weren't burned. I've just had coffee from that pot, and it's like bathwater."

I have to admit I was trembling inside, wondering what I'd do if he didn't leave. A lot of folks, including me, were surprised when Smitty glanced out the plate-glass windows in front, where Willie and Tyrone slouched on the sidewalk, and gave me the devil's own smile. "Sure, Judge. Anything you say." The way he swaggered out, I half expected a patter of applause. Art slunk to the kitchen, his face still red.

Buddy joined us just then. "Glad you were here, Judge. Thanks."

I didn't reply. I was too busy hurrying to the corner booth. As I had feared, the notebook was gone. Smitty had created a most effective diversion.

⧽ 10 ⧼

I asked, but nobody had seen who took it. I tried to call Ike to tell him to pick up the trio. He didn't answer. When I called headquarters, the dispatcher said, "I'll give somebody the message, but almost every officer we've got is over at the school, and the rest are tied up with a bad wreck out where they put up the new four-way stop signs. You and I both know nobody remembers those signs are there."

Disgusted as much with myself as with Smitty, I motioned for Myrtle and pushed my cup her way. "Bring me a fresh cup, as hot as you've got it."

As she brought it, Martha and Cricket returned. Buddy and Garnet walked with them, chatting. Buddy carried his paper neatly folded, but Garnet's unzipped book bag hung precariously on one shoulder. She was still pale.

"Did you get the picture I mailed you?" Cricket was asking Garnet.

She nodded. "I loved it. Thank you." Her bag slipped and she automatically shoved it higher.

Buddy frowned. "Zip that thing and put in on properly, before you spill everything."

He wasn't the only man right then who wanted to run her life. "Put my picture on your wall," Cricket commanded, "and I'll send you my new one when it's done. It's going to terrorize you!" He climbed onto the bench, picked up his crayon, and started coloring industriously.

Seeing Garnet's startled look, Martha explained, "That's his new word for *scare*. And by the way, that thing we were talking about after class yesterday? It's getting checked."

Buddy had moved toward the register, but turned back. "What was that?"

"Nothing." Garnet gave Martha a warning look, biting her lip so hard I was afraid she'd draw blood.

Martha waved one hand to show how unimportant it was. "Just something I promised Garnet I'd check on after I spoke to her class yesterday."

"Okay. Come on, Garnet, let's go. I want to drive by the high school. We seem to be the only two people in town who haven't seen it today." He turned to me for confirmation. "Sounds like they said some pretty nasty things about De-Wayne Evans."

Considering how much Garnet admired DeWayne, Buddy could have been more tactful. Cricket had perked up his ears, too, so I quickly said the first thing that came to my mind. "Speaking of DeWayne, Buddy, have you talked to him? He came by my office yesterday and said there's something he needs to discuss with you."

Before he could answer, Garnet's book bag finally fell. Books, notebooks, pens, and loose papers flew all over the floor. "Oh!" She knelt, her face pink with embarrassment. "I'm sorry."

When Art came rushing to her assistance, the pink deepened. She seemed real glad when Cricket slid off his bench to help, too, although his glare at Art was ferocious.

Except for a frown when it happened, Buddy acted as of nothing was going on at his feet. "Yeah, DeWayne came by the office early this morning." He leaned closer to me and said so no other table could hear, "Did he tell you who he really is? Little Gerrick Lawton. We used to play together as kids." He shook his head ruefully. "He used to be littler than me. I could pick him up. Now he could give me three inches and a good fifty pounds. I sure hate for his sister to bring all that up again about his daddy, though—especially after what happened this morning. Well, gotta run." He headed for the register again, calling impatiently, "Hurry up, Garnet. I need to get back to the office."

By then Art and Cricket had collected her books and papers. When Art walked her toward the front door, Cricket climbed back onto our bench, picked up his yellow crayon and drew a circle, pressing so hard he snapped the crayon. "This bee is going to sting those two mean old dogs."

Art stayed with Garnet only a second, before Myrtle's frown sent him back to work. Garnet gave Buddy a quick sideways look, then hurried back to us. "Could Cricket come home with me for the day? I don't have anything to do, and I'd love to have him." She wasn't dumb, that girl. With Cricket along, Buddy wouldn't be as likely to fuss.

Cricket, of course, was enchanted. He swaggered out like a prince consort. While they waited on the sidewalk for Buddy to finish paying, I signaled Art for another cup of coffee.

"How many cups is that, Mac?" asked Martha the Nurse with a frown.

"I sent the tepid one back, and I'm gonna need all the stimulants I can get when Ike and Chief Muggins hear what I've done." Since Cricket was gone and I could talk freely, I told her about the notebook. "I had it in spitting distance and let it get away."

She reached out and touched my hand. "There are some things we cannot fix no matter how much we want to. You know that. So stop worrying. There's bound to be another way to find out who painted the school."

"Tell that to Ike. He's coming in the door."

He hurried over to our booth, apologizing before he reached us. "Sorry to be late. We had a crash on the highway, and most of our folks are tied up over at the high school, so I had to go. Where's the notebook?"

I felt sick as I described how cleverly Smitty had engineered its retrieval. Ike listened glumly. "I'll get a warrant to search their houses. Maybe we'll find it, but I doubt it." He sighed. "That Smitty's got more smarts than a bee sting."

"Smitty is slime," I corrected him.

"Sure he's slime, but he's smart slime. He's cut from the same cloth as generals or corporate CEOs. If somebody had taken charge of him early—say in the hospital nursery—"

Martha shook her head. "Sometimes I doubt that the womb would have been early enough for Smitty."

"Did you get Tyrone's jacket?" I asked.

He shook his head. "He claims he lost it. I've got deputies alerted to check out Dumpsters, but the force is spread pretty thin right now. Don't take this personally, Judge. We can't win them all."

"At the moment," I pointed out, "we aren't winning any."

⸨ 11 ⸩

I felt pretty useless as I left Myrtle's. "Is there anything I can do to help here?" I asked, but the Almighty was slow with inspiration, so I strolled toward the office. I was barely paying attention to items in shop windows until a ceramic cat in the Second Chance Thrift Store caught my eye. He was black and white, with a pink bow around his neck and a look on his face that said, "You needn't look for the cream. I already found it." Bethany collects ceramic cats, and I knew she'd love that one.

I went into the store and greeted Wilma Roberts, who is almost as tall as she is wide and has kept that store going for twenty years in spite of garage sales and competition from a shop run by the Church of Full and Complete Righteousness across town. She wanted three dollars for the cat, which was probably more than it had cost new. She accepted two, which was all I had left in my wallet. While I paid, I asked, "How's business?"

"'Bout like usual." She shoved bushy brown hair off her forehead. "Some folks give me stuff I can sell and some use me to get rid of junk. Just before you came in, I was unpacking the clothes barrel I keep out back, and somebody put a jacket in there that's so filthy I don't know if I can ever get it clean enough to put on my rack. Looks like it's been worn to paint in."

I've lived long enough to know answers to prayers come

in many forms, but it took all the self-control I possessed not to dance a jig or burst into the "Hallelujah Chorus." "Could I see it? I've been needing a painting jacket."

She broke out with the gasps and wheezes that meant she was laughing. "This one would swallow you whole. It'd be big even on Joe Riddley."

"Could I just see it?" I restrained myself from pushing past her into the back room.

Wilma shrugged. "Sure, but you ain't gonna want it." She waddled through the door and came back almost at once, carrying a khaki jacket. She was right about how filthy it was. She was also right about the paint. It was blue.

"I know somebody who would just love that," I told her honestly. "I'll take it."

"Oh, Judge, I can't sell it to you until I get it cleaned up a little, and I honestly don't know if I can get the paint out. Can you come back Monday?"

"I want it just like it is. I can get it cleaned." I whipped the jacket out of her protesting hands. "I'll give you a check. I don't have any more cash." I also wanted to leave a paper trail.

She grabbed it back and clutched it to her more-than-ample chest. "I ain't priced it yet."

"I'll give you five dollars for it."

Wilma studied that jacket like it had suddenly turned to gold. "I don't know. That's gonna be a mighty fine coat once it's cleaned."

"You said it's junk. I'll give you seven." I whipped out my checkbook.

"You couldn't make it ten, could you?"

"Nope, I've already written the check." If Wilma didn't come down on her prices, shopping at a superstore might be cheaper.

She folded the jacket like it was made of cashmere and put it in a plastic bag recycled from one of our two grocery stores in town. The logo read SHOP SMART.

"I did," I assured the Boss Upstairs as I headed toward the police station.

Isaac appreciated the joke and assured me the jacket was enough to pick up Tyrone for questioning. I just wished we could find some evidence on which to pick up Smitty. Was there anybody who might know if he could draw?

My question was answered that afternoon when Ridd flopped down in my wing chair in a manner guaranteed to eventually shatter its legs. "Some days, it's a good thing I don't believe in firearms, or I'd shoot somebody's head off," he growled, sounding just like his daddy.

"Got a particular head in mind, or will anybody's do?"

"It's not a joking matter, Mama."

"I know it's not. Did you see DeWayne?"

"Yeah, but he'd already seen the school before I found him. He was shaking so bad he could hardly stand up, and he's threatening to pack his bags and move. I told him he needs to stand and fight, but he says he's already gone through people staring at him and whispering behind his back, and he isn't up to doing it again."

Ridd sounded so dejected, I offered him a sliver of hope. "Ike's closing in on the perpetrators. We're pretty sure it was Smitty's gang."

One corner of his mouth lifted. "It sure wasn't Smitty who drew the picture. I had him for geometry, and he can't draw a straight line. Tyrone might have, now. The graphics-art teacher says he's got a lot of talent. He did caricatures for last year's yearbook, and they were incredible."

I described the notebook, and immediately Ridd said, "That's Tyrone's. He carries it everywhere, in his jacket pocket."

I can't tell you how bad that made me feel. I liked Tyrone, but he'd gotten himself into some pretty hot water. "How long's he been running around with Smitty?"

"Not long—since spring, I think. Tyrone's not bad. He's just easily led."

I reached for the phone. "Drawing those pictures on the school was bad, son. He didn't have to follow Smitty's lead. Do you still have last year's yearbook?" He nodded as Ike answered the phone.

Before I could say a word, Ike crowed, "We got the note-book, Judge! Found it in a Dumpster over by the school. The cover's been wiped, but the inside pages have Tyrone's prints all over them. Found somebody who sold Willie Keller the spray paint, too."

"There's got to be evidence somewhere pointing to Smitty. You and I both know Tyrone and Willie didn't think up all that mess."

"Smitty may have thought it up, but he wasn't there—at least according to Willie. Willie swears Smitty was over at his house playing video games from six last night until four this morning, then crashed on his living-room sofa—which alibis Willie, too, of course."

"Wet Willie would swear a black horse was white if somebody put him up to it."

"Maybe, but we can't disprove it this time. Willie's mother corroborates that Smitty was asleep on her couch when she got home at eight after working the night shift at the nursing home. She's an aide." Ike sighed. "At least we got Tyrone. He's at the youth detention center until his hear-ing tomorrow."

"You and I both know Smitty had to put him up to it. Have you asked him about that?"

Isaac would never have snapped at me if he hadn't been under pressure. "Of course I asked him, but he's not talking, and you know as well as I do that we can't bring Smitty in without evidence or a witness."

"I have another question. How could our patrol cars miss seeing somebody painting that building? It must have taken well over an hour." Isaac didn't answer. "We do still have night patrols, don't we?"

Ike was quiet so long, I thought he'd hung up. Finally he

admitted, "Not right now. The chief feels they are an unnecessary expense. Says we don't get much crime at night."

"Then how come I get called out of bed to go down to the jail several nights a week? And what does he call last night's episode—a party?" We both knew I was just letting off steam. Ike would never say anything derogatory about a senior officer.

"How's Chief Muggins using all that money he's saving?" I knew the answer as soon as I asked the question. Good thing, because Ike wouldn't have answered that, either. He didn't have to. It was as clear as my newly washed window that Chief Muggins was able to drive a fancy new cruiser because he was leaving our town unprotected at night.

Later that afternoon I held a probable cause hearing for a woman who had set a county record in passing bad checks. Afterwards, I ran into Judge Roland, a juvenile-court judge and an elder in our church. When we'd exchanged those little pleasantries that grease the wheels of civilized society, he asked, "You know Tyrone Noland, don't you?"

"A little. He used to sweep up for us to earn spending money."

Judge Roland shook his head in dismay. "I sure was sorry to get a call about him this afternoon. I had him in a Webelo Scout troop years ago, soon after his daddy left. When I heard his name, all I could think of was 'Why haven't I kept up with that boy all these years?' "

"Does it ever feel to you like we're letting kids slip through our fingers around here without noticing? We all get so busy. Years pass—"

"—and a child doesn't have many years before he's an adult. What bothers me most is, I look back and wonder what I've been so busy doing that was more important. Tell me, Mac, given that most of the evidence is circumstantial but real good, would you have released him to his mother, or kept him until his detention hearing tomorrow?"

I thought it over. "Sending him home would really mean sending him right back to the boys who got him into all this trouble. I think I'd have put the fear of God into him, sent him to the youth-detention center, and then gone home to pray."

He clapped me on the shoulder. "I did the first two, but hadn't thought to do the third. Let's both pray for Tyrone. He needs it."

The problem is, once I've prayed for somebody, I begin to feel responsible for him. So when I had to go to the jail late that afternoon to set bond in a marijuana possession case, I found myself swinging by the YDC—better known as juvey—on my way back to the store. Tyrone was sitting by himself in one corner of a common room that had seen a lot of living.

His hair hung down beside his face like a black shade. He didn't look up when I moseyed over and said, "Hello, Tyrone. They treating you all right?"

"I'm okay." He picked at a scab on one finger.

I looked around. A bored guard was sitting near the door. Two kids were sprawled on a sagging couch watching TV. I figured it was turned that high to accommodate their damaged hearing. Another three were playing cards at a table so beat up it could be sold as distressed furniture. "You got everything you need?"

He shrugged. "I need to get out of here."

I was tempted to say something quick and reassuring and head back to work, but the slump of his shoulders made me perch on a very lumpy chair. "I can't ask you if you painted the school, but I saw your notebook. Why'd you throw it away?"

His face flushed. "I didn't! I haven't seen it since I left it at Myrtle's."

"Nonsense. I saw you all come back for it. Smitty drew our attention while you and Willie picked up the notebook."

He hung his head. "We didn't get it. Somebody else already took it."

"That won't wash," I told him flatly. "I was there."

"You didn't see me get that notebook," he persisted stubbornly.

We weren't getting anywhere, so I changed direction. "You're a real good artist. Do you know that?" All I got was another shrug. "Ridd says your art teacher thinks you could become a professional if you want to."

A glint of something like pride flickered in his eyes, but it quickly died. "I'd have to go to college. I ain't got the grades or the money."

"You're not dumb," I reminded him. "You used to make all A's. You showed me your report cards, remember?" He used to come stumbling in, hardly able to get inside before waving them at Joe Riddley and me.

He flushed again, probably embarrassed I'd brought that up. Boys hate to be reminded of their childhoods. "High school's real hard."

"How about if I make you a deal?" He slewed his eyes my way, but he didn't say a word. "Since it's a first offense without weapons or danger to yourself or others, they'll probably just make you work around the school a few hours. Someday soon, I want you to come to my office and we'll talk to Joe Riddley. Maybe we can give you a job after school this next year and help you bring up your grades— even help you figure out a way to go to art school. If that's what you want," I added hastily. I wouldn't worry right then how we'd hire somebody else if the superstore took a chunk of our business.

"That'd be all right." Knowing teenage boys, I translated that into ecstatic acceptance.

"The only stipulation will be that you stop hanging around Smitty. He's poison and we both know it. If he was part of that mess over at the school, you tell the judge. You hear me?"

Tyrone pulled away as if I'd prodded him with an electric rod. "Smitty's okay." He didn't look at me when he said it, though.

"He's not okay, and it's not okay for you guys to keep protecting him. He's using you. Can't you see that?"

He looked over his shoulder at the kids playing cards. "Smitty's okay. He wasn't there." He spoke louder than he had before. I saw one of the cardsharps look our way, a boy with a hard face and smoldering eyes. His gaze flicked Tyrone like a whip, then returned to his cards.

I leaned closer. "One of his friends? You still need to talk, Tyrone. Somebody's got to. If they don't, this will go on for years and years. Believe me, I know. It takes courage, but—"

"You don't know jack." He gave the card table another quick, nervous look. One foot drummed the floor. I could tell he was wishing I'd pack up and leave.

I stood. "I know more than you think. Do you need anything?" He shook his head. "Maybe another notebook and a pen?" His nod was almost imperceptible, but I patted his shoulder. "You got it. I'll bring them by on my way home tonight. Hang in there."

I was halfway across the room before I heard one hoarse word behind me. "Thanks."

That June was cooler than usual, so the gnats weren't too bad. Hopemore lies south of the Georgia gnat line, so we spend a lot of summer evenings fanning away those vicious little no-see-ums. As Joe Riddley and I climbed into bed that night, the sweetness of new crops and fresh-mown grass floated in our open windows and our sheets smelled like sunshine and fresh air.

"Tell me something from a man's point of view," I asked before Joe Riddley could fall asleep. "What would make a big, strong boy like Tyrone scared of a weasel like Smitty?"

"Smitty either has something on him—something Tyrone is scared people will find out—or he's threatened somebody Tyrone cares about. His mother, maybe. You think Tyrone's scared?"

"I don't know. But I do know Tyrone is sitting in juvey right now lying for Smitty. We've got to do something before Smitty takes over this town. If he's this bad at seventeen, what will he be like at thirty?"

"Dead. That sort don't live to see their grandchildren. But let's think about it tomorrow." He turned over and faked a snore. Poor thing, he didn't have the energy or the stamina he'd had before he got shot.

I wasn't the least bit sleepy, though. "I sure am sorry for folks who never open their windows or hang out their clothes." If I could get him to talk a little, maybe I'd get sleepy, too. "They sure miss a lot of good smells."

He turned back over. "You want good? I'll show you good." He held out one arm and I rolled happily toward him. Forget what I said about his stamina.

❧ 12 ❦

Saturday morning, Joe Riddley got up before seven, banging around getting ready for our church's monthly men's prayer breakfast. He hates to get up any day, and when he has to be somewhere early on a Saturday, he wants the world to give him credit. I was wide-awake by the time he left, so I figured I might as well go down and eat.

I was enjoying my second cup of coffee, feeding scraps of toast to Lulu while Bo ate on his own place mat, when I heard a car turn in. In a minute, Ronnie carried in an overflowing laundry basket. Clarinda puffed in behind him with another.

"More laundry with this boy at home," she complained. "I'd have done it yesterday, like usual, but I went from here to a Sisterhood meeting and didn't want my underwear on display if somebody went in my trunk." She's real sensitive about anybody seeing her underwear. If my bras were that size, I'd wave them from the housetop.

While she put a load in the washer, I fetched Ronnie some coffee. "Did you and Yasheika get everything sorted out? I heard she was upset with you on Wednesday."

He stirred sugar in his coffee with a wry grin. "So what's new? That woman was born under an upsetting star. She came down here yelling that I couldn't work for a white man who put her daddy in jail. I didn't know her daddy. If he's anything like her, maybe he deserved to go—whoever sent him." He stopped and peered into his coffee like he'd lost something precious at the bottom. I knew we were both thinking of his own daddy right then. "But she drove off in a manner guaranteed to get her arrested, killed, or both, and I knew that either would upset DeWayne, so I went after her and at least got her calmed down enough to admit it's none of her business who I work for. Did you know her daddy?"

I was surprised at that sudden twist in the conversation.. "Yeah. He was convicted of killing a little girl, Buddy's best friend." I was filling him in on the story when Clarinda came back.

"You talking about Gerrick Lawton? What's got you on to him all of a sudden?"

"DeWayne and Yasheika are his children."

"Lordy!" She breathed out the word like her lungs were collapsing, and her legs must have collapsed at the same time, because she dropped heavily into a chair. As I told Ronnie the story, she kept up a constant stream of "Lordy, lordy, lordy"—the Clarinda Standard Version of what the Bible calls "prayers too deep for words." When I finished, she pooched out her lips like she does when she's thinking hard. "That girl was the little one with all those braids Janey used to keep?"

I nodded.

"Lordy!" She added to Ronnie, in a normal voice, "you 'n' her used to play real good."

"I got smart since then." He stood. "I've also got things to do. When do you want me to come back for you?" Before she could answer, his cell phone rang. "Hey!" he said as soon as he heard a voice. Then he gave a sharp cry of disbelief. "Did you call the police? Okay, you call them and I'll get over there." Wherever he was going, he didn't sound real thrilled.

He hung up and headed for the door, calling over his shoulder, "Got to go. I'll call you in a little while."

Clarinda and I collided, trying to follow him out the back

door at the same time. "What's the matter?" we called in unison. We truly have been together too long.

He was already getting in his car. "That was DeWayne on his cell phone. Somebody's painted up his house. He saw it as he was leaving for school. He has a meeting and has to get ready for Monday, so he can't stay, but he's calling the police and he wants me to go stay with Yasheika until the police get there." He backed down the driveway and spurted gravel as he roared toward the highway.

Clarinda hurried inside, grabbed my pocketbook and thrust it at me. "Go after him. He don't know the first thing about dealing with somethin' like that. And you know how they fight. That girl could kill him before he tells her why he's there."

I am so used to following her orders, I was at the highway before I remembered I don't know the first thing about dealing with "something like that," either.

I called Ridd on the way, to get directions. Naturally, he wanted to know why I needed them and was as appalled as the rest of us, by the news. "I'll come as soon as I can," he promised.

DeWayne was renting a pretty yellow house with two tall poplars, lots of azaleas, and mounds of red, coral, pink, and white impatiens along the walk. The house wasn't pretty right then, though. Nasty red and blue words were sprayed all over the front, interspersed with swastikas. Yasheika and Ronnie stood on the narrow concrete porch, arguing. The way they both waved their arms, it looked any minute now one of them would take off and fly. I sure wished they got along better. It would make DeWayne's life a lot simpler, for one thing. However, I wasn't there to make peace, I was there to—what? I had no idea what Clarinda thought I could do, but I'd better climb out of the car and start doing it.

Chief Charlie Muggins's supercruiser wailed in behind me as I opened my door. I saw curtains twitch up and down the street, but nobody came out. I figured the neighbors didn't want any more contact with the police than necessary. Given some of Charlie's biases, they were wise.

"Mornin', Judge." Chief Muggins tipped his hat just enough for me to see the gleam of his yellow hair, then swaggered ahead of me up the walk. "You folks got some trouble?"

Yasheika was mad enough to cry. "*I've* got some trouble." She glared at Ronnie to make sure he didn't claim a share. "Look at this mess." She stepped aside and I saw the worst of all: four bloodred words sprawled on the door's white face: *Leave town or die!*

I felt just sick. Hopemore needed DeWayne and Yasheika a lot more than we needed whoever had made that mess.

"It had to have happened after one." Her eyes flickered with a fear I could identify with. I'd have been terrified to know I'd been sleeping inside while somebody sprayed that much hate all around me. "DeWayne and I went to Augusta after ball practice. It was one when we got back, and the house was all right then."

Chief Muggins glanced at the door and scanned the rest of the house, looking about as concerned as if he'd been called out to inspect the gutters. "You didn't hear anything?"

"No, sir. We went straight to bed. Our bedrooms are at the back and we have window air conditioners that make a lot of noise. I've told DeWayne a dozen times to get a dog, but he says they're too much trouble."

Chief Muggins hitched up his pants and looked around. "Where is he?" He'd always rather deal with a man than a woman.

The way her lip curled, Yasheika knew that already. "He left before I got up. Summer school starts Monday, and with all the ball practices, he's late getting ready. He didn't wake me, but he didn't need to go calling Ronnie, either."

"He was worried about you." Ronnie turned away, but I saw how scared his eyes were, too. He'd grown up in Hopemore and had never seen anything like this. What was this epidemic in our little town? And what must it be like for

Yasheika and Ronnie, knowing somebody out there hated them so much for nothing but the color of their skin? I literally could not imagine. But I sure could worry. It might be Clarinda's house next, or Isaac's. I took a few deep breaths to calm my stomach.

Chief Muggins touched the door gingerly, but the paint was dry. "Tyrone Noland got out of YDC yesterday. We'll talk to him. You keep watch tonight to see if they come back." He turned on his heel and nearly knocked me down in his hurry to get back to his car.

"That's all?" Yasheika yelled in disbelief. "You aren't going to check for fingerprints or look for footprints or anything?" He climbed in and drove away like her voice was a puff of wind.

"Welcome to Georgia." Ronnie took Yasheika's elbow. "You can't stay here. Grandmama is down at Miss Mac's. I'll take you there, then come back and start painting."

She jerked away from his grasp. "I can paint as well as you, if that's what's called for, but I think the landlord ought to be notified first."

I ignored their squabbles and reached for my cell phone. "Chief Muggins doesn't represent all of Georgia, and you both know it," I said angrily. In a minute I had Isaac on the line.

"I can't go over the chief's head," he protested when I explained.

"Tell him you heard the newspaper is coming over. You just did, because I'm about to call them. A couple of deputies investigating would make a better picture for next week's paper than an angry young woman complaining that the police didn't do a thing."

The police arrived just ahead of the reporter, and I was glad to see they immediately strung yellow plastic tape and took the crime scene seriously.

Ridd pulled in behind them and surveyed the damage with disgust. "Is there anything I can do here?"

Yasheika looked at the deputies and at Ronnie, then shrugged. "Not that I can think of."

"Is DeWayne still over at the school?" When she nodded, he climbed back in his car. "Then I'll go see if he's all right."

"I'll be right behind you." I headed to my Nissan.

If you're asking, as Chief Muggins eventually would, why I went with Ridd, I don't know. But I couldn't just go on to work as if nothing had happened.

Anybody who believes teachers work only during school hours doesn't know a thing about teaching. In an hour or so, the high school would fill with teachers getting ready for summer school. That early, though, the faculty parking lot was empty except for DeWayne's blue Honda and a white car belonging to school security. Only a few smears remained on the brick front to show where paint had been, but that caricature was permanently etched in my memory. It's not easy to get rid of a picture of evil once you've seen it.

"We'll have to go in the front door. That's the only one they open on Saturdays," Ridd said, and he headed off at a fast lope. My boys keep forgetting their legs outgrew mine.

I have never liked jogging, particularly after breakfast. As I thudded along after him, my whole body kept up a steady protest. I went in the door a minute after he did, panting so loud I was embarrassed to see Clint Hicks, the security guard, propped on the hind legs of a folding chair in the front hall. Ridd was already over at the faculty mailboxes, automatically pulling out a handful of fliers.

"Good morning, Clint," I said, trying not to gasp.

Clint had graduated two years before with plans to join the Hopemore Police Department, in spite of a spectacularly unimpressive high-school career. I'd heard he had flunked his test and was currently working school security. The way he was propped in the chair cleaning his fingernails with a key, I could tell he didn't consider it the career of his dreams. He grunted, but didn't bother to look up. If we'd been burglars coming for the computers, I got the impression he'd have let us take them so long as we didn't ask him to carry anything.

"You know where Mr. Evans is?" Ridd asked.

Clint's fingernails required most of his attention, but he managed to jerk his head in the general direction of the math and science wing the school board had tacked on behind the gym a few years before. "Came in a little while ago and headed thataway."

Ridd and I headed thataway, too.

That stale, empty school scent of chalk dust, sweaty children, musty books, and bathrooms was as thick as water as I ploughed through it. I could hear my breath coming short and fast. Up ahead, Ridd's running shoes made a soft *thud, thud, thud* while my own square heels clattered and echoed on the hard tile floors. The effect was downright eerie, and the place seemed enormous without students. I wished Ridd would wait up for me. I got to the corner just in time to see him taking the shortcut through the gym. A broad band of sunlight lay across the hall where he'd at least left the door open for me.

He went around the edges of the floor like he was supposed to, but I was feeling obstreperous enough to walk straight across, defying the voices of long-dead gym teachers who shouted in my head, "Get off that floor in your street shoes!"

Maybe today's gym teachers weren't that strict. Somebody had left the end of a coil of yellow rope dangling across the floor.

I got to the back hall in time to see Ridd entering a room halfway down, calling, "DeWayne? DeWayne!" I could tell by the way his voice echoed that there wasn't anybody there.

I followed him anyway, to a large classroom with wide black Formica lab tables and stools instead of student desks. I paused at the door, puzzled by the faint smell of smoke. Ridd, who is not always the most observant of people, was sniffing, too. "He must have been using the Bunsen burner.

DeWayne? DeWayne!" He opened a connecting door to the next classroom and called again. "DeWayne?"

I followed my nose toward the front lab table, which ran crossways to the others. A pile of ashes still sent up faint spirals of smoke in the bottom of a metal wastebasket. On top was one small unburned piece of notebook paper with the letters *ped* still clear, in purple ink.

"What are you doing?" Ridd demanded irritably.

I straightened up and pressed one hand against a stiff place in my spine. "Checking to be sure this fire is out. Where's DeWayne?"

Ridd looked around the windowless room. "Maybe he went back to the house and we just missed him."

"He could have used that door." Unlike the days when I was in school and the school had two exits, this new wing had been built to fire codes and had an exit door in every other room, always kept locked, but with a safety bar to open it. I moseyed over and peered out the window. It looked onto a grassy side yard and a sidewalk that led to the street running beside the school. I saw no sign of DeWayne, nor any reason he'd have gone out that way.

"He's left his wallet and keys," Ridd reported.

I turned and saw them on the desk. "Not real smart, if Clint's the only security in the building."

"You got that right. Maybe he's in the boys' locker room. It's got the nearest bathroom. I'll check. I hate to leave without making sure he's okay."

After Ridd headed down the hall, I felt uneasy. Surely I was too old to feel like a student hanging out in a classroom she wasn't supposed to be in, so what was bothering me? The wallet and keys. Why would anybody leave them lying out like that? I strolled over to the desk and saw a folded piece of paper beneath them, with Yasheika's name on it in block letters. That scared the living daylights out of me. Why would DeWayne be writing Yasheika when she was two miles away?

I was battling temptation to read the note and about to

lose when I heard Ridd pull open the heavy door of the locker room and call, "Anybody in here?" That brought me to my senses. I sure didn't want DeWayne coming in and finding me reading his mail. I headed to the hall in time to see Ridd stick his head in the door as he called again, "Anybody he—?"

He cut off midword, gave a lurch, and clutched the door for support. "No! Oh, God, no!" He clung to that doorframe and his knees buckled.

I will never know how I covered the distance so fast, but I caught him before he slid to the floor. That was enough to stiffen his knees just a little. I held him tight around the waist and peered past him.

I'm no expert on locker rooms, particularly boys' locker rooms, but this one seemed extremely gray, high, and dim. The only light came from a skylight. Pipes ran along the ceiling.

From one of those pipes DeWayne Evans hung at the end of a yellow rope. He was still swinging.

❧ 13 ❧

The world blurred around the edges and my lungs forgot how to function. I let Ridd go and held on to the other side of the door, unable to breathe.

Do you know how long a woman can live without oxygen? That's how long I stared at DeWayne swinging from that yellow rope. I know it was yellow, because I kept looking at it so I didn't have to look at his poor swollen face. Finally I managed to suck enough air into my lungs to think halfway straight. Was he dead, or merely dying? There was little doubt he was dead. Urine had darkened the front of his jeans, and his face—well, he was almost certainly dead. But somebody had to make sure, and Ridd was busy throwing up all over the locker-room floor. He's always had a sensitive stomach.

DeWayne's right arm was still warm, but limp. I found no pulse, but shoved up the expandable watchband on his left arm and tried that wrist to be sure. Behind me Ridd was still retching.

I reached for my cell phone and called 911. The dispatcher promised to send help right away. *Help?* It was an unfortunate choice of words. Poor DeWayne would never need help again. Yet as I looked up through a blur of tears, I couldn't help thinking that death gave him freedom and dignity, too. Nothing could ever hurt him again.

I was a sopping, sobbing mess by that time.

"Go home," Ridd said weakly. He rubbed a hand across his mouth and looked in embarrassment at the mess on the floor. "I'll—"

"Get some towels to clean that up."

He stumbled toward the sinks and I stepped back into the hall to get away from the foul smells in that close air. The building seemed bigger than ever, and emptier. What if De-Wayne hadn't killed himself? It wouldn't be the first murder made to look like suicide. Given how warm he was, a killer hadn't had much time to get away. Had he heard us? I pressed my back to the wall and nearly wore my neck out trying to watch both ends of the hall at once. Where was Clint? Why hadn't he come running when he heard Ridd's cry?

Running apparently wasn't one of Clint's speeds. It was several minutes before I heard him call through the gym, "Hey! You folks all right? I thought I heard a yell."

"We're fine," I called back, "but Mr. Evans isn't. The emergency squad is on its way." I went down to the gym door and saw him in the doorway across the way.

"Is he sick? I'm not supposed to leave the door after I open up, you know." He eased a couple of steps toward me, then craned his head, listening—maybe in case a crowd had arrived in the past half minute.

"He's had an accident," I said.

Clint rocked on his shoes, torn between curiosity and responsibility.

"Go back to the front to let in the EMTs. We'll take care of things here," I promised.

"I could come for a minute, if he needs me." He sidled another step my way.

"He doesn't need you," I told him honestly. "Go back to the door." When he took another step, I flapped a hand at him. "Go on." He obeyed, but I could tell he didn't like it.

I found Ridd on the floor with a wad of wet paper towels, smearing the mess worse. He had his back to DeWayne, but that's where his mind was, because his first words were, "You don't reckon DeWayne was lynched, do you, Mama?"

The question shocked me, but once he'd said it, I had to admit it was possible. Something real ugly had been unleashed in Hopemore that week. "I sure hope not, hon. But can you think of any reason DeWayne would want to kill himself?"

"Seemed to me like everything was going great—until Thursday. He said then that he couldn't stand to have people pointing at him and whispering behind his back. Maybe he saw his house this morning and it was just too much."

"I can see that making him mad, or convincing him to move, but do you really think it would be enough to make him do—this?" I waved a hand toward DeWayne, then let it drop.

Ridd looked down at the wet mess on the floor like he couldn't quite figure out what to do next. "Maybe some dry towels?" I suggested, heading to the sink.

Silently, we cleaned up his mess together. When we'd finished, we stood and looked without a word at the figure above us. Ridd moved so close to me I could feel his body heat through his shirt. I felt cold, and I pressed against him to get warm. He shuddered.

"M-Mama?" He choked on the word. When I looked up, tears were streaming down his face. Several thoughts popped into my head, but none of them would provide one speck of comfort. I pulled him to me like he was two years old, and we sobbed together.

Sirens wailed in the distance. I jerked two tissues from my pocketbook, mopped my eyes with one and handed Ridd the other. He blew his nose and we headed through the gym to show the police where to come.

Chief Muggins and a deputy strode down the hall in our direction. His first words were, "You sure get around, Judge. What's your problem now?"

I stepped behind Ridd. "It's your problem. We just found it. Tell him, Ridd."

"Come to the locker room," he said, leading the way.

Chief Muggins opened the door and whistled. "Isn't that the fella whose house got messed up, the one who's been coaching the Honeybees? Did he do himself in, or did somebody string him up and hope we'd think it was suicide?" He looked at me and narrowed his eyes—probably calculating whether I had the strength to haul DeWayne up by the neck.

Chief Muggins closed the door and got on his phone to summon his crew. Then he folded his arms and stared down at me. "So why'd you come over here?"

I looked at Ridd so he'd take the lead again. "We came to see how DeWayne was taking it that somebody painted his house," he explained.

"Well, now you know," Charlie said callously. He whistled through his teeth, which I guess was supposed to impress us that he was thinking. "Seems like a pretty strong reaction, though, doesn't it? Has anybody meddled with the body?" He was looking at me again.

"I checked his pulse," I admitted.

"You didn't touch anything else?" His voice implied I'd tromped all over the scene dragging a string of red herrings across his trail.

"Just both wrists, to be sure he was dead. And I moved his watch up a little. But before we found him here, we were in his room. His wallet and keys are there along with a note to his sister."

"You read it?"

"Of course not." I spoke with more heat than I intended, and knew I was getting pink. Heck, I felt as guilty as if I *had* read the darned thing, when all I'd done was consider it.

Thank goodness a deputy stuck his head around the corner right then. "Slade Rutherford is here, from the paper. Can he come back?"

Chief Muggins nodded. "I'll talk to him in a minute." He turned back to Ridd and me. "I'll see that Mr. Evans's sister gets her note. You all come by the station later and give statements." I knew why he wanted us gone. He didn't want to share his glory in next week's *Statesman*.

The arrival of real police had galvanized Clint. He was standing when we got to the front door, and he held up one hand. "I'll need to take your names and phone numbers in case the police want to contact you. There's been an accident."

"Cool it, Clint," Ridd said shortly. "We talked to them already."

Clint looked wistfully down the hall, which had yellow crime tape across it now. Poor thing, it wasn't fun being just outside the action. "Keep up the good work," I encouraged him.

The parking lot was beginning to fill with folks who wanted to know what was going on. I saw Art Franklin peering out the window of a desperately old Ford at the front curb. Smitty and Willie slouched against a poplar over in one corner of the school yard. Brandi's family clustered under a big oak. Even Sara Meg was on the edge of the crowd, peering over heads.

Wonder of wonders, Ridd walked beside me all the way to my car and held my door. "I guess I'd better go tell Yasheika." He sighed. "You going on to work or back home?"

"Work, I guess. I can't think of anything better to do right this minute. And don't narrow your eyes at me like that, hon. It makes you look like Chief Muggins."

"You won't start poking around or anything? You'll let them take care of this? I don't want you meddling. You nearly got yourself killed last spring, remember." Ridd never has been fond of what he calls my "messing around with murder."

"I'm not meddling." Maybe my voice was a little testy, but that was the second time in a very short time that somebody had accused me of meddling. Still, Ridd had no call to back away holding up his hands like I was dangerous.

"Don't get your dander up. I just don't want you getting yourself in trouble."

"I told you, I'm going to work. You go tell Yasheika. And

tell her if she wants to sleep at our place tonight, she's welcome."

Maybe I did spurt a little gravel as I drove away, but he had no right to speak to me like that. I wasn't going to do any investigating, except on the computer. Any sensible person would want to know if there was anything on the Internet that DeWayne didn't want folks to know about.

I didn't see much else to investigate except what it is that makes people so hateful to other people, and folks a lot smarter than me have wondered about that for a very long time.

⊰ 14 ⊱

I didn't get to the computer right away, because Bethany met me as I came in the side door. Her hair was messy, her yellow T-shirt streaked with dust. "Hey, Me-mama, I'm done. And you know what? Our team is gonna be fantastic, even without Hollis. Coach Evans says we have a good chance to win the district."

I stared at her, appalled. I'd forgotten who else needed to know about DeWayne besides Yasheika: his team.

Bethany had volunteered to come in that morning to finish the inventory that Monday's storm and Thursday's graffiti had interrupted. Her blue bike was propped next to our office door, so she must have ridden over early and gone straight to work. I didn't want to blurt out my news in front of clerks and customers, so I put an arm around her waist and steered her toward the office, asking the first thing that came to mind. "Why isn't Hollis on the team? You were both picked."

Bethany made a little noise of disgust. "She *says* she's got too much to do, but I don't know the real reason. She's acting real weird right now. Hardly ever leaves her house except to drive Garnet to class and go to work."

"Wasn't everything okay Thursday?"

"Not really. I rode with her to take Garnet to school and hung out at the pool while she taught swimming lessons. After that, she said she had to go get Garnet, so we drove

back to the college, but Garnet wasn't there. Hollis got furious. She drove so fast going home, I was scared, and when
we got to their house and found Garnet coloring with
Cricket, of all people, Hollis really yelled at her. Garnet said
she'd gotten a ride from school to Myrtle's and brought
Cricket home from there to play for the afternoon." Bethany
interrupted herself to say in an accusing voice, "They said
you and Mama were over there eating pie."

"We do that occasionally," I agreed. "I'll take you sometime."

"Okay. Well, then Hollis decided to go back to work, but
we couldn't talk while she was on lifeguard duty. Afterwards, at her house, we went up to her room while Cricket
and Garnet played the piano, and I asked what was the matter, but she wouldn't tell me. She got mad that I even asked."
Bethany sighed. "She's weirder than Garnet right now.
You'd think she was hiding out or something." She reached
for her bike. "Well, I better go. Mama's working, and I told
Daddy I'd watch Cricket this afternoon so he can cut hay."

I steered her toward the office door. "Come in a minute,
first. We need to talk."

She gave me a puzzled look. "I did the inventory exactly
the way you said."

"This isn't about the inventory. Come in and sit down." I
held the door.

Bo squawked a welcome from the curtain rod. Cricket sat
in my chair, drawing. Joe Riddley looked up from a seed
catalogue. "Help, Crick, we're being invaded by female re-
lations." He added, for my benefit, "Ridd lit out somewhere
this morning, and Martha got called in to work early, so
we've got a helper until his daddy comes looking for him."
I could tell Joe Riddley hadn't heard about DeWayne any
more than Bethany had.

Cricket gave me a quick glance and bent back to his
crayons. "I'll be finished in a minute."

I picked him up and headed for the door. "You're finished
right now. We need you out front. Charlene? Don't you need

a helper at the counter?" Cricket got a kick out of standing on a chair at the register, taking money and putting it in the right places in the drawer. Charlene, whose grandchildren lived in Atlanta, kept assuring us she liked having his help.

"Don't you mess up my picture," he warned as he headed to work.

Bethany dropped into the wing chair. "What's the matter?" Her eyes were wary.

I closed the door and sat in my own chair. "I've got something to tell you both. DeWayne Evans—" I started to say "died" but that wasn't the truth and Bethany would hear it soon enough. I'd rather she heard it from somebody who loved her. "DeWayne Evans hanged himself this morning."

Her shoulders hunched to shield her from what I was saying and she gave a yelp of disbelief.

Joe Riddley swivelled my way. "What happened? How'd you find out?"

"Ronnie brought Clarinda to do her wash this morning and DeWayne called him to say their front door got painted last night, like the school."

"No!" Bethany clenched her fists to shut out this further pain. Tears trembled on her lower lids and spilled over. "Who'd do a thing like that? And why would he—he—"

"We don't know yet. The police are checking things out. I went with Ronnie to see the house, and your daddy came over and said we ought to go see if DeWayne was—all right." My voice wobbled. "So we went to the school, and we—we found him." I had to stop. My lungs weren't working again.

"Daddy knows? He knew and he didn't come tell me? He didn't have the decency to come tell me?" She shook with rage. "It's not true! It's not! It's not!" She flailed her arms so, Bo swooped overhead, in danger of hurting himself. I held up my arm for a perch while Joe Riddley pinioned Bethany's arms to keep her from flinging herself to the floor.

He scooped her up like she was three years old. "Come here, sugar." He held her on his lap like he used to, a big sprawling thing now with a tiny girl's broken heart. As she wept against his shoulder, he stroked her hair.

I stroked Bo's back and set him gently on my desk when he grew calm. My own eyes stung. When I finally trusted myself to speak, I said, "We need to think about the rest of the team. Somebody needs to get them together and tell them before they find out some other way."

That quieted Bethany. She has always been good at thinking about other people as well as herself. "They're gonna die," she whispered, then realized what she'd said and gasped. "He can't have done that, Me-mama. Somebody must have killed him. He didn't have any reason to do it. He didn't!" She took a deep breath and wailed, "I want my mama!"

I nudged Bo away from my phone and dialed the emergency room. "Martha? I know you're working, honey, but we need you real bad at our office right now. Bethany's just heard that DeWayne Evans killed himself this morning, and she's pretty upset."

"DeWayne?" Even Martha, who sees a lot of violence, was shocked. "I heard about his house—one of the deputies came by for coffee—but nobody said a thing about De-Wayne." Our law enforcement officers drink so much coffee in the emergency-room nurses' station after they bring folks in, they tend to stop by for breaks on other days, too. Martha often brags that good coffee keeps her abreast of the news.

This time her sources were late. "He wasn't found until half an hour ago. I know, because Ridd and I found him. It wasn't the best morning either of us has had lately."

"Tell Mama to come," Bethany whimpered from her granddaddy's lap. "I need her."

"Did you hear that?"

"I heard it. As soon as I can get somebody to cover for me, I'll be right over."

Once she knew her mama was coming, Bethany calmed down and accepted my offer of a Coke. Then she asked, "Could I use your cell phone for a minute, Me-mama?"

"There's a phone right there." Joe Riddley nodded toward his desk.

"Yeah, but this is kinda private." When I handed her the phone she left the office, already dialing. I heard her voice faintly through our thin old walls. "Hello, Todd? The awfullest thing has happened." We didn't see her again until her mother arrived.

Bless Martha's heart. While she was waiting for her replacement to come in, she had called somebody from the school who was trained in grief counseling. "He's going to call all the team, have them meet at our house, and tell them together," she reported when she arrived. "He'll be there when we get home." Her face had been serious, but now it broke into a wry smile. "I saw my younger offspring running the store. Can you keep him awhile longer?"

"We'll keep him until suppertime," Joe Riddley offered. "Good counter help's hard to come by."

Bethany might be five inches taller than her mother by now, but she clung to Martha's arm as they left.

Joe Riddley waited until the door closed behind them, then demanded, "How come you always land up in the middle of these things? That takes real talent."

"Don't you fuss at me, or you'll have me crying on your lap like Bethany."

"Not to worry. Not to worry," Bo begged anxiously.

Joe Riddley held out his arms. "In that case, I'll fuss. Come here."

I didn't climb in his lap—that wouldn't look dignified if somebody passed our door and looked in. But I did go over and rest my head on his shoulder for a while. Some days are heavier to carry than others.

Clarinda doesn't work Saturdays, except to do her own laundry if she hasn't gotten to it sooner, so we generally eat dinner at Myrtle's. That day, I couldn't stand the idea of meeting people and hearing them talk about DeWayne, so I suggested that Joe Riddley and Cricket go down to Hardee's

and bring back hamburgers to eat in our office. As soon as
they left, I turned to the computer.

The Internet is a fearsome thing. It holds enough dirt
about people to create another planet and spews it willingly
for anybody able to work a mouse. All I had to do was type
in *DeWayne Evans* and it referred me in seconds to twenty-
two articles. Nine were about the right DeWayne.

Two were from recent editions of the *Statesman*. I
preened to think our little paper went all over the world via
the Internet, whether anybody read it or not. The next article
was about DeWayne's previous baseball team winning the
state championship. I doubted he'd killed himself over any
of those, so I pulled up the next listing. That's where I found
what I was looking for: COLLEGE ATHLETE ACCUSED OF RAPE.

I had to get a Coke to help me through the next four articles. They reported that when DeWayne was a college
freshman, he was accused of slipping something into a female student's drink and raping her after a fraternity party.
She wasn't shy about telling her story. A large picture
showed her, a slender white woman with straight blond hair
falling in front of her face, clutching the arm of a male
friend (also white) for support. I had only one article to read
when Joe Riddley and Cricket got back, and I went off-line
at once. It wasn't just that I didn't want Joe Riddley catching me reading up on DeWayne and accusing me of
sleuthing. I simply couldn't read any more. The way I felt, I
didn't want a hamburger, either.

While Joe Riddley and Cricket prattled on about nothing,
I sat there wondering why our school board hadn't found out
about all that before they hired DeWayne. Why was he still
permitted around young girls? Did Tyrone and whoever else
had painted the school know, or was that caricature a well-
aimed shot in the dark? That half-hour lunch seemed to last
as long as Moses wandered in the wilderness. Finally
Cricket stood up. "I has to go now. Miss Charlene needs me
to run the register."

Joe Riddley went down to the nursery to start getting

ready for our Fourth of July sale. I paid a few bills, but all the time I was working, I kept seeing pictures in my head: a shy little boy with a big round head ducking and smiling as I handed him a cherry sucker. Coach Evans in his uniform proudly watching another Honeybee streak home. DeWayne in a yellow shirt sitting in Joe Riddley's chair, trembling so hard he could not stand. The face of that young blond woman whose life had been so brutally damaged.

Tears filled my eyes again and again, and I drank so many Cokes that afternoon, their stock should have gone up five points.

You needn't think I was getting much productive work done. I had about decided to go on home and bob around in the pool—one of my favorite places to wash off troubles—when the phone rang. "Mac, it's Martha. We've had a good meeting, but the girls don't want to go home. They're crying and holding each other and say they can't stand the idea of being separated tonight. I'd invite them all to sleep here, but—"

I knew what she didn't like to say. Ridd and Martha lived in a small bungalow with two bedrooms downstairs and one they'd put in upstairs for Bethany after Cricket was born. It only had one bathroom—nowhere near enough for twelve girls overnight. We, on the other hand, had five bedrooms and two bathrooms upstairs, plus another bathroom and a den with a sofa bed downstairs. We also had a swimming pool.

"Why don't you take them down to our place tonight? You and Ridd can stay in our room and we'll stay at your house with Cricket."

"That would be marvelous." She sounded so relieved, I knew she had hated to suggest the idea but had been holding her breath until I did. "I'll tell them to go get their suits and pajamas and meet us down there."

Before I could hang up, she said in a tentative voice, "There's one more thing."

Martha knows good and well that Joe Riddley and I will

give almost anything we've got to somebody who needs it, and she wasn't generally nervous about asking. So I was surprised when she came to a flat-out halt.

"What do you need?" I figured she wanted to know if she could raid our freezer for supper, and I was trying to remember how much hamburger we had, when she sighed.

"It's Hollis. She wasn't at the meeting, and Bethany says she didn't accept DeWayne's offer of a place on the new team. Oh, darn, we'll need to call those girls, too—"

"Ridd can do that. You'll have enough to do, getting the Honeybees fed and bedded down for the night."

"I guess so. But somebody needs to tell Hollis what's happened. Bethany says she's scarcely left their house all week, but one of the few times she went out was to talk to DeWayne on Wednesday. She doesn't need to hear about this by accident. I'd do it, but I can't leave the girls."

I'd rather have volunteered for an experimental case of West Nile Virus, but I said as willingly as I could manage, "Okay, I'll go. I'm not getting much done around here anyway."

❧ 15 ❧

On my way over, I tried to think how to tell Hollis what had happened. I'd seen her have a conniption over a rip in a new shirt, so I decided to take it in stages. First I'd tell her De-Wayne died. Then I'd tell her he killed himself. I hoped to high heaven she wouldn't start flinging her arms around like Bethany did. Hollis wasn't tall, but she was sturdy. We might both wind up on the floor.

I also wanted to sound her out about whether DeWayne had ever made improper advances toward any of the girls. Could that be what had been bothering her this past week? If he had and had thought it was about to come out, he might have preferred suicide.

If I had thought he laid a hand on Bethany or Hollis, I might have killed him myself.

With those sentiments, regrettable for a magistrate and a Christian, I pulled into the drive.

The afternoon was delightful, so I expected the Stantons' front door to be wide open to let in the breeze and save on air-conditioning. Instead, the door and all four porch windows were closed. From the front walk I heard a soprano run up and down a scale. Hollis must be practicing her voice lessons. I hated to interrupt, but I pressed the bell.

She peered through the glass, then fetched a key, unlocked a bolt, and slid off a chain. Few folks in Hopemore lock doors in the daytime if we're home. Nobody I know puts on a dead bolt except at night. Only our most timid citizens use a chain.

When she finally got the door open, she stood there barefoot, wearing a T-shirt so long I could only guess she had on shorts underneath. Her hair was limp and dim as a dirty penny, and instead of greeting me with a tidal wave of talk, she stood there without saying a word.

"Was that you singing?" I asked. "It sounded real good."

"Could you hear it plumb out in the street?" Getting her dander up when embarrassed—now, that was more like the old Hollis we knew and loved.

Relieved, I said, "Oh, no, just from the walk. May I come in a minute?"

Her eyes grew wary, but she'd been raised right. "Yes, ma'am." She stepped back for me to enter. "We can go to the living room." She sounded like it was the best she had to offer, but it wasn't much. I saw at once what she meant.

When Sara Meg inherited the house, it had a boring yard, pallid rooms, heavy drapes and a few good Persian rugs. When she and Fred married, they poured their hearts into the place. He painted the chalky green exterior shiny white. She planted flower beds and laid a curved brick walk. While he painted inside and refinished the floors, she sewed curtains and slipcovers and painted lovely pictures for their walls. The living room, particularly, was such a happy place. The fabric on the sofa and a big overstuffed chair looked like somebody had flung daisies, daffodils, irises, and tulips all over them.

Fred painted the dining room buttercup yellow; Sara Meg hung white sheers and brought down a red and yellow rug from the attic. "It's the color of mustard and ketchup," she had joked. "Nothing the girls spill will show."

Back in those days, Sara Meg's life was her family, her house, and her community work. By far the youngest member of our Hopemore Garden Club, she had loved for us to meet at her place. She had always served cookies that she and the children had baked and told us with a laugh that in a year or two they'd redo the old-fashioned kitchen.

As soon as Fred died, Sara Meg dropped the Garden Club and started neglecting her yard. I doubted that she had ever redone her kitchen, and I wondered how long it had been since she'd had the time or energy to bake. The place was swept and dusted, but it had that neglected look that said nobody's heart was in the house anymore. Fingerprints showed up on the cream newel post at the bottom of the stairs. Through an archway down the hall, I could see the den piled high with newspapers and sewing projects. To my left, the dining-room sheers were limp, and behind the glass doors of a mahogany sideboard, silver trays were black with tarnish. The once-vibrant rug was hidden beneath papers, and the table was covered with books, hinting that Garnet studied there.

In the living room, sunlight straggled through unwashed windows to rest on a baby grand piano and a stack of music in the overstuffed chair beside it. The piano had been polished until it shone, and the navy rug was striped where somebody had recently vacuumed, but the now-faded flowers on the slipcovers looked wilted and dying. A grubby afghan slung over the couch only partly covered a rip it was supposed to hide. It made me sad to see the place looking so unloved.

Hollis shifted the stack of music to the top of the piano. "Won't you have a seat?" Generally, Hollis either loved or hated things. She was so apathetic today, I wondered if she'd already heard my news. If so, she was taking it mighty calmly.

I perched on the front of the chair and she sat at one end of the couch and drew her feet up on the cushion in front of her. Green shorts peeped from beneath her shirt. "Did Bethany send you?" Her toes wiggled, like they were wondering, too.

"Not exactly. But she's been missing you."

Hollis twisted a long strand of hair. "I—I've had some things to do."

"You're not mad at her for any reason, are you?" Grandmothers stalk right in where others hesitate to tiptoe.

"Oh, no, ma'am. I've just been real busy. Stuff I left undone during the school year, you know? And Garnet's been—uh—sick this week, so I've been staying with her." She picked her way through that story like a child climbing barefoot through blackberry briers. I suspected she was making it up as she went along, especially when she gave me a real earnest look and added, "Mama couldn't leave the store."

"Garnet looked okay Thursday at Myrtle's, and she said she'd been to class. Cricket even came here to play that afternoon."

"Oh, yes, ma'am. Garnet's real dedicated. She wouldn't skip classes, no matter how she felt. Besides, she felt a lot better Thursday. And she's not contagious or anything. You don't have to worry about Cricket catching it."

"I'm not worried about that. I came to tell you something important."

"I'm going to call Bethany, honest. I've just been so busy—"

I held up a hand to stop the flow. "It's not about Bethany. She's over with the rest of the Honeybees—"

"I'm not on the new team. Like I said, I'm real busy, and—"

The only thing to do was shove my prow against her waves. "They called the team together to tell them that Coach Evans died this morning." I steeled myself for a storm.

Instead, Hollis stiffened and turned so white I was afraid she'd gone into shock. I cursed myself for being too blunt while she sat examining her toenails like they were some new and fascinating appendage. When she clutched her calves in the circle of her arms and started rocking back and forth, she still hadn't made a sound.

From rocking, she went to shaking, and she shook so hard, you'd have thought she had a bad case of malaria. I took the afghan and tucked it around her. I wanted to hold her, but people are funny about adults touching children these days—with good cause. Adults who touch inappropriately have defiled honest, caring hugs.

Hollis clutched her knees closer to her chest, like she was afraid she'd shake apart if she didn't hold herself together. Finally she whispered, "How was he killed?"

I was so sorry I hadn't been clearer. Children raised on television expect violence. "He wasn't killed, honey. He hanged himself."

Her feet flew off the couch and hit the floor with a thump. "He killed himself? For real?"

I nodded.

"Oh." What an odd little puff of relief and dismay.

She grew still again, but it was a different stillness. Before, she'd seemed frightened. Now she seemed to be letting it sink in. In a minute or two she unwrapped the afghan and flung it to the floor. "That's too hot." She spoke angrily, and when she looked across at me, her eyes were full of furious tears. "He shouldn't have done that. We loved him. We loved him so much."

The last two words were a loud wail. Her face crumbled and she fell forward, face buried in her hands, boohooing like a small child.

Once Hollis let herself go, she cried a river and a stream. She got up and paced the room, dripping tears on the carpet. She belly flopped onto the sofa, buried her face in her hands, and wailed some more. I handed her every tissue in my pocketbook, and they weren't enough. Finally, I went to the powder room under the stairs and brought back the whole roll of toilet paper.

She cried so long and hard, I was afraid she'd make herself sick, but whenever I tried to calm her, she waved me away. How the dickens had I let Martha talk me into this?

And what had scared Hollis when she first heard DeWayne was dead?

She finally stood up and roamed the room again, touching things lightly. I'd done that myself. It was a kind of reassurance—if they were still there, you must be, too. Finally, she asked, "You don't reckon he did it because of what they wrote on the school, do you? Under the picture?" She plopped back into the chair across from me, her freckled hands clenching and unclenching on her bare thighs.

Something clicked for me. Tyrone drew that picture and he obviously liked Hollis. Did she like him back? Bethany had never mentioned them in one breath, and I couldn't imagine why Hollis would favor a big, beefy fellow who hung out with Smitty Smith, but stranger things have happened. I watched her closely as I asked, "Do you think Tyrone Noland drew it?"

Before that afternoon, I would never have believed Hollis had such a talent for stillness. She clenched her fists tight and didn't answer. Stubborn. That was the word that came to mind. Or my mama's favorite, "bullheaded."

"I saw a notebook of his drawings, and they looked a lot like that one," I prompted.

Nothing.

"Tyrone seemed to like you last Saturday."

That jump-started her engine. "Oh, no, ma'am! We just used to be friends, until he started hanging out with Smitty. Tyrone lives down the road, so we walked to school together before I started driving or riding with Bethany." She wrinkled her nose. "I can't stand Smitty Smith."

Were they friends until he started hanging out with Smitty, or did he start hanging out with Smitty after she found another way to get to school? Losing a friend like Hollis could take a sizeable chunk out of a young man's life.

She added in a rush, "Tyrone wouldn't do bad things unless Smitty made him. Somebody ought to lock Smitty up for the next *millennium*." She glowered at me as if I were personally refusing to put Smitty behind bars.

"I wish they could," I agreed, "but they can't even accuse him of helping Tyrone paint the school, because Willie Keller says Smitty was at his place all that night."

"Wet Willie would say *anything!*" She glared at me, and a silent challenge was flung across that room: *I can't believe you grown-ups are dumb enough to believe him.*

The weight of adult impotence sat heavy on my shoulders. I wanted to explain that adults can't do everything we hoped to when we were young, that years of accumulated evil and human folly make a very thick hedge that hems us in on every side. I wanted to plead that all any generation could do was chop through in little places, as God gave us grace and strength. But Hollis wouldn't understand. I wouldn't have, either, at her age. Youth is what God gives humanity to remind grown-ups they should try harder.

But how much harder could I try? I had been so busy since we found DeWayne, I hadn't even had time to grieve. I yearned to go home, float in my pool, and cry. But I couldn't go home. The place was swarming with girls. Instead, once I finished here, I had to go feed Cricket his supper, read him a story, and hope my tears would wait until I had a minute to myself.

In the middle of my pity party, I remembered I was there to comfort Hollis, persuade her to join the Honeybees at my house, and find out if she suspected DeWayne had messed with any of the girls. I might as well get on with it. "When you saw Coach Evans Wednesday—"

Her eyes widened. Shock? Guilt? Fear? "How'd you know I saw him?"

"Bethany said you couldn't eat lunch with her because you were meeting Coach Evans."

"Oh." She lowered her head and fiddled with the edge of her shorts.

"Is there anything somebody should know about that conversation?"

Now she was edgy again. She nibbled the end of one

grubby thumb. "No, it was private." Her eyes searched mine. "Are they positive he did it himself?"

I nodded and reached for my pocketbook. Whatever Hollis was worried about, she wasn't going to discuss it with me. I might as well get on with my program. "The team is spending the night together down at our place. They want you to come, if you will. If you'll grab your bathing suit and toothbrush, I'll drive you down."

"I can't leave Garnet." Her voice was wistful.

"Don't be stupid." Garnet stood in the doorway, hands on her slender hips, looking like a dancer in a black cotton T-shirt and black pants. Her skin was so pale, she seemed more like a wraith than ever. A furious wraith. "Go on. I can take care of myself. You don't have to hang around all the time." She gave Hollis a glare that would have felled a lesser woman, then noticed her sister's spiky lashes and tear-washed eyes. "What's the matter? Why are you crying?"

Before either Hollis or I could answer, somebody pounded on the back door. The girls jumped and exchanged a look I couldn't interpret, but it was certainly a blend of fear mixed with uncertainty and a grim determination.

The pounding continued.

I looked from one to the other. "Don't you think you should see who it is?"

"It's nobody. Don't worry." Hollis flapped a hand at me. Garnet stood, clutching her shirt with one hand.

Whoever it was pounded again. I got up. "I'll go."

A crash in the kitchen was followed by the tinkle of falling glass.

❧ 16 ❧

I grabbed my cell phone to call 911. "Quick—out the front door!"

We heard a furious roar. "Why is this door bolted? Let me in!" With relief I recognized Buddy and that tone of voice. My boys still get irritated like that if we lock a lock to which they don't have a key. What is it about young males that makes them expect to walk right into their old homeplace whenever they like?

Hollis looked sheepishly from Garnet to me, then jumped up and headed down the hall. "All right, already," she yelled. "You don't have to take the house down. I'm coming." Garnet followed, so I joined the party. Hollis fetched a key from the top of the refrigerator and turned the lock.

"Why did you bolt that door?" Buddy demanded when Hollis swung it open. "And why aren't you at work?"

"We forgot to unlock it," Garnet explained.

"I wasn't feeling so good," Hollis replied. She ignored my look saying she ought to get her stories straight about who was sick around there and added virtuously, "It's dangerous not to bolt doors. You don't know who might come in. Mrs. Yarbrough—I mean Judge Yarbrough—is here."

Buddy and I both noticed that unfortunate juxtaposition. He gave me a grin. Then he lifted one loafer to examine slivers of glass stuck to his sole, and his smile became rueful. "Sara Meg will kill me, but I was afraid something had hap-

pened. Not that anybody would notice a little glass under-
foot, with all this mess. Get a broom, Garnet."

Now that he mentioned it, the kitchen was worse than the
rest of the house put together. Dirty dishes filled the sink and
countertops, and clean ones filled the drainer and sat among
the dirty ones, like somebody found it too much trouble to
put them away. Remains of cereal, sugar, milk, and orange
juice littered the table, and an archeologist could probably re-
construct their past week's menus from scraps on the kitchen
floor. Buddy looked very out of place, fresh from a shower,
smelling of aftershave, and wearing clean white jeans and an
olive polo shirt.

I was surprised to notice, though, that Sara Meg *had* redone her kitchen, and not long ago. The walls were creamy
and bright, the floor covered in rust and cream vinyl squares,
and the stove, refrigerator, microwave, and dishwasher were
new. They all looked more expensive than I'd have expected
her to buy, given that she still had two girls to put through
college.

"It's Hollis's week to clean in here." Garnet yanked the
broom from beside the refrigerator. "She always puts it off as
long as she can, and I refuse to do her work." She skillfully
avoided a piece of lettuce and a crust of bread, sweeping up
only glass.

"I'm going to do it. I just haven't had time," Hollis grumbled.

"Get the dustpan," Buddy told her curtly. From the look
he gave me, I knew he was embarrassed I'd seen the place
looking like that, but what he said was, "You know your
mother doesn't like to see it looking like this."

"It's not Mama; it's you," muttered Hollis, heading for the
dustpan.

At the same time Garnet demanded, "When is she ever in
the kitchen?" She jerked back a chair to reach a piece of glass
under the table with her broom.

Buddy didn't answer either of them, but when Hollis
banged the dustpan down on the table, he ordered, "Do those

dishes right now. Your mother can't keep up with all this. She has to count on you."

She and Garnet both looked at the floor, united in shame. Then Hollis moved to the counter and started putting clean dishes away in a manner that suggested that at least one plate or glass wouldn't survive the experience.

Buddy asked Garnet again, "Why did you bolt that door?"

She shrugged. "I told you—we forgot to unlock it. We hadn't gone out it all day."

Remembering the chain on the front door, I knew she was lying, but I had no idea why. Whatever those girls were afraid of, they didn't want their uncle to know.

Having deployed the troops, he turned to me. "Did you need the girls for something, Mac, or was this just a friendly visit?"

Before I could answer, Hollis muttered over one shoulder, "She came to tell me Coach Evans"—she paused, and her voice grew thick—"he—he killed himself."

"What happened?" Buddy demanded. "I just talked to him this morning!"

Before I could ask when and why, Garnet's broom clattered to the floor. Her dark eyes moved from Hollis to me. "How? When? Where?" The questions came out in little puffs of air, leaving no space between for me to answer. "Are you sure?"

"He hanged himself early this morning over at the school. That's all I know so far," I said.

Garnet's shell cracked and crashed around her. With a shriek, she whirled and dashed down the hall, whimpering, "No! Oh, no, no, no!" We heard her burst into tears just before the powder-room door slammed.

Hollis started slinging dishes into the dishwasher, then stopped with that job half-done, turned the water on full force and squirted too much detergent into the dishpan.

As she plopped in a couple of pots with burned bits stuck on them, Buddy said, "Man, just when I was looking forward to getting to know DeWayne again. I called this morning to invite him to play golf and he said he'd get back to me."

"When was that?"

He thought and shrugged. "Sometime around eight, maybe? He was on his cell phone going to school."

Hollis finally deigned to look around. "Where'd you know him from before?"

"He used to live in Hopemore when he was little. He and I played together until—"

"—he moved away." I shot Buddy a warning look. We didn't need to be rehashing DeWayne's past right then.

We chatted a few more minutes, until I noticed that my watch said four o'clock. "I came to invite Hollis to spend the night down at our place with the rest of the Honeybees," I told Buddy, "so they can grieve together. They're having a sleepover, with Martha and Ridd to chaperone. I know Hollis doesn't like to leave Garnet when she's sick, but—"

"I'm not sick." Garnet stood in the doorway, looking exactly like a ghost with the flu. Her eyes were still wet with tears, but the shell was around her again. Buddy reached out and felt her forehead. "What's the matter with you?"

She backed away. "Nothing. Really. I was feeling yucky a few days ago, but I'm okay."

"I sure hope so. I heard this morning that we can play in the doubles tennis tournament down in Savannah next month. That's what I came over to tell you. If we're gonna knock their socks off, we'll need to practice a lot."

Garnet bent for the dustpan full of glass, looking about as thrilled as if he'd asked her to swallow it. "I don't know. I've got lots of studying to do."

At the sink, Hollis muttered, "I'm not leaving you here."

Garnet glared at her, then turned to me. "Could you drop me at the store when you take Hollis? I can help Mama close up."

"If you're sick—" Buddy dropped a hand to her shoulder.

"I feel fine." She backed away again, looking as fine as a ghost ever looks—wan and not quite present.

He frowned down at her. "You aren't being bothered by anybody, are you? Has that Franklin fellow been over here?"

Hollis gave a snort that might have meant anything. But the way Garnet pressed herself against the refrigerator as she exclaimed, "Oh, no!" and the way she stared at the floor after that made me wonder if Art *had* been bothering her. Maybe Hollis had decided to guard her.

Buddy looked from one to the other uncertainly. "If he bothers you, you let me know, okay? Don't worry your mother. I'll deal with him." When she didn't reply, he repeated, "Don't worry your mother, now."

Garnet turned away to get a glass of water. "I won't."

Hollis turned from the sink, her face red and blotchy. "We *never* bother our mother."

At the rate Hollis was doing the dishes, we'd never get away. I told her, "I need to get going, or Joe Riddley's going to wonder what's happened to me."

"Get your things," Buddy told her. "I'll do the dishes after I fix the glass."

"Great!" Hollis scampered up the stairs like she'd been let out of jail.

He looked ruefully at the broken pane. "I'd better go get some glass and putty to fix this, or Sara Meg will be air-conditioning the whole outdoors. Good to see you, Mac."

I gave him a hug. "Good to see you, too. And Garnet and I'll finish the dishes." Garnet wasn't excited by that prospect, but after he left, she scrubbed pots while I loaded the dishwasher.

When the phone rang, Garnet reached for it like she was afraid to answer. When she heard who was on the other end, her relief was obvious. "Oh, hi, Martha. You did?" She listened, then sat down in a nearby chair. "Oh, no."

I wouldn't have believed Garnet could have gotten paler than she already was, but she did. Tears welled in her eyes and she turned her head so I couldn't see them. For several seconds she sat, listening. Finally, she sighed. "I guess you're right. But I'm sure gonna miss her." She listened again, then said, "Yeah, she's right here. We're waiting for Hollis to pack. Okay. And—thanks." She said the last word reluctantly, then handed me the phone.

"Everything going all right over there?" Martha asked.

"As well as can be expected. We're about to head out. I'm dropping Garnet off at Children's World, then I'll bring Hollis down."

"That's good. And listen, Mac, be extra nice to Garnet. I just gave her some real sad news. Last week after my lecture to her psych class, she told me she wondered if one of her piano students was being molested. The child seemed to know more about sex than a child that age should, and that's one of the symptoms I mentioned in my lecture. I had the situation checked out, and Garnet was right. The child's mother's boyfriend was molesting her. She's been sent to live with an aunt."

Just the piece of news I needed to round out a perfect day.

While I was talking to Martha, Garnet finished the dishes like an efficient ghost. As I hung up, before I could say a word, she silently led the way back to the living room. We sat in awkward silence, her in the chair and me on the sofa. I watched dust motes dance in the sunlight and wondered what I could say to bring Garnet the most comfort.

She broke the silence. "Did Martha tell you what she told me?" I nodded. She murmured, more to herself than to me, "She was only nine. Nine years old." She reached up and brushed away a tear that had started down her cheek, but it was followed by another.

"You saved her, honey. If you hadn't said something, it could have gone on and on."

She bent her head. "I know. But I'll miss her. I hope they have a piano wherever she's gone." Her shoulders shook with sobs. This time I didn't hesitate. I went to sit on the arm of her chair and held her head tight against my shoulder.

Gradually her sobs stopped. I felt her shoulders tense, and she looked up with a new hardness in her face. "I need a job," she said fiercely. Seeing that she had startled me, she added,

"I don't make enough money teaching, and now I don't have enough pupils. It doesn't take enough time, either. I only have morning classes. Do you all need anybody?"

Regretfully, I shook my head. "I'm afraid not. Things are slow with us, like they are with everybody. Couldn't your mother use you?"

She shook her head. "No, I've asked her several times, but she says she just doesn't have the money to hire anybody right now."

Seemed to me like Sara Meg had her priorities wrong, putting so much money into a kitchen she seldom used, but that wasn't the time or place to say so. "What can you do?"

She sighed. "Not much, really. I'm pretty good with computers, but I've never worked except to help Mama sometimes."

"Well, if I think of anything, I'll let you know." If the new superstore was built, she could probably work there. But where else? The answer came like an answer to an unvoiced prayer. "I've got one idea. Can I use your phone?"

"It's in the den." She rose and led the way. Walking behind her, I wasn't surprised Art Franklin was attracted to her. She was grace in motion, and her hair was spectacular. Unlike Hollis's, it was clean and shining, lying in a heavy mass against her back.

I dialed the number for MacDonald Motors, which was owned by a good friend of mine. If anybody could bring Garnet Stanton to life, it would be Laura MacDonald. And if Garnet was still grieving her daddy, Laura would understand that, too. Both her parents had died in February.* Her deep voice sounded delighted to hear from me. "Hey, Mac, what's up?"

"Garnet Stanton wants a job, and I wondered if you needed somebody to help you in the office. Did you ever replace Nicole out front?"

"Not yet. Can she answer the phone, type letters, and do data entry?"

*Who Left That Body in the Rain?
•

"Sounds right up her alley. Can I bring her by your place in a few minutes to discuss it?"

"No time like the present."

Bless Laura MacDonald's big heart.

Garnet hurried upstairs and came back wearing a dark green skirt and a white blouse. She had caught her hair at the nape of her neck with a green ribbon. "You clean up real good," I complimented her. I expected a smile. I got a shrug.

Hollis clattered down the stairs out of breath, wearing jeans and a cute purple top, carrying two stuffed bags. "You moving in with us?" I asked.

"It's just clothes and stuff," she assured me.

"Mostly stuff," said Garnet with disdain.

We let Garnet off at Laura's, and she said she'd walk from there to Children's World. I dropped Hollis off at my house into a swarm of red-eyed, red-nosed Honeybees who poured from the house to engulf her. At last I took time to stop by the church chapel for a private half hour to myself, to pray for DeWayne and all who loved him. Then, feeling better, I stopped by Myrtle's for a quick piece of pie, since I hadn't eaten much lunch.

Art Franklin waited on me, and it didn't take a genius to see that he was excited. "Did you hear that Coach Evans—the chemistry teacher over at the high school—hung himself this morning in the boys' locker room?" he asked as he brought my coffee.

The way he looked, he'd be willing to sit right down and discuss it if I invited him. "Sure did," I said shortly. "You got any chocolate pie?" If I sounded callous, I didn't care. I hate it when people get excited over other people's tragedies.

When Art brought my pie, he licked his wet lips a couple of times and said, "Did you hear how he did it? I mean, did he stand on a sink and jump, or what?"

I stared at him. "I haven't the foggiest." It was a good question, though. As far as I could remember, there wasn't a thing to stand on where DeWayne was found.

Getting no satisfaction from me, Art dashed over to another new customer with his coffeepot. I heard him ask, "Did you hear that Coach Evans . . .?"

I punched in Ike's private cell-phone number. "I doubt you're conducting the investigation into DeWayne's death," I began.

"What investigation? Chief Muggins says it was a clear case of suicide."

"Maybe so, but I found DeWayne, remember? And as far as I can recall, he was a mighty long way from the sinks or toilets, so what did he stand on to jump from?"

I heard silence while Ike thought that over. "He left a note, I understand."

"Well, it might bear some thinking about."

Ike gave a disapproving grunt. "Mac, haven't you had enough murders in this town for one year? We don't need to be looking for murder every time somebody dies."

"I'm not looking for murder, Ike. I am merely asking whether there was, in fact, any way for DeWayne Evans to do what he seems to have done."

"I'll tell you what. I have to go by the high school to pick up my little brother, who's helping one of his teachers set up. How about if I wander back to the locker room and have a look?"

"How about if you do? Thanks, Ike."

"Anytime, Mac. You just save me a front-row seat at your own funeral if Joe Riddley or Ridd learn I'm doing this." Speaking of Joe Riddley, it was about time I headed back to the store to see if he and Cricket were ready to knock off for the day. I felt pretty proud of myself right then. Everything was under control.

That's because I had plumb forgotten something real important.

❧ 17 ❧

As soon as I walked into the office, Joe Riddley said, "Call Clarinda. She called wanting something, but I forgot what. You know how bad my memory is since I got shot."

"Your memory is fine until you don't want to remember something." I dropped my pocketbook near the desk and reached for the phone.

As soon as she recognized my voice, Clarinda started right in on me. "Is this the person who couldn't be bothered to call and tell me what she and Ridd found? Of course, it's not as if DeWayne Evans was important to me or anything, although I reckon he was one of my grandson's favorite people, all the time over at our place. Maybe that doesn't count. No reason to put yourself out to give me a call so I would know what Ronnie and that poor little thing were going through and what everybody else in town already knew. No reason at all. No reason for you to call and explain so I'd know why Ronnie sent one of his buddies over to drive me and my wash home, either. No siree—no reason—"

I hoped that wherever DeWayne was, he knew that his death had moved Yasheika up in Clarinda's roster from "that girl" to "that poor little thing." But I needed to stop Clarinda's horse at full gallop or she was capable of going on through the night and well into morning.

"I forgot," I admitted. "Flat-out forgot. After we found De-

Wayne, it was all I could do to get back here and sit down without passing out. Then I saw Bethany—"

"You spent the afternoon down at Stantons'." Her tone implied we'd been carousing around a piano. I'd be hearing about this for weeks. Clarinda is a champion grudge bearer.

"I went to tell Hollis what happened," I explained.

"You coulda swung by here. Not that it matters—"

"I thought Ronnie would tell you." At least, that's what I would have thought if I'd given Clarinda any thought at all. "I reckon he did, since you called."

"Oh, Ronnie finally told me when he called a little while ago to say why he was so late. The reason I called was to find out when you want him to bring Yasheika down."

Southern hospitality can get you in bubbling hot water sometimes. Like when you invite a person to spend the night, then forget and give away your house. I doubted that Yasheika wanted to join the Honeybees for their grief-a-thon.

While I was still trying to figure out whether I could ask her to sleep up in Bethany's room with the bathroom all the way down the stairs, Clarinda took another lap around the track. "I'd love to have her over here, of course, but you know I haven't got but the two bedrooms and one bathroom, and—"

"—and she and Ronnie might throttle each other if you turned your back."

"Oh, they've called truce while we're dealing with De-Wayne's passing. Right now, Ronnie's taken her down to the po-lice station to pick up his things."

She paused—probably to give me time to adjust to that amazing development. Instead, I found myself wondering why Clarinda and a lot of older black Americans pronounce "po-lice" with an accent on the first syllable. Could it be because, in their experience, the "po-lice" were so painfully connected with "po' folks"?

I tuned back in as she said, ". . . back here for supper, but I doubt she'll eat a bite. She's real cut up, poor little thing. After supper, he's driving her to Atlanta to pick up her mother and

her auntie. They're flying in. The real reason I called was to
ask if you can put them up, too."

I caught my breath in a quick hiss. Clarinda caught it at
once. "Of course, if you think it's too much trouble, they can
always go to a motel or something."

She knew as well as I did that the only motel anywhere
around was up on I-20, miles away. We had four bed-and-
breakfast places in town, but they tended to be pricey, or so I
had heard. (With five bedrooms, I'd never needed to use
them.) I was also having one of those real uneasy moments
white southerners sometimes still get, wondering how welcome a local bed-and-breakfast might make black guests.

"It's not that they'd be any trouble," I assured Clarinda.
"It's that we aren't staying at our place. Martha and Ridd are
taking the Honeybees down there tonight, and we're keeping
Cricket at their place. Yasheika can have Bethany's room, but
you know they don't have any spare beds."

"Oh, well, if your house is full of a teenagers' slumber
party—"

"It's not a slumber party. It's DeWayne's team. They're real
upset, and Martha feels they ought to be together to grieve. Her
house isn't big enough, so I said they could use ours."

"Where's DeWayne's family gonna grieve, then? You
gonna make them poor women stay in a motel? They can't go
back to his house, not with nasty words written all over it."

"You saw it?"

"Sure, I saw it. Told Ronnie's pal to swing by there on our
way home. It's real scary."

I was ashamed of myself. I'd been so focused on De-
Wayne's death, I had forgotten that somebody was still loose
in town with a can of spray paint and a hate-ridden heart, rous-
ing fear in every black friend I had.

"It is scary, but the police are gonna find out who's doing
that and stop it," I said firmly. "They've already arrested Tyrone Noland as one of the perpetrators down at the school. If
they can persuade him to talk, maybe we'll get them all pretty
quick."

"Tyrone Noland? That little fat boy who used to sweep up for you? The one you brought down here one day for dinner and he ate up most of a whole chicken? That sweet little boy ain't painting hate words all over town." As far as Clarinda is concerned, anybody who likes her cooking is too nice to commit a crime.

"I'm afraid he is. At least, he's admitted he painted the picture on the school. I don't know about the words. And I don't know if he painted DeWayne's house, but I intend to find out."

Clarinda heaved a sigh that nearly took down the telephone lines. "I sure hate for DeWayne's mama to see all that nastiness. Ronnie wanted to go paint over it before she got here, but the po-lice said leave it until they get through."

"You're right that his mother can't stay there. That's for sure. Let me think a minute and call you back."

"Okay. And one more thing. Tell Martha not to let the girls use your dryer. When Ronnie's friend came to get me, I went off and left my underwear still in it."

I had no more than hung up when Joe Riddley swung his chair around. "What about Walker's place? They've got scads of room. And since you're already watering their plants, taking in their mail and feeding their menagerie, what difference will it make if we use their beds for a couple of nights? They aren't coming back all month, are they?"

I gave him a look that would have withered him if Joe Riddley hadn't developed thick skin over the years. "If you had that figured out, why didn't you fix that up with Clarinda? You could have saved me a lot of grief."

He had the gall to laugh. "I wouldn't have missed that for the world."

Bo added a cackle straight from hell.

I spent a little time letting them both know they were in my black book, but Joe Riddley was right. Walker, his wife, Cindy, and the bank—with the bank as major partner—own a huge house in the wealthy part of town. Worry about how they could afford the mortgage, decorators' fees, bills for new furnishings to augment Cindy's family heirlooms, two new cars, private school, and frequent weeks at Hilton Head would have put gray in my hair if I hadn't had a great beautician.

"I hate to use the house without asking," I said slowly. "Maybe I ought to call them."

"I figured you would. It's as good an excuse as any. Give the kids my love."

I felt exotic picking up the phone to call Hawaii. What a let-down to find it was no more complicated than calling Atlanta.

The kids and Walker were at the beach, but Cindy didn't even hesitate. "Of course you should all stay there. Use anything you find in the refrigerator, pantry, or freezer. I'm so sorry about DeWayne, and we're delighted to help." Her kindness touched me. I'd just begun getting to know Cindy the previous winter, and I regretted wasting fourteen years holding this daughter-in-law at arm's length because her elegance intimidated me. Even if she wasn't as comfortable to be around as Martha was, she was an equal treasure in our family.

Cricket bounded in while we were talking. I covered the mouthpiece. "Do you want to talk to Aunt Cindy in Hawaii?"

He grabbed the receiver. "How are ye in How-are-ye?" He burst into giggles.

He wasn't so enchanted with us when he heard our new plan for the evening. "I want to go to your house. I want to swim." His lower lip slid out like a drawer.

"You can swim another day," I promised.

"I don't want to swim another day. I want to swim today. You never let me swim. You always say 'another day.' I never get to play with Lulu, or swing on the swing—"

Joe Riddley bent down and lifted him up. "There's swings over at Uncle Walker's. Come on. Let's go get your things while Me-mama calls Clarinda."

After I explained the plan, Clarinda had to think a minute before she admitted, "That'll work. When my cookies come out of the oven, I'll bring them over to Walker's and make beds."

"I can make beds," I assured her, "but you can come help if you want to." We've been together so long, I knew she didn't want to be left out of the program. Clarinda has a big heart. She also thrives on being in the inner circle whenever there's a tragedy.

However, I was more than a little miffed when she arrived at Walker's, set warm cookies on the counter, and announced, "I'll come over early and get breakfast."

"I fix breakfast every morning," I reminded her.

"Not for comp'ny. Burnt eggs and dry toast don't cut it for guests."

Granted, I perpetuate the myth that I cannot cook. It ensures that we eat out on Sundays and nobody expects me to come home from work and stand over a hot stove. When we have guests, we usually ask Clarinda to come fix a special meal so I can enjoy the party, or we take them to a restaurant. Still, Clarinda knows I am perfectly capable of putting a full meal on the table if I need to, and my breakfasts are as good as hers. Almost.

"I have never in my life served anybody burned eggs," I said. "Besides, Cindy's bound to have a few Sara Lee coffee cakes in the freezer. I can put them in the microwave, make coffee and pour juice as well as you can."

"Don't you be using stuff from Cindy's freezer. I'll bring what I need. I wish I could have them all at my place. I know exactly what his mama is going through." She turned away, but I saw her brush away a tear.

My eyes blurred as I remembered the day her Janey died. Maybe that's why I relented. "I'll cook, but you come eat breakfast with us."

She turned back, all business again. "No, you feed them breakfast and I'll send Ronnie to get them right afterwards. I want them at my house the rest of the day. Okay?"

"Fine. But if they want a nap in the afternoon, you bring them back here."

Two generals who had completed a battle plan to our mutual satisfaction, we marched upstairs to make the beds.

*   *   *

Fireflies were dancing in the dusk before Ronnie's car pulled into Walker's drive. Ronnie looked worn out as he ushered three heartbroken women in through the den, and it occurred to me he hadn't had time to grieve privately, either. From the way he and Yasheika edged away from each other and Ronnie hurried back out to bring in their cases, I also deduced their day together hadn't been all sweetness and light.

Yasheika looked like she'd been running marathons for several days. Her mother looked like all her stuffing had been removed. The aunt, whose name I didn't catch the first time around, looked at the elegant rooms full of Cindy's grandmothers' furniture, rugs, and silver, and demanded, "Who did Ronnie say you put out on our account?"

"It's my uncle Walker's," Cricket bragged. "He's gone to How-are-ye, so we can sleep at his house and play with the LEGO if we feed Tad's guinea pig and newts, Jessica's fish, and Aunt Cindy's dog and her cats."

My face grew hot. We had so very much, and right this minute they had so little. Then Cricket added, "Uncle Walker doesn't have any pets, but he plays with theirs. You can, too." And he handed Yasheika the golden kitten he'd been holding. When it purred and started climbing up her blouse, it brought smiles to all our sad faces.

As Yasheika cuddled it to her neck, Joe Riddley and Ronnie took the bags upstairs and I led the women toward the living room. I could tell they were doing their best not to impose their grief on the rest of us, but when I told Elda, "You cry if you want to. I'm a mama, too," she turned and broke down in my arms. That made me cry; then Yasheika and her auntie started sobbing. Between us, we created a new tributary for the Savannah River.

"Pop, come down here!" Cricket roared at the bottom of the stairs. "These wimmen is crying and crying and Yasheika's 'bout to drown Aunt Cindy's kitten."

३ 18 ६

Everybody went to bed early, but I couldn't sleep. I lay there until one-thirty, then sighed, sat up, and fumbled for my slippers beside the unfamiliar bed.

"Where you going?" Joe Riddley mumbled.

I felt around for my robe. "Down to get some warm milk and see if they've got some graham crackers." Walker loves them almost as much as I do, so it was likely he'd have a box.

Joe Riddley turned his back and pulled the sheet over his ears. "Just like a baby. Need a full stomach to sleep."

"If it works, don't knock it." I padded downstairs in the dark.

I turned on the den light and startled Yasheika, who was standing by the window in a red silk robe trimmed in gold. Tears glistened on her cheeks and her nails were *scritch-scritching* against the soft silk as she clenched and un-clenched her fists.

"Oh, honey!" I flipped the light back off and went to stand beside her in the dim glow of a streetlight. "Having trouble sleeping?"

She was trembling. Even her voice shook, but it was low and furious. "I'm having trouble believing this has happened. I keep thinking it's a mistake, a bad joke. He had no call to kill himself. He didn't! I loved him so much. Why wasn't it enough?"

Surely those are the saddest words in the world.

I didn't know what to say, but I knew it's not words that comfort people who are grieving, it's touch—just having somebody there. I started rubbing gentle circles on her back. She edged closer and I slipped my arm around her waist. She was a good six inches taller than me, but she bent her head to my shoulder and sobbed.

"Why didn't he tell me what he was thinking?" she raged. "He talked all week about other things—how much he used to love this place, things he used to do, people he knew. But not a word about this. He should have *told* me." Her voice trailed so low I almost couldn't hear. "Maybe he tried and I didn't listen."

I gave her a squeeze of reproof. "Don't talk like that. It won't change what's done, just make you feel worse. From what I hear, people who are determined to take their own lives are going to do it, no matter what others do."

She stepped back and sniffed. "But he *wasn't* determined to do it. After practice last night, he was real excited about the new team. Said he was sure we could win the district and go to state. And he went to school to get his room ready for summer school. Does that sound like he was planning on killing himself?" She sniffed again.

"No," I admitted. I found a clean tissue in my pocket and handed it to her.

She blew her nose before asking, "So what changed?"

"I don't know." I hesitated. Joe Riddley and Ridd would call me nosy, but I preferred the word "interested." I'd been interested all day in that piece of paper DeWayne left on his desk with Yasheika's name on it. "I don't guess he left a note?" That wasn't a lie, exactly. You don't have to guess about something you already know.

"He did, but it didn't say a thing." She reached in her pocket and pulled out a piece of paper. "Read it." She thrust it at me. It was rumpled and damp, like she'd read it and cried over it many times since somebody first handed it to her.

I groped my way through the dimness to a lamp by the

couch, and blinked in the sudden light. I sat down on the couch and held the page at arm's length, but I didn't need my reading glasses. There was only one word, written in careful black block letters: SORRY.

I looked across the room at Yasheika, standing forlornly by the window. "You're right. It doesn't say much." It didn't explain why he'd done what he had. It didn't even explain the burned papers in DeWayne's wastebasket. Now that I'd seen the Internet articles, I suspected the unburned letters might be the end of the word "raped." If I'd found those articles easily, somebody else could have, too, and sent them to DeWayne with a note written in purple ink. Was that what DeWayne had burned?

"Was there anything DeWayne was scared of people knowing besides what happened to your daddy?" I asked. "Could somebody have gotten hold of something and threatened him with it?"

"Oh, my God!" It was a gasped prayer. "But nobody around here knew. How could they?"

"Knew what?" I reached up and turned the light out again so she couldn't see my face. I felt pretty small, pretending I didn't know when I did. Besides, I was afraid my face would show my disgust at what she was about to tell me. Part of me still admired and respected DeWayne Evans, but most of me was plumb sick to think we'd put him in charge of young girls after what he'd done.

Yasheika began pacing, an agitated shadow that passed back and forth in front of the window. "DeWayne's first year in college, he went to a party and got a little drunk. Afterwards, a white girl claimed he raped her. DeWayne said he didn't even know her—thought maybe he'd danced with her once at the party. But she described what happened in lurid detail."

I was listening the way I listen on the bench when perpetrators' families claim their son or daughter is innocent. I've heard it too many times to believe it. But Yasheika surprised me.

"At the trial, DeWayne's lawyer got the girl to admit she had lied, that her boyfriend had put her up to it because De-Wayne had made the baseball team and he hadn't. He hoped if DeWayne got expelled—well, anyway, DeWayne was completely exonerated and she and the boy were expelled instead. Charged with perjury, too. But before she confessed, the story was in the papers, with DeWayne's picture and everything. Everybody on campus read those stories." Her voice grew bitter. "A lot more than those who read the little paragraph saying he'd been cleared."

Including me. I was so ashamed of myself for stopping without checking that last Internet article. Mama always said it's human nature to be more willing to believe bad things about a good person than good things about a bad one.

Yasheika was still talking. "DeWayne told me later that going through those weeks were like reliving the bad time with Daddy all over again. People whispering behind their hands, pointing at him, turning their backs. For months he had nightmares, shakes, the whole nine yards. Missed a semester of college. He even transferred colleges and lived at home until he graduated. He said he couldn't stand going back to people staring at him and talking about him."

No wonder Yasheika had gotten into Yale. She went right on to figure out what I was getting at without my saying another word. "You reckon somebody found those articles? If they threatened to spread that story around—" She didn't have to finish. I knew how people would talk, the way they would avert their eyes, wondering how much was true. I knew it as well as she did. Maybe better—I'd lived in Hopemore all my life.

She said real low, to herself, "If he'd had to go through that a third time, it would have killed him." Then she realized what she'd said and pressed one hand to her lips.

But Yasheika was a fighter. She was soon muttering to herself, figuring things out. "Somebody had to have talked to him after he left for school—or sent him something there.

Nothing came to the house—I got Friday's mail, and yesterday's mail hadn't come before he left—so if there was something like that, it must have gone to the school. You didn't seen anything like that on his desk, did you? I heard you were the one who found him." Her voice dropped and she looked down at her hands, twisting and untwisting in her lap.

I sighed. "Something I will always regret. But no, I didn't see anything like that on his desk." There was no point in telling her I'd seen burnt ashes in his wastebasket, since I hadn't poked through them and wasn't positive what they had been. Having lived with Joe Riddley while he was a magistrate and now being one myself, I have a lot of respect for being real accurate when giving evidence.

She flipped on another light. "I won't sleep until I know if the police found anything like that. Do you know where your son keeps his phone book?"

"Honey, I know the police number by heart." I called out the numbers as she dialed. After she told the officer on duty who she was and what she wanted, she listened, then dropped the phone into its cradle without saying good-bye. When she turned, she was shaking as bad as DeWayne had in my office, and she spoke in little gasps.

"They found ashes in DeWayne's wastebasket. They've been sent to the lab for analysis—but he said . . . he said they looked like Internet printouts. You know it's those stories—it has to be, doesn't it?"

"It seems pretty likely."

She stumbled back to her chair and fell into it, still shaking. "Poor DeWayne. He must have found them there this morning right after he saw the front of the house. No wonder he went over the edge. He thought it was all going to start again." Tears glistened in her eyes and she swiped them angrily away. "Whoever sent them as good as killed my brother!"

I had one good candidate. Smitty might look like something from a horror movie, but if he played computer games, he knew how to use the Internet. "Do you know if DeWayne taught Smitty Smith—the kid with the shaved head and one long string of hair, the one who made those rude remarks at Myrtle's last Saturday?"

She collapsed against her chair and laid her head back in pure exhaustion. "Was that just last Saturday? It feels like a year ago."

I agreed, but I didn't want to lose our train of thought. "Could DeWayne have flunked him? Could Smitty have a grudge against him?"

"I don't know. I don't even know if DeWayne taught him. What makes you think it could have been him?"

"One of his gang confessed to painting the picture on the school, and I think Smitty planned that whole thing. A witness gave him an alibi for that night, but he's probably lying. We know he's a racist, so if DeWayne flunked him—"

Her lips twisted. "That kid looks like a lot of teachers have flunked him. You think the kid would want to *kill* DeWayne for that?" Disbelief and anger rose in her voice.

"The intention may not have been to kill DeWayne," I reminded her, "just scare him, or run him out of town."

A soft drumroll filled the room as she pounded the arms of her chair with both fists. "If he sent DeWayne copies of clippings from that trial, he as good as tied that noose. Have you told the police this?"

"Not yet. It's just an idea, so far." I wondered how far Ike had gotten in looking at the locker room and whether he'd decided that DeWayne could have or could not have, in fact, hanged himself. But why would somebody send the clippings, then kill DeWayne? And how had anybody gotten in the building without passing Clint Hicks cleaning his nails in the front hall?

Something else had been bothering me all day. I spoke more to myself than to her. "What I really don't understand is why he would hang himself. He had a lab full of chemicals."

Yasheika gave a sad little snort. "It's not that easy to kill yourself with chemicals. DeWayne talked about that a lot. Most stuff either maims you or kills you slowly and painfully." She clenched and unclenched her fists, and her voice grew bitter again. "If he wanted to do it, I guess he didn't want to take the time to figure out what would kill him fast. Besides, if he'd mixed gas strong enough to kill him right away, it most likely would have killed whoever found him, too."

I pictured Ridd sticking his head in the locker room with fumes rolling out to greet him. Trembles started in my shoulders and moved down my whole body. "Dear God," I breathed, not knowing if I was voicing terror or thanksgiving.

We sat in silence until the hall clock chimed three. Then I pulled myself to my feet, feeling like my body had added a hundred pounds since I sat down. "I'm exhausted, and you look like I feel. Let's don't talk about this any more tonight, okay? I came down to get some warm milk and graham crackers to help me sleep. You want some? Or some wine? Cindy is sure to have wine."

"I don't drink milk, but I wouldn't say no to a glass of wine."

We raided Cindy's kitchen like two conspirators. Yasheika chose wine, cheese, crackers, and an apple she found in the refrigerator vegetable bin. I put a mug of milk in the microwave and found graham crackers and peanut butter. We both felt a little lighter as we carried our loot to the table. As I sat down, Cindy's Irish setter, Red, lumbered over from his basket to doze on my feet. Trying to talk about anything except DeWayne, I asked, "How long have you known you wanted to be a lawyer?"

Yasheika turned her wineglass around in front of her. "I never wanted to be a lawyer. I wanted to be a phys-ed teacher, or an accountant like Ronnie. I love sports and math pretty equally. But I'm becoming a lawyer to get my daddy out of jail."

"You could be a phys-ed teacher or a rich CPA and hire a lawyer," I pointed out.

She shook her head. "Nobody would work as hard on his case as I will."

I drank the last of my milk. "Well, after you've become a lawyer and gotten your daddy out of jail, maybe you can become a gym teacher. You're real talented in working with a team, and not everybody has that gift. Not everybody keeps the same job all her life, either." I started to push back my chair. "We better get up to bed. Ronnie's coming early in the morning."

"Yeah."

Her tone dismissed him as unimportant, which made me mad. "Don't be rough on him, honey. He spent all day yesterday driving you around, and he's hurting, too. You lost a brother. He lost one of his best friends."

She thought that over, tracing a design on the tabletop with one long slender finger. Finally she gave a short nod. "I know I ought not to be so mean to him, but it gets me, the way he's always so nice. He's just like DeWayne—never fights anybody for anything. Lets people walk all over him with that great big smile."

"Not always," I corrected her. "He was on the high-school debate team and did real well. Joe Riddley suggested Ronnie become a lawyer, too, but Ronnie said he didn't want a job where he had to be fighting somebody all the time."

"See? That's what I told you."

"Did DeWayne tell you about Ronnie's family?"

"No, but I know his grandmother. She doesn't have any trouble fighting."

"You got that right. Clarinda makes everybody toe the line, including me. But I meant his mother and daddy. You didn't hear about them?"

She shook her head and didn't look real interested, but I told her anyway.

"Ronnie's daddy beat his mother all their married life.

Beat Ronnie, too. Broke his arm when he was just a baby."
I had her attention now. "Finally, one night Buck took his
gun and shot Janey, right in front of the child. Killed her, and
died in the electric chair for it."

I gave her a minute to let that sink in, then added, "Ronnie has a sweet nature, yes, but he also used to have a terrible temper. He'd throw a fit about anything that didn't go his
way. That memory you have of him giving you the ball with
a great big smile? The next minute, he probably grabbed it
back and bopped you with it. You just don't remember. But
one day down at our house when he was about seven, he got
so out of control, he took a stick and started beating our dog
because it wouldn't fetch a toy he'd thrown. That's when we
all took him in hand. We taught him that he may have been
raised to hit and fight, but he didn't have to live that way.
And Ridd and Joe Riddley taught him that hitting a woman
is something no nice boy would do." I licked peanut butter
off my fingers. "So don't think because Ronnie's gentle,
he's a wimp. He's not. He knows what he is capable of and
chooses not to let that control him." I'd said more than
enough on that subject, so I changed it. "Before we go to
bed, I have one more question. In all that talking DeWayne
did this week, did he mention Hollis? She went to see him
Wednesday."

Yasheika gave a small snort that was close to a laugh.
"She sure did. Nearly embarrassed DeWayne to death."

"Can you tell me what it was about, or is it too private?"

"It was sort of private, but it was so vague, I'll tell you.
She wanted to know what a hypothetical person should do
if she thinks somebody she knows is sleeping with somebody she shouldn't be sleeping with. Should that person
tell, or is it none of her business? And what if the person
would get in bad trouble if she tells?"

"The person who told, or the person she was talking
about?"

"I asked DeWayne that. He said she wasn't clear on that
point."

•

I tried to think that out while Yasheika drained the last drops of her wine and set the glass on the table. "I sure wish she had come to me instead of DeWayne. He's—" She stopped, gulped, and went bravely on. "He *was* shy, and after what happened to him in college, he had a hard time talking about sex at all. Talking about it with a teenager in a miniskirt?" She gave me an impish grin. "Ooo-ee! He said he didn't know where to look. Besides, he said he had no idea who she might be talking about, and he didn't want to know private things about her mother, her sister, maybe Bethany, or even me."

"Bethany?" That upset me so much, I jumped. Poor Red, napping on my toes, gave a low woof of portent.

"Or me," Yasheika reminded me, "although I don't know who DeWayne thought I could be sleeping with. I don't know any guys in town except Ronnie, and we certainly aren't on those terms." At least this time she didn't say his name like it was poison.

She got up and went to wash her plate and glass. "DeWayne worried all evening about whether he'd handled it right. Kept feeling like he'd let her down, that he should have had a good answer when he didn't."

"What did he tell her?"

She turned and leaned against the counter. "Said he needed to think it over and he'd get back to her. He wanted me to tell him what to say, because he didn't have a clue. After what he'd been through, he didn't want somebody accused of something they weren't doing."

I was so bothered that Hollis might suspect—or even know—that Bethany and Todd were messing around, I scarcely noticed when Yasheika picked up my dishes and went to wash them, too. Was that why Hollis had been avoiding Bethany? Should I mention this to Martha?

Yasheika's chuckle rolled over her shoulder. "The end of their talk was real funny. DeWayne said Hollis flew right off the handle. You know how everything's either hot or cold with that girl? Well, she said that folks are all the time saying if you think something's wrong, you're supposed to tell a grown-up you trust, and he wasn't helping her at all. Then she flipped her hair at him and stomped out. Poor De-Wayne." I heard a sad smile in her voice.

I got up to put away the milk. "He never talked with her again?"

"Not that I know of, except when he called to tell her she'd made the all-county team. When she made up some excuse not to play, he figured she was still mad."

That might explain Hollis's flood of tears. Did she regret the way she'd ended their last conversation?

Yasheika yawned. "I think I can sleep now. Thanks for talking. And please don't think badly of DeWayne. He never was strong after Daddy went to jail."

"I don't think badly of him, honey. He was a fine man with some deadly wounds." I went to give her a hug. "Starting tomorrow, I will do all I can to help find the person who drove him to do what he did."

She headed for the stairs, but paused at the door. Her voice was low and venomous. "You better find him before I do."

❧ 19 ❧

Sunday I woke early and lay in bed trying to figure out how to casually ask Ridd if DeWayne ever taught Smitty without his suspecting why I was asking. Joe Riddley and the boys get so upset when I investigate things, I have to tiptoe around them the whole time. Mama used to say, "No woman worth her salt lets her menfolk know half of what she *is* doing or a quarter of what she *can* do." I used to accuse her of being a hypocrite and a manipulator and swore I'd never grow up to be like that. I sure wished now I'd asked her to teach me how.

I also tried to figure out how I could talk to Tyrone. I had a hard time believing he'd have painted DeWayne's house the night after his hearing, but Smitty seemed to have a strong hold over him. Somehow, we needed to break that hold.

For starters, I had to haul myself out of bed and prove to Clarinda that I could cook.

Ronnie arrived before we finished eating. He didn't look any more rested than Yasheika did, and she looked as terrible as a pretty girl can look. Wan and weepy. But I noticed her glancing at him when she thought nobody was looking. Finally he took them to Clarinda's and the rest of us went to church.

Have you noticed that in this entire dreadful week, I hadn't seen Sara Meg? When she walked into church with Buddy, I felt like one of us must have been on a long trip. According to the bulletin, the youth choir was singing. Garnet always played for them. That morning, Hollis was supposed to sing a solo, but I doubted she or Bethany would appear.

Buddy looked real spiffy in a tan seersucker suit, the kind my daddy used to wear. Poor Daddy never looked that good in his, though. Sara Meg wore a beige linen shirt with huge wooden buttons down the front and a long matching skirt. On me, that outfit would have looked like feed sacks sewn up to clean house in. On her, it looked chic.

I waved for them to come sit with Joe Riddley and me. As they slid into the pew, Buddy leaned across Sara Meg and said softly, "I still can't get over DeWayne. Everybody's going to miss him."

I nodded sadly and swallowed a lump in my throat. "I guess Hollis and the others on the team won't be singing."

Sara Meg surprised me. "Oh, yes, they will. Hollis came by this morning for her Sunday clothes. She said all the Honeybees in the choir decided to sing in honor of Coach Evans."

Listening to Hollis practice octaves hadn't prepared me for what a lovely voice she had. She opened her mouth and soared on the high notes, her face flushed with pleasure. I leaned over and whispered, "I didn't know you had *two* musicians in the family."

Sara Meg glowed with pride. "They got it from Fred," she whispered back. "We Tanners could never carry a tune."

During announcements at the end of the service, Joe Riddley looked at me and asked a silent question. We've been married so long, I knew what he wanted. I didn't feel a bit like eating with people, but I nodded, so he wrote a note and passed it to Sara Meg. *Little Bit is feeling rich today. Join us and Ridd's crew for dinner? Buddy, too.*

Sara Meg started to nod, then passed the note to Buddy for his opinion. He smiled their acceptance. A single woman in the pew ahead beamed back, then colored when she realized his smile wasn't for her.

We decided to eat at a place down by the river and, as we often did, Martha was going to ride with me while Joe Riddley rode with Ridd and Cricket. Bethany decided to ride with

Sara Meg, and Buddy told Garnet to come with him so he wouldn't be lonely. She nodded, then bent impulsively to Cricket, "Would you like to ride with Uncle Buddy and me?"

Cricket abandoned his daddy and granddaddy without a backward look and climbed happily into Buddy's backseat.

"Didn't those kids do a fine job this morning?" Martha asked as I headed out of town.

"Yeah, but Bethany, particularly, still looks awfully pale. She seems to be taking DeWayne's death real hard."

"That's not all. She and her daddy had a real row last night. She had told us earlier that she and Todd were going with another couple to a movie, but after she heard about DeWayne, she decided she'd stay with the other girls. When she called Todd to tell him, he got furious. Came down to your place and dragged her out into the backyard to yell at her. Ridd didn't like that, so he went after them and heard Todd telling her it was going to be a great party and she had to come. That was the first we'd heard about a party. At least Bethany stuck to her intentions and said she needed to be with her team right then, but that made Todd so mad, he took off fast and spun a rut in your driveway as he turned onto the road."

"I'll send him a bill," I joked. The truth was, he could have dug a pit in my driveway if that meant he was too mad with Bethany to come back.

"But that wasn't the worst. Ridd started reading Bethany the riot act for telling us it was a movie when it was really a party, and she got furious with him for eavesdropping. Then he told her she wasn't going out with Todd any time he'd been drinking. She insisted Todd hadn't been drinking and Ridd insisted he had, and they got so loud, I finally ordered them down to the barn. Poor Bo had to listen to them yell at each other for nearly an hour."

"Anger's a great way to forget for a little while that you're grieving," I reminded her.

"I know. Ridd finally realized that and told her he was sorry. They both came back to the house crying. But Bethany has good cause to be pale. Between her daddy fussing and

Todd yelling at her, she had quite a night even without De-Wayne's death."

Luckily, we had arrived. It sure wasn't the time to mention that Hollis was worried that somebody she knew was sleeping with somebody else.

The restaurant we'd picked was known for its fried catfish and hush puppies, but the hostess was so skinny, I could have used her shinbone for a needle.

Joe Riddley leaned down and muttered in my ear, "I hope she's not an advertisement for the quality of the food." I smacked him lightly, but she hadn't heard. She was explaining to Ridd that there would be a thirty-minute wait for a table for ten, but they could immediately give us one table for four and one for six.

Ridd waved toward the smaller table halfway across the room. "Okay, kids, you eat there, behave." I wondered if Garnet would rather eat with the adults, but she seemed happy enough to take Cricket's hand and go with him.

"We'd better watch those two," I joked to Sara Meg as we headed to our own table far across the room. "He's got a serious crush on Garnet."

Buddy laughed, but Sara Meg said wistfully, "He'd be the first male she ever looked at. I used to picture making my girls prom dresses and wedding gowns, but Garnet has no interest in boys whatsoever. She even skipped her senior prom. And Hollis—" She sighed and shook her head. "Sports, sports, and sports. That's all she thinks about."

"Skipped her prom?" That seemed an odd way to put it.

Martha and Ridd had already reached the table and taken chairs across from each other at one end. Joe Riddley had gone around to sit by Martha, so I headed for the chair by Ridd as Sara Meg replied, "She was invited by a real nice boy—"

"—but bad old Uncle Buddy didn't realize it was prom weekend, so he had rented a condo at the beach," Buddy finished as he gallantly held my chair. I motioned for Sara Meg to sit by me. I hadn't seen her in a long time, and I wanted her close.

"*Sweet* old Buddy had also found somebody to keep the store Saturday to give me a little break," Sara Meg added as she sat down, "but Garnet had a choice. I told her we'd let Buddy go alone if she wanted to go to the prom. She said she'd rather go to the beach." She picked up her menu and added absently, "I was real put out with her, to tell the truth." She looked at Martha over her menu. "I wanted to see her all dressed up, coming down the stairs." She sounded so wistful, I wondered if what she really wanted was a memory of her own mother watching her come downstairs in a prom dress. Some hurts never heal.

"You've still got Hollis's prom and two weddings to look forward to," Martha consoled her.

"And pay for," Ridd added glumly. We all laughed.

As the waitress distributed our drinks, Buddy looked around the table and said, "This sure is peaceful after a week in the war zone."

I thought at first he was referring—rather crudely—to the two episodes of graffiti and DeWayne's death, but Sara Meg gave an embarrassed little laugh and explained, "The girls have been fighting more than usual. Pick, pick, pick at each other, all week."

"What's it about?" Martha wondered.

Sara Meg felt around in her purse and brought out reading glasses. "I don't have a clue. I asked, but you know how kids are. They slide away from questions like fried eggs on a buttered plate. Garnet says she's tired from summer school and Hollis says she has some stuff to think about that she has to figure out on her own. I tried to make Garnet tell me if Hollis is in some kind of trouble, but Garnet said not that she's aware of." Sara Meg tried to laugh again, but her heart wasn't in it. "Of course, Hollis could be six months' pregnant before Garnet looked up from her book and noticed. I don't mean that, of course," she added quickly.

"I don't think any of us have any worries on that score," Ridd assured her.

I held up my menu to hide my face and hoped Hollis *hadn't* been talking to DeWayne about Bethany. Most of the time I think of myself as a modern mother, but I sure didn't want to bring that up with Ridd and Martha.

Martha asked, "Does Hollis even have a special boyfriend right now?"

Sara Meg shook her head, and Buddy added, "Not since she stopped hanging around with Tyrone Noland. Boy, that was a relief."

"He wasn't a boyfriend," Sara Meg protested, "just a friend. And he used to be real nice."

I turned to Ridd and asked softly, "Did DeWayne teach Tyrone or Smitty?"

"Tyrone, yeah, but I don't know about Smitty."

I was feeling real clever until I realized that meant it was Tyrone, not Smitty, who might have a motive for murdering DeWayne. Then I didn't feel good at all.

Our waitress returned and we all ordered catfish, but I pointed out to her that whoever decided to have "all you can eat" that day should have added a footnote: "except for Yarbrough men."

Martha asked Ridd, "Are you going, or shall I, to make sure Cricket doesn't order french fries, mashed potatoes, and a baked potato as his three vegetables?"

"You go. I've got to stay here and make sure Mama doesn't embarrass me by telling stories from my childhood."

"Do you have any influence over your mother?" Buddy asked. "Nobody else does."

I expected Ridd to laugh, but he gave me a very solemn look. "We'll see. I'm going to try to influence her. I want her to find out who killed DeWayne."

Nobody was more surprised than I was. After what he'd said the day before about "poking my nose where it doesn't belong" and "meddling," I wanted to bop him.

"DeWayne killed himself," Joe Riddley said firmly, pouring himself a second glass of tea. He always claims going to church is thirsty work. "It's real sad, but true. So you all just let it go at that, you hear me?"

"Are they sure?" Buddy wondered. "I mean, DeWayne seemed to be on top of the world, between the team doing so well and having a job he liked. He came by Thursday morning and told me he really liked being back in Hopemore."

"Nevertheless, the police are satisfied he killed himself," Ridd said gloomily. "Chief Muggins told me so last night. However, I think somebody had to have pushed his buttons to make him do it, and in my book, that counts as murder. I just don't know how we'll prove it."

Joe Riddley leaned across the table and pinned him with the glare he used to use when Ridd was eight and declaring he wasn't going to church that week. "You all aren't *going* to prove it. That's what we pay police officers for. MacLaren has no call to go mixing in stuff like that." He never calls me that unless he's upset.

"Ike can figure it out," I said in a soothing voice. "He's a lot smarter than me." When Joe Riddley relaxed, I figured maybe I'd learned a little bit from Mama after all.

We went on to talk of other things, but in a few minutes I noticed Ridd pounding one fist lightly on the edge of the table. That was unusual—Walker is generally the pounder in our family. I leaned over and asked, real low, "What changed your mind, son?"

I had to bend even closer to hear him. "I saw Chief Muggins last night at the Bi-Lo. We'd run out of snacks and he was getting his groceries." Chief Muggins had been getting his own groceries ever since his wife made one too many trips to the emergency room with a broken bone and decided she'd be safer in Atlanta. "I asked if he had any leads yet, and he said he isn't looking for leads—it's a clear case of suicide. When I protested that somebody had to have driven DeWayne to do it, he shrugged and said, 'I got more important things to do than try and figure out what makes those people do what they do.' " Tears reddened Ridd's eyes. "You know as well as I do that if DeWayne had been white—"

"Hush," Joe Riddley growled. "Don't say things like that in public. She's a magistrate."

"And that still takes some getting used to." Buddy's eyes twinkled across the table. I gave Ridd a warning kick. We'd talk later when nobody was listening in.

I tuned in to Martha, who had come back and was telling Sara Meg about talking to Garnet's psychology class. "She asked a real good question, too."

"Oh? What was it?" Any mother likes to hear about it when her child has been bright.

"I talked about child abuse, particularly sexual abuse, and described symptoms and various treatments. Garnet asked the one question I'd failed to cover: 'What happens to victims of abuse when they grow up?' "

"What did you say?" I asked, intrigued. Martha knew a lot about a lot of things, but this was one subject I'd never heard her discuss.

"Some remain victims, repeatedly seeking out others to abuse them in various ways. Some manage to get enough counseling and support to function pretty normally. We call those survivors. A few become thrivers—people who are strong enough to reach out and help others in similar situations. Some thrivers even become professionals—pastors, counselors, or psychiatrists." She sighed. "But those are the rare ones. Most bear scars the rest of their lives. This class had an extra-good outcome, though. Garnet told me afterwards about a little girl she suspected was being abused, and it turned out she was right. The child has been sent to a safer place."

"Who?" Buddy, Sara Meg, Ridd, and Joe Riddley spoke in unison. In a town like Hopemore, it's easy to think that things like that can't happen. We know our neighbors and pretty much what goes on in our neighborhoods. A lot of folks, for instance, suspected Charlie Muggins was beating his wife. It just took our youth pastor a while to convince her she could safely leave. I, too, wondered who the child was. The idea that she had been going through that kind of horror and we hadn't suspected was intolerable.

"I can't give her name, but it was one of Garnet's piano pupils. I had the Department of Family and Children's Services check it out, and they removed the child at once." Martha heaved another sigh, one that seemed to come from far under the earth. "If we had the space, I'd love to take in kids like that. I can't stand to think there are children who don't have a safe, happy place to sleep at night."

"Me, neither," Buddy agreed, setting his glass exactly in the ring where it had been.

"I'm glad Garnet told *you*." Sara Meg emphasized the last word, sounding more sad than glad. She added wistfully. "I don't even know who her piano pupils are. I didn't know she was taking psychology. She tells me nothing. If you have a lecture on secretive daughters, I'd like to hear it sometime."

"Introductory psych is such a waste of time, though." Buddy sounded like he was the world's foremost authority on the subject. "It teaches kids just enough to make them think they're messed up without giving them tools to fix themselves. Take me, for instance. I took it, and I'm still a mess." Everybody laughed. I appreciated his lightening things up a bit.

"Maybe Garnet will become a psychiatrist," Joe Riddley suggested thoughtfully. "She can try to fix Buddy, and even if she fails, she can support you both in your old age."

Everybody laughed except Sara Meg. "Somebody may have to," she said in an unsteady voice. "Have you all heard they're definitely putting a big superstore out on the edge of town?"

Joe Riddley nodded. "They've already started bulldozing." He slewed his eyes toward me and sent a silent message: *See? I told you Sara Meg never notices a thing.*

I frowned at him. I didn't want her seeing that look. I said, "At least, if Garnet works for Laura she can help out a bit. Did she get the job?"

Sara Meg nodded, but before she could say anything,

Buddy leaned across the table with a worried pucker between his eyes. "I wish you hadn't suggested that, Mac. Garnet's not real strong, and she's already got a lot on her plate."

"It's not hard work," Sara Meg protested. "She's at a desk all afternoon, and Laura told her she can study when things are slow."

"But we agreed she'd concentrate on school," Buddy reminded her.

"I know, but she wanted to give it a try. . . ." Her voice trailed off uncertainly.

"At least she told you about the job," Joe Riddley pointed out. "That's a good sign."

Sara Meg brightened. "It is, isn't it? Of course, she was real excited about it, and I was the first person she saw. If she'd run into Buddy or Hollis first—or anybody else she knew—I wouldn't have heard a word. Still, she did tell me. And like Mac said, it will help to have her earning something." Now it was her forehead with the worry pucker. "What are you all going to do? I don't know whether to try to sell out now or wait to see if the store can make it. I'd feel real dishonest selling to anybody if it's going under, but if I try to make it and can't—" Her voice dropped to a whisper.

We all said what we could to reassure her—it would take months to get their store up and running; she didn't have to make a decision right away; maybe something else would come along. None of us sounded real convincing. Maybe it's because we weren't convinced.

Finally, Ridd leaned across me and suggested to Sara Meg, "Maybe you ought to marry a rich man. Have you considered that?"

Martha reached over the table and smacked him lightly. "Men! You think you're the answer to all our worries."

That, finally, brought back Sara Meg's smile. "Find me an eligible millionaire, and I'll marry him tomorrow. Hollis would be thrilled. She's thrown every single man in town my way."

"What about Garnet?" I wondered. "Would she mind?"

"I don't know. What do you think?" Sara Meg asked Buddy.

He considered the matter, then shook his head. "I don't know, either. Garnet and Fred were real close."

Martha decided this was an opening for what she wanted to say. "I'm not sure she's come to terms with his death. Has she ever gotten counseling?"

"No." Sara Meg looked distressed. I'd be distressed, too, if I figured other people worried about one of my children, but she wasn't reluctant to discuss it. "Lately she seems even quieter than usual, and I've caught her crying a few times, but when I ask about it, she bites my head off." She hesitated. "I found her daddy's picture under her pillow last week when I was stripping the beds."

"The local counseling center has some good grief groups," Martha suggested. "She might benefit from talking to somebody and maybe joining one."

"Maybe so." Sara Meg sounded like the idea had never occurred to her. "Sometimes I think she blames me for Fred dying. And between finding that picture and watching the two of them circling each other these past few days like dogs ready to fight, I'm getting crazy myself. Did you ever feel like you could happily give your children away?"

"I tried several times," I told her. "Took out ads and everything, but nobody would have them. Speaking of kids, here come four good-looking specimens searching for a home."

Garnet and Cricket arrived first. I hadn't had a chance to talk to the girls after church, so I told her, "You look mighty pretty today," although she'd have looked better in something brighter than that brown skirt and a beige cotton sweater. "You look almost as good as your mama."

She brushed a hair off Sara Meg's collar. "Yeah, she looks pretty good *today*." If we hadn't known better, we'd have thought Sara Meg was an ordinary woman with a pretty face she wore on Sundays.

As Hollis came up to the table, Joe Riddley said, "Fine job

today, honey. I didn't know we had a budding singer among us."

She turned such a happy pink that her freckles almost disappeared. "Thanks. I wasn't sure I could hit that A without squeaking, but it came out all right, I think."

"It came out great," Bethany corrected her. She looked happy, too, so I guessed that whatever had been wrong between them was fixed.

"And you played beautifully," I told Garnet, trying to include her in the conversation.

She shrugged. "It's easy playing music for folks to sing to. Nobody notices your mistakes."

"She likes playing Art's songs." Hollis drew out the last two words as only a little sister can. "He wrote her one that's actually not bad." Ignoring Garnet's quick, angry motion, she sang softly, " 'I once saw an angel in a forest glen, walking with her hair ablaze. She turned to give me a winsome grin, and—' "

Garnet elbowed her. Hollis elbowed her back. Bethany pulled her away.

"Who's Art?" Sara Meg asked the rest of us.

"He's a poet," Hollis drawled, sticking out her tongue at her sister.

Garnet seized her shoulder and shook her in fury. "You have no business going through my things."

"Garnet!" her mother cried. "Stop it!"

Garnet stopped, but she spoke with venom. "She keeps going through my private stuff and you don't do a thing about it." She looked at the floor and added sullenly, "That song was a class project. Art's taking a poetry class and wanted me to set it to music." She stomped off toward the door, then turned and looked back.

I looked quickly at Hollis to make sure she hadn't been blasted into outer space by that glare. Like the angel in Art's poem, she was grinning.

❦ 20 ❦

Joe Riddley and I decided to go back to our place for a Sunday-afternoon nap. Ronnie had a key to Walker's if the women needed a snooze. I could have slept a lot longer if we hadn't gotten a frantic call from Martha.

"Cricket's missing. Bethany went home with Hollis, and the rest of us came home and slept. When Ridd and I woke up, he was gone. He isn't on the property." That's better than an alarm clock for any grandmother.

I shook Joe Riddley. "Cricket's gone off somewhere and Martha can't find him." He had on his pants and shoes and was clattering down the stairs before I got my hair combed.

I snatched up my pocketbook as he grabbed his cap. Those things are so much a part of us, our boys tease us that they're going to bury Joe Riddley in his red Yarbrough's cap and me with my pocketbook. I tell them to buy me a new one for the occasion.

"You look around downtown. I'll swing out toward the nursery," Joe Riddley ordered as we ran to our cars. We took off like we were part of a movie about a high-speed car chase. I beat him down the drive by a hair.

My heart was pounding as I clutched the steering wheel, frustrated I couldn't soar over the trees looking for that precious small boy. In far less time than it takes to tell it, I'd pictured him hit by a truck on the highway, struck by a car in the Bi-Lo parking lot, and swept into a van and carried off to California. As I passed Spence's pasture, I scanned it, but thank God, it was empty. The cattle pond is mighty tempting to small males. Just ask my two sons.

I was almost to the highway when I saw Cricket coming my way, pedaling his little bike with a lot of difficulty on the gravel. I screeched to a stop and jumped from my car. Joe Riddley skidded to a stop behind me. "You scared us all to death," I stormed. "What on earth are you doing all the way down here? It's over a mile. And how did you get across the highway?"

His face was pink with exertion and sweat matted his hair, but his grin was proud. "I looked both ways and nobody was coming. It's boring at our house," he added.

"Not anymore it isn't," I told him grimly. "You scared the living daylights out of everybody. You can't go riding off—"

"Easy, Little Bit." Joe Riddley put a hand on my shoulder. "Taking a ride, son?"

"Coming to swim, actually." That was a new word, and he was proud of it, too. "Mama and Daddy are sleeping," he added, as casual as if he rode down every day.

"You aren't allowed to swim without grown-ups," his granddaddy reminded him. How on earth did that man stay so calm in times like this? It drives me crazy sometimes, but it's one of the things I love about him and depend on.

"You were home," Cricket pointed out. "You're grown-ups."

"We might not have been home. We're staying over at Uncle Walker's, remember?"

Uncertainty flickered behind his brown eyes. "Oh, yeah, that's right."

I jumped in. "And you don't come to swim unless you're invited." I hoped my heart would soon get out of my throat and let me catch my breath.

Cricket's lower lip trembled. "Bethany got to swim. And all the Honeybees. It's not fair."

Joe Riddley squatted down and looked him in the eye.

"Do you think it's fair to scare your mother and daddy? They're real worried. They don't know where you are."

"Call and tell them. *Then* we'll swim." He set his right foot against his pedal again.

His granddaddy picked him up, bike and all. "Don't you have a rule about leaving your yard?" Cricket looked down and didn't reply. "Can't swim today, then. We can't reward you for breaking the rules. But I'll take you home and we'll fix a time when you can come swim. Okay?"

Cricket's lips tightened and he got a mutinous look in his eyes. "You got that pool every day of your life, and I don't ever get to swim."

"Keep that up and you're heading in that direction," I warned.

Joe Riddley separated boy from bike, stowed one in the trunk and held the door for the other to climb in. "He's fine, Little Bit. You can relax. Call Martha and tell her we're coming."

"Tell her not to spank me," Cricket ordered. "I'd have asked," he added virtuously, "but I didn't want to bother her when she was sleeping."

Ridd chuckled when I told him that over the phone; then he sighed. "I don't know what we're going to do with him. Bethany never wandered off, but that's the third time he's left our lot this month."

"Bethany stayed down here until she started school," I reminded him. After Cricket was born, Martha arranged her schedule to be home more. Cricket also went to nursery school, because his parents felt he was too much for Clarinda to handle. "I warned you when you bought that house that it's too near the highway."

"Well, it's the one we've got, so Cricket's got to learn to live in it, under our rules. I don't remember you and Daddy having this much trouble raising us."

You boys grew up in this house, at the end of a road with lots to do and space to roam, whispered a nagging voice that lives somewhere at the back of my head. Joe Riddley's folks moved to town when Walker was born, telling us the big house was getting to be too much for them. We moved in, and our boys grew up in the same house Joe Riddley and three other generations of Yarbroughs had—the big blue one his great-great-granddaddy built. *You and Joe Riddley have talked about looking for another place,* added that pesky voice.

Other things keep coming up, I reminded it. Maybe Cricket's bicycle adventure was a wake-up call. I'd think about that as soon as I got time.

To Ridd, I said, "The operative phrase is 'I don't remember.' I clearly remember somebody thinking he could fly from the roof of our barn and a few discussions with the palm of your daddy's hand about Hubert's cattle pond."

"Yeah, well—"

"Yeah, well. But listen, did you mean what you said about us looking for whoever drove DeWayne to do what he did?" I wasn't ready to mention my question about what he might have jumped from. There was no point in Ridd thinking it could be murder unless he had to.

"If we can do it without Daddy killing us both."

"I thought of a few things we could check on. Could you find out whether DeWayne gave a bad grade to any of Smitty's gang, somebody who might be holding a grudge? I'm going to talk to Tyrone again, if I can find him, and see if he knows who painted DeWayne's house. You got any other bright ideas?"

"Not right now, but I'll think it over. I'm coming by the store tomorrow to pick up some more begonias, and then Yasheika and I have to decide what to do about the team. She wants me to coach it, but I don't know. . . ."

The specter of DeWayne hanging in the locker room floated between us. "I'll see you tomorrow, then." Mothers do what we can, but some decisions a man has to make himself.

*   *   *

I'd barely hung up when Clarinda called. "Why didn't you tell me you were going home? Are those women supposed to move all their stuff down to your place?" She sounded as aggrieved as if we had taken off for Mars and left guests without food or water.

"We didn't 'go home.' We just came by for a nap. I'm heading back to Walker's right now. There's no point in all of us moving unless we have to. Are the women back there?"

"Yeah, they went back after dinner to lay down awhile. Now they're real upset and need you. Elda got through to Gerrick—at the prison, you know?"

"I know." If Gerrick weren't in prison, DeWayne could have grown up in Hopemore and become the strong young man he was created to be.

"He wants DeWayne buried out at Mount Olivet, in his family plot. Elda and her sister want to take him back up to Washington to bury him there. Yasheika is all confused, wanting to honor her daddy's request but not feeling real kindly about Hope County—"

"—for which we can't blame her—"

"—so Elda doesn't know what to do. You need to get on over there."

I have never been an expert on where other people ought to bury their dead, but I know better than to try to reason with Clarinda in that mood. "As soon as I feed the animals."

I gave Bo food and water in the barn and fed Lulu and put her in the yard dogs' pen. I could hear her complaints all the way to Hubert's. Beagles are never shy about telling you when they've been insulted, at full voice.

On my way, I called Joe Riddley over at Ridd's. "Why don't you drive them up to Mount Olivet?" he suggested. "At least they can see the place."

Ronnie was at Walker's, too, and said he'd like to drive out to the cemetery with us. Yasheika gave him a look that said as plain as day that he was horning in where he wasn't wanted, but I remembered that his mama was buried there.

I could tell by the way Yasheika's aunt—whose name
was Doris—climbed into my small backseat that she wasn't
crazy about driving five miles and back in cramped quarters
on what she considered a fool's errand. When Elda got in the
front, Yasheika looked at the available remaining space and
announced sourly, "I'll take my own car. You want to ride
with me, Ronnie?"

"Sure. My life insurance is paid up."

As we drove through the countryside, Elda pointed out
houses and barns she remembered from when she used to
live in Hopemore. She told me they'd been raised down near
Wrens, but she'd come here to work in the meat-packing
plant, which is where she'd met Gerrick.

Mount Olivet was a little white frame church with a squat
steeple, sitting in a bare-ground parking lot. Tall pines
shaded the church and surrounded the cemetery, which lay
up a slight rise to the east. It was a lovely burial ground,
smelling of pine and honeysuckle, with grass full of sunny-
faced dandelions and mockingbirds singing overhead. People had placed vases of flowers beside many stones, and if
they were plastic, at least they were bright and showed
somebody cared. It was the kind of place I'd feel better
about leaving one of my children, if I had to leave him anywhere. From the look in Elda's eyes, I could tell she was
now leaning in the same direction.

Ronnie went quietly toward his mother's grave. Yasheika
prowled, shredding a dandelion. I got the feeling she hadn't
spent much of her life roaming cemeteries. Some folks do,
some don't.

"There's your grandparents." Elda pointed out a tombstone with *Lawton* carved on it.

Yasheika gave the stone one look and shrugged. "That
doesn't mean a thing to me. DeWayne and I never knew
them. You know what, Mama? I don't think he'd want to be
buried way out here, miles from nowhere."

"It's mighty pretty. And I thought you wanted to do what
your daddy wants."

"I'm changing my mind. DeWayne wouldn't want to be out here in the sticks."

"This isn't the sticks, honey. It's lovely. Real peaceful under the trees." Elda's voice had lost its Washington sharpness and was getting softly Southern again out in that cemetery.

Yasheika's was sharp enough for them both. "I don't want DeWayne way down here and us up there."

"Maybe you ought to think about somebody else for a change."

Uh-oh. They were starting to yell. This is where Clarinda expected me to play peacemaker and help them come to a good decision. I sure was glad when Ronnie strolled back and said, "Like DeWayne told Mr. Tanner the other day, you have to get over things the best you can. Seems to me like it's not a matter of what DeWayne or even Gerrick wants at this point. DeWayne's not going to care, and Gerrick's not going to be visiting him anytime soon. You all need to do what will most comfort *you* in these coming months."

Yasheika turned and glared at him for horning in again.

I said quickly, "Your mother's buried here, isn't she?"

"Yes, ma'am." He looked toward her stone again. "I don't get out here as much as I'd like to, but it always makes me feel better to drop by."

Elda took Yasheika's arm. "He's right. Your daddy isn't going to be doing any visiting, so let's put DeWayne where it will do *us* the most good."

Yasheika jerked away. "Daddy is going to get out, Mama. Can't you get that through your head? He is going to get out if it's the last thing I ever do. And if he wants DeWayne here—"

"Don't talk about the last thing you'll do when your brother's just died," her aunt Doris snapped.

Yasheika turned so we couldn't see her face. "Sorry. But Daddy *is* going to get out, so it makes me mad when Mama won't believe it. And if he wants DeWayne here, we ought to put him here." She sounded, however, like they'd be abandoning DeWayne to a fate worse than death. The little cemetery hadn't worked any magic on her spirit.

"We'd never see his grave again," Elda protested. "Never get to put flowers on it or say a little prayer beside my baby, never just stand beside him and remember all the things he used to do . . ." Her voice broke and she turned away, sobbing. Doris went to take her in her arms.

Ronnie stepped next to Yasheika and spoke so low, I almost couldn't hear. "When your daddy does get out, you think he's gonna want to come back to Hopemore? More likely, he'll wind up in Washington where you all are. Put DeWayne where it will do everybody the most good."

"Where he'd do me the most good is right here, alive and well." Yasheika turned and stomped off toward her car.

Ronnie took a step after her, but I grabbed his arm. "Let her be for a minute."

Doris and Elda were wandering around finding names they recognized, giving Elda time to recover a bit. I asked Ronnie to show me his mother's grave.

As we stood there, I asked, "When did you hear De-Wayne say that thing to Buddy about getting over things the best you can?"

Ronnie bent down, pulled a grass stem, and started chewing it. He'd learned that from Ridd when he was five and spent that whole summer with grass between his lips. I pulled up a stalk of my own. The tips are real sweet. But I looked at him to show I wanted an answer.

"Thursday morning," he said reluctantly. "DeWayne came to our office, and my desk is in the main room, not far from Mr. Tanner's door."

I smiled to hear that Buddy was "Mr. Tanner" now that he was also boss.

"What else did you hear?"

"Not a lot. I was waiting for somebody to get off the phone and show me what to do." He flung a stone toward the horizon.

As a little boy, Ronnie had given new meaning to the

word "nosy." He had outgrown most of that, but surely he had wanted to know what his best friend wanted with his boss. "Did you hear DeWayne tell Buddy he was Gerrick Lawton?"

"Well, yeah, I did hear that. They didn't close the door right away. I didn't know who Gerrick Lawton was, and it was such a strange thing for him to say that I did listen a bit."

"What did Buddy say?"

"He gave a little whoop—you know how he does—and the next thing I knew they were hugging and laughing and slapping each other on the back. Then they talked for a while—stuff like, 'Do you remember the time we painted the crosses and Sara Meg made us scrub it off?' and 'Remember how we used to play house, with Anne as the mama and you as the daddy and me as the little boy?'—stuff like that. Then they talked softer for a while, until DeWayne raised his voice a little and said that thing about everybody needing to get over things the best they can. Then he told Buddy that Yasheika was planning to bring all that back up again, and you thought he—Buddy—ought to know, and Buddy said that was kind of you. They noticed the door was cracked around then, and somebody closed it. When DeWayne left, they stopped by my desk and Buddy said, 'Ron, you won't believe it, but this man used to be one of my best friends.' He showed DeWayne to the door and they were laughing and cutting up all the way. As he left, DeWayne gave Mr. Tanner his card and said, 'Call me sometime,' and Mr. Tanner said something about he'd talk to Hollis. Then they hugged again. That's all."

It didn't exactly fall under his earlier category of "not a lot," but it at least explained how Buddy got DeWayne's cell-phone number. I'd wondered about that.

We ambled back to the cars. Yasheika sat in her driver's seat. As Ronnie went to the other side, I saw her give him a secret look of grudging respect and say something only he could hear.

He turned and said to Elda, "Yasheika agrees you ought to take DeWayne home. Why don't we drive you to the funeral home right now, to make arrangements?"

"They haven't released the body yet, have they?" I hated to ask, but I also hated for DeWayne to get shipped back to Washington before all the investigating that could be done had been done.

"Not yet," Elda said sadly, "but we might as well make what arrangements we can for whenever they let us take him home."

Before they left, I took Elda's hands in mine. "Before you leave town, I hope you'll have a memorial service here. There are a lot of people who would like to pay their last respects."

Her eyes filled with tears. "We sure will. Thank you so much."

I handed her a tissue from my pocketbook. She was still dabbing her eyes as they drove away. I was, too.

ࢫ21ࢭ

Monday morning Ridd dropped into the chair by my office window, stretched his long legs in front of him, and poked the arm with a puzzled look. "I thought this was red plaid."

"It was until Christmas. That's when I had it re-covered." The chair and valance over our window were now dark green, decorated with game birds.

"Guess I'm a little slow in the noticing department."

"I guess you are. I reckon you haven't noticed anything that might help us figure out who drove DeWayne to do what he did, either?"

"Nope, but I did find out that DeWayne taught Smitty. DeWayne flunked him last semester, in fact, which is why he has to go to summer school."

"Do you reckon Smitty cares whether he passes or fails?"

"Oddly enough, he does. He usually gets A's and B's. Smitty's not dumb, just wicked."

That certainly might give Smitty a motive to paint up De-Wayne's house and send him the clippings, but I shared Yasheika's uncertainty that he'd kill a teacher who flunked him. I needed to talk to Smitty, that much was certain. But first, I wanted to know what Ridd told Yasheika about the team.

When I asked, he sighed. "I was planning to tell her that I wouldn't do it, that we'd have to call in one of the other coaches from the county. But Bethany and Hollis carried on so about how we have to do this for DeWayne's memory and how he'd want me to do it for him, that I guess I'll do it. Hollis even says she'll catch now. I wish Yasheika would come back to help but she's not real crazy about Hope County right now."

"Which we can all understand. But maybe if you sic Hollis and Bethany on her and point out that DeWayne's rent is paid through the end of the month, and if you say that somebody will pay her airfare so she can fly up for DeWayne's funeral, then come back—"

"Is that an offer?"

"I think the team sponsor can come up with a plane ticket if she will use it."

We sat in a few minutes of silence. Ridd was the first to speak. "You know, Mama, something's got to be done about Smitty. Kids at school are scared to use the lunchroom if his gang is in there. Teachers are nervous about giving any of them a bad grade. They've taken over Myrtle's corner booth like it's their private dining room, and the way they acted about DeWayne, Yasheika and Ronnie being in the place ought to be illegal. Can't you do something?"

"They're juveniles," I reminded him. "Magistrates don't deal with juveniles."

"What's the point in having a mother who's a judge if she can't help you out?" He pulled himself to his feet. "If we can prove Smitty drove one of the best friends I ever had to take his life, I'm going to deal with him real good."

Now I knew how Joe Riddley felt when I headed off investigating a murder. "Be real careful, son. He's mean."

"So am I." From the back, he looked a whole lot like his daddy on the warpath.

After that, I signed warrants for four deputies who came in so close together I didn't have time to think. Then, just as I was catching my breath, I got a call from Slade Rutherford down at the paper. Slade and I hadn't hit it off when he first came to town, but after I had alerted him to a few news stories Chief Muggins had been trying to conceal, and he had liked my monthly gardening column so well he'd moved it to a better location in the paper, we'd become better friends.

"I've got something here that baffles me," he greeted me.

Just then, Joe Riddley came in. For forty years my husband has persisted in believing I can talk on the phone and listen to him at the same time, so he started right in explaining something about a shipment of roses. I said quickly, in my most charming, apologetic voice, "Listen, I'll come right down to check that ad. Joe Riddley's just come in. He can hold the fort here."

Slade chuckled. "I'd hoped you'd come. I just hadn't gotten to that. See you in a few minutes."

I grabbed my pocketbook. "Be back in a little while. I need to look at next week's ad for the paper. There may be a problem with it." I hurried to my car before he could ask how I'd missed the problem, since I wrote the copy.

The person working the *Statesman*'s front desk that morning was Chancey Carter, their circulation manager. Chancey was a large woman who seemed to hover over a desk rather than sit behind it. She was so conscientious, Slade sometimes joked that if he'd let her, she'd hand deliver the papers to be sure they got to the right destinations.

She wore thick glasses and a big bun of hair as black as it was when we started first grade together. In Hopemore, you don't pass an old schoolmate without speaking, so I asked how her mother was. Mrs. Carter was one of the crabbiest old women God ever made. At ninety, she was the bane of our local nursing-home staff, but Chancey remained devoted to her even on days when she thought Chancey had come from the IRS to take all her nonexistent money.

"She had a little turn on Wednesday, so I had to leave • early and spend the night with her," Chancey told me in a gush of worry. She started a long droning story about how her mother's bowels wouldn't move, and then when they did—"right on the stroke of twelve!" in case I was interested in that intimate detail—the aide didn't come for the bedpan because she was down the hall, fighting with her son, who had come to ask for money, and Chancey had to empty the thing herself, and what were we paying those people for if they didn't do the work? There were other people who would love to have a job if they'd quit. By then I was a bit numb.

"Is she any better now?" I asked to stem the tide.

"Oh, yes. She even knew me yesterday. How's Joe Riddley?"

"Ornery as ever, but pretty much back to normal. Slade in?" I tried to sound casual.

. She nodded. "He sure is. But your ad is fine. I checked."

"People who listen in on phone calls are apt to hear things about themselves they'd rather not," I warned.

"I picked up by mistake, trying to call and check on Mama." She and I both knew she had listened in on purpose. All her life Chancey has thrived on knowing other people's secrets. When I went into Slade's office, I shut the door firmly behind me.

He looked up and grinned. "I see you know Miss Chancey."

I nodded. "Since first grade. She hasn't changed a bit."

Going to see Slade was always a pleasure. He had the kind of dark good looks that made a woman look better just being in his vicinity. That morning he was right handsome in tan slacks with a rust cotton sweater. He leaned back in his chair, locked his fingers, and stretched his arms over his head. "You and Ridd found DeWayne Evans's body, I understand. Want to tell me how that happened, for the record?"

"Yeah, but just say Ridd found him. He'd gone over to the school to see how DeWayne was taking the mess somebody made of his house. I hope you got pictures of that."

"We got them, but I was out of town at the time. I was just getting in when I picked up the call about DeWayne." Back in the winter, Slade had fitted his car with a radio that picked up the police band.

"That's two major incidents we've had at night since the

police discontinued our night patrols," I pointed out. "The school and DeWayne's house."

He raised his eyebrows and reached for a pencil. "Discontinued night patrols? I hadn't heard about that." He jotted a note. "So, tell me about finding the body."

I gave him the gory details, reminding him again not to use my name.

"An anonymous source, that's you. Was anybody else around besides you and Ridd?"

"Only the security guard at the front door. I don't think you'll get much from him. What was it you wanted me to see?"

He jerked his head toward a credenza behind his desk. "All this came in Saturday's mail, and I just opened it this morning."

He had spread out a number of computer printouts and a note written in purple block letters on a sheet torn from a spiral notebook. A large manila envelope was propped against the credenza on the floor. I got up and went to see what he had.

The first clipping was three columns, and the picture showed Gerrick Lawton shackled and being taken to jail. The others were stories about Anne Colder's death, Gerrick's trial, and—as I had suspected—copies of the stories about DeWayne I'd read on the Internet. I got out my reading glasses to be sure, but Slade didn't have that little paragraph Yasheika mentioned about DeWayne being cleared.

I didn't need my reading glasses for the note. Its letters were big and square.

YOU DON'T KNOW IT ALL. DEWAYNE EVANS'S DADDY KILLED A WHITE GIRL. DEWAYNE EVANS RAPED A WHITE GIRL. PEOPLE WANT TO KNOW WHY HE'S IN THIS TOWN. DO WE REALLY WANT HIM HERE, HANGING AROUND OUR WHITE GIRLS?

There it was: the word "raped" with the same three purple letters I'd seen on the burned page. Bile rose in my throat.

Slade was watching me closely. "You aren't surprised, are you?"

I shook my head. "I saw ashes in DeWayne's wastebasket, and bits hadn't burned. I knew about Gerrick, of course, and when I got back to my office, I checked the Internet and found the rest."

"Including this one they didn't bother to send, I presume." Slade laid one more printout beside the others, the article saying DeWayne had been cleared.

I shook my head. "Yasheika told me about this later, but I stopped reading one article too soon," I confessed. "I'm glad you didn't."

"No newsman worth his salt would presume those were the only clippings about that story."

I couldn't say a word, but I think he could tell from my face how proud I was to know him. He took back his article and asked, "You got any idea who sent that bunch?"

"Ideas, but no proof. I've also got a lot of anger at whoever it was. You may not know it, but DeWayne never got over the terror of seeing his daddy pulled from their car and hauled off to jail. Just thinking about it was enough to give him the shakes, so the idea of all this being spread around town, even though he was innocent, may well have been enough to drive him over the edge. Whether the law ever admits it or not, if he took his own life it was still a kind of murder. Are you going to mention all this other stuff when you report DeWayne's death?"

Slade shifted in his chair. "Well, like the letter said, people want to know."

"What you really mean is, this will sell more papers. I'm a big believer in freedom of the press from political oppression, but I don't think the Constitution intended to give papers license to print things that are nasty or hurtful. I don't even think people really want to know."

"If it bleeds, it leads. You know that." But he had the grace to look embarrassed.

"Somebody ought to check up on all the damage done to

people by that philosophy." I picked up my pocketbook. "At least point out that both times, DeWayne was the victim—and now he's been made a victim again. Have you called the police yet about this?"

"I'm going to call them as soon as I write the story," he promised. "Maybe they can trace the note or the envelope."

I gave the note one more look and felt sorrow clutch my heart. I was pretty sure they could trace it, all right, to Tyrone Noland. That child was in a whole lot of trouble.

"Call Ike, not Chief Muggins." I didn't need to explain. Slade knew them both.

"One more thing," he said, reaching for another envelope on his desk. "This came in today's mail. What do you recommend I do with it?" He handed me a poem titled "Justice."

> *Othello! Look not on her with desire,*
> *Let not eyes burn with unholy fire.*
> *God roars with fury, earth feels his ire.*
> *Oh, come, sweet justice!*

I wondered if the end of the poem was so abrupt because the poet ran out of rhymes. I mentally ran down the alphabet: "byre," "choir," "dire," "fryer"—when I got to chickens, I brought myself back to the problem at hand.

Slade was finishing a sentence I hadn't heard him begin. ". . . both know who and what that refers to. I'm going to get every racist crackpot in town chiming in before this is over." I handed him the poem and he slung it back on his desk in disgust.

"Write your story and call Ike," I urged him. "This has got to stop."

As I passed Chancey's desk on my way out, she waved a copy of our upcoming ad in my face. "At least take a squint at it. It'll make an honest woman out of you."

*   *   *

I had to hold traffic court down in south Hope County late that afternoon. Coming home, I had just gotten back inside our city limits when I saw blue lights flashing. Disgusted at myself, I pulled over. I do speed sometimes, but generally I keep a weather eye out for troopers. I was downright embarrassed when the cruiser's door opened and Ike climbed out. This was going to be awkward for both of us.

"I was late getting back from traffic court and not paying attention," I started as soon as he came to my window.

He held up one huge hand. "For a wonder, you were no more than five miles over the limit, Judge. I pulled you over because I have some news for you that I knew you'd want right away, and I suspected you wouldn't want Joe Riddley to hear. Come sit in my car a minute."

I shifted the paraphernalia he had spread out on his passenger seat and settled in, expecting him to say Slade had called him. Instead, he said, "As much as I hate to admit it, you were right. DeWayne Evans did not kill himself. He was murdered."

For a minute I was so shocked I couldn't think of anything to say. Finally I managed, "Are you sure?"

"Real sure. I started where you suggested—looking at where DeWayne was hanging. He was near the lavatories, but I took some measurements, and the rope wasn't quite long enough for him to have stood on the lavatory to jump. He'd have choked himself first. You understand?"

I grimaced. "Well enough to picture it."

"So I called in the forensics folks and they started looking at things we hadn't checked when we thought it was suicide. They found several curious things. Two doorknobs were a lot cleaner than the school janitor ever keeps them— both the one from DeWayne's room to the hall and the one on the outside door to his room. Part of that doorjamb was wiped, too. And the knobs to the locker room on both sides were smudged like somebody was wearing plastic gloves."

"Gloves?" I blurted. "It was premeditated, then?"

He nodded.

"But how?"

"We think he was killed in his own classroom. They found traces of urine and feces in the seat of his desk chair—which had been carefully cleaned, by the way, just not quite enough—which makes us suspect he was choked there, then taken to the bathroom to be strung up. The hall was pretty much a mess—nobody had bothered to preserve it as a crime scene, since nobody thought it was part of anything—but forensics picked up a couple of traces that look like his heels were dragged."

I sat there trying to take it in. "So he wasn't even hanged?"

"Not in the technical sense. He was choked by the rope, then hauled over the pipe when he was dead. Not a pretty way to go, but better than twitching at the end of the rope waiting for the end."

"But DeWayne was so strong. Who could—?"

"We don't know, but it would have to be somebody who both surprised him and had the strength to hang on until his air was gone."

I couldn't help picturing bulging biceps with dragons crawling up them. "Could it have been Smitty? Ridd says DeWayne flunked him last semester."

Ike shrugged, which was hard when you were his size and sitting behind a steering wheel. "We'll check his alibi for Saturday morning, but you can be sure he'll have one, and we'll have a tough time breaking it."

I climbed out of his car feeling two hundred years old. "Thanks for filling me in, but what the heck is going on in this town?"

He shook his massive head. "If I knew, Judge, I'd put a stop to it. You know I would. Looks like the devil got tired of hell and has decided to take up residence in Hopemore."

⊰ 22 ⊱

Talking to Tyrone was now my number-one priority, but finding him took a while. Finally, Tuesday afternoon, on my way back from the jail where I'd held a bond hearing, I stopped by the Bi-Lo. Tyrone's mother, Florence, worked in the produce department.

When I asked if I could talk to her a minute about Tyrone, she didn't stop putting apples in rows in a bin. "I don't see enough of him anymore to recognize him on the street." She'd never been a beauty, but back when she was in high school with Walker, she'd had nice blond hair and a figure she took pains to show off. Now her hair hung limp and shaggy around her face, her body carried a lot of extra weight, her shoulders slumped, and she spoke in a perpetual whine.

"You were at court with him Friday, weren't you?" Surely she hadn't missed that.

"Yeah. That was one of the worst ordeals I've faced since the night he was born. I never thought I'd see the day when my son would stand in front of a judge and admit he defaced a school. And did you see what he drew?" Her eyes were so pitiful, I hated that I had to nod. "He wasn't brought up like that—you know it. We have all sorts here"—her eyes wandered to the registers, which were currently staffed by two African American women, a Mexican woman and a white woman—"and we get along just fine. I never taught Tyrone

to think bad about anybody." She sighed. "But now, everybody probably thinks I did."

I patted her husky shoulder. "I'm sure everybody knows
where you stand. We do the best we can, but none of us is
responsible for the way our children turn out. Do you have
any idea where I can find Tyrone?"

She dropped an apple. "Is he in more trouble?"

"Not that I know of. I talked to him Thursday and we
didn't finish our conversation."

She bent to retrieve the fruit with obvious relief. "You
might try Smitty's. Tyrone's been hanging out with him
some lately, and to tell you the truth, it worries me to death.
Something's got to be done about Smitty, Judge, and that's
God's own truth, or he's going to take over this whole
town."

"I keep hearing that," I told her. "You got any idea what
anybody can do? He's never been convicted on any charge."

She shook her head. "He's slippery like a water moc-
casin, and twice as bad."

"Do you have any idea where he lives? I don't."

"Yeah, he 'n' his mom live in that trailer out on the
Waynesboro Road. The one that looks like it might fall
down any minute, but somehow never does."

That was as good a description as anybody could give. I
recognized it as soon as I saw it sitting in what must have
once been a small pasture surrounded by piney woods. This
was definitely a trailer—far too old to have ever been called
a mobile home, much less a modular home. It sagged in the
middle. Its screens were torn and patched with duct tape.
The steps were cement blocks and had been there so long
that a determined yellow flower grew between them. The
lawn was adorned by two rusting lawn mowers, an abandoned washing machine, and a pile of beer cans and bottles
at exactly the right angle to have been tossed through the
door.

I parked by the chain-link fence—which also sagged—
and headed for the gate, listening to see if a dog would crash

around the corner and make my life difficult. I heard nothing except a television turned up way too loud. I rattled the gate. Still nothing. I took a hesitant step inside.

That's when it occurred to me to wish I'd brought somebody with me. I generally don't walk into risky places alone, even in broad daylight, but I had been so focused on finding Tyrone that I hadn't stopped to think that the most likely person I was going to find at Smitty's was Smitty. Or Smitty's mother—whose first language was profanity and her second, threats. I was fixing to go back to town and return with a deputy when I heard a shot.

I fell into the tall grass flatter than one of my infamous cakes. I lay belly to the ground, head down, and thought I remembered that if you hear a shot, you won't get hit, because the bullet reaches you before its sound. That might not be true, though, and wasn't particularly comforting anyway, since whoever shot once was probably reaching for the trigger again right that minute.

Besides, the way my ears were pounding, I could die of other causes. Fright, for instance.

"It's Judge Yarbrough," I called without raising my head. "Don't fire. I'm looking for Tyrone."

A bullet whizzed by to my left. It hit the ground with a thud, and I shook so hard, the grass above me must have waved like little flags. I strained to listen, but I heard nothing except the TV and a cardinal calling *cheer! cheer!* somewhere over in the woods. I am much older than you think, because I lay in that grass without moving for at least a hundred years.

Finally I heard a snicker. "You can get up. I ain't shootin' at you. Was shootin' squirrels."

I looked up cautiously. Smitty leaned against one corner of the trailer, a rifle resting across one arm. It was probably a .22. Lots of boys around Hope County owned them for hunting squirrels and rabbits or killing rats around their parents' farms.

Three of his buddies stood off to one side, all grinning.

Smitty jerked his head down the yard. "Them squirrels been botherin' our peaches."

I raised my head and looked that way. At the far end of the yard stood a scrawny tree with small hard peaches clinging to the branches by sheer determination. They would never be any good, because that poor tree probably hadn't been fertilized since Smitty was born.

Why was I worrying about peaches at a time like that? To avoid worrying about Smitty with a lethal weapon, in easy killing distance.

I climbed slowly to my feet, aware that his dead gray eyes were watching my every move. His friends looked edgy and excited, waiting to see what he'd do. At my age, getting up off the ground is an accomplishment. Getting up gracefully is practically impossible. I heard another snicker, but it stopped when Smitty snarled something over his shoulder.

Shaking like I was, I was amazed I could stand at all. "I'm looking for Tyrone." A car passed behind me. The driver probably thought we were having a neighborly visit.

Smitty sighted and fired a couple of yards to my right. "Squirrels are real bad this year." He was having himself a fine old time.

"Stop that!" I yelled. "You could hit somebody on the road." One of the boys drew back a little, so I must have sounded right fierce, but I was no Genghis Khan. My hands trembled so badly, I had to clutch my pocketbook to my chest to keep from dropping it, and my knees were about to drop me.

Strengthen the weak hands and make firm the feeble knees. We'd just studied that part of Isaiah in Sunday school. It came to me like a prayer. I tacked on a verse of my own: *Help!*

No angels descended to take away Smitty's gun. I did hear that voice that lurks in my head, though: *He wouldn't kill you on his own property with three witnesses.*

How reliable do you think those witnesses would be in

court? I demanded. *Anybody can have a hunting accident.* I sure hated to go to my grave murdered, labeled an accidental death.

He won't have a hunting license, the voice insisted. *Face him down. Don't drop or run.*

He's on his own property, I pointed out. *You know any officers of the law zealous enough to arrest somebody this far outside the city limits for scaring squirrels away from his peaches? They'd have to arrest half of Hope County.*

Don't let him know you're afraid.

With that last piece of advice, the voice disappeared. I felt unexpectedly bereft, considering that it and I seldom agree on anything. Still, I didn't have any better advice to offer myself, so I straightened my shoulders, lifted my chin, and repeated, "I came looking for Tyrone."

"He ain't here." Smitty fished in his pocket for more shells and reloaded. He glanced up and down the road, sighted along the barrel, and aimed straight at me.

I'd learn some time later that Smitty considered me a gutsy lady, that he told folks, "She faces a gun cooler than any woman I ever saw." I would preen a little at that accolade. And I wish I could tell you I stood there calmly because I was ready to receive my heavenly reward. I'll never get it, however, by lying, and the truth is, I wanted to run, even if that meant getting shot in the back. The trouble was, my body had petrified. Even my head had petrified. I didn't feel a thing while Smitty fired off another shot over me, grinning all the while.

Help came from an unexpected source. "Stop that!" Tyrone clomped down the trailer steps, clutching his pants in front of him. "Stop it! She's a judge!" He reached Smitty faster than either Smitty or I knew he could run and wrested the gun from Smitty's hands. The others watched in astonishment as he yelled, "You stupid, dumb—" I won't repeat the rest of what he said. It's not language I generally use, but it was certainly language Smitty understood.

To give him credit, though, he didn't cower, just snick-

ered up at Tyrone. "I wasn't hurtin' her—just shooting squirrels." Several of his henchmen guffawed. Tyrone stomped
away from him and glared, his big face flushed and furious.
He still held the gun in one hand and clutched his pants with
the other.

Smitty turned and swaggered toward the backyard. With
a jerk of his head he drew those puppets after him. "She
came to see you, anyway," he informed Tyrone over one
shoulder.

Tyrone laid the gun on the steps and lumbered over to
where I was firmly planted in the soil and sending down
roots for support. "You okay?" He peered down at me between two ripples of long black hair. His worried face
looked very like his mother's.

"A little shook up," I admitted. "I was afraid he might
miss a squirrel and hit me."

"Oh, no, he's a real good shot." Pride flickered in his
eyes, which was then chased away by shame. "He shouldn't
have scared you like that, though. I was in the bathroom and
the TV's on. I didn't know the shots were real at first." He
looked down and saw he was still clutching his unzipped
pants. He turned bright red, showed me his back, and zipped
up. "Excuse me."

"Honey, I'll excuse you anything. I expect you just saved
my life."

"He wouldn't have hurt you. He was just foolin' around."

My laugh was pretty shaky. "He sure fooled me."

"Were you really lookin' for me?" His breath came in
short, anxious gasps. I wondered how he could breathe at all
with those tight leather strings and beads around his thick
neck.

"Yeah. I wanted to talk to you, but right now we're both
having trouble getting our breath. Ride back into town with
me."

He cast a quick look toward the trailer. "I better stay here.
We're havin' a meetin'."

"You're in a heap of trouble, and it's getting deeper all

the time. I need to ask you some questions, and I don't want Smitty listening in. Come on. Ride back to town with me."

"I can't." If ever a boy looked miserable, it was Tyrone. "He—he'll—I just can't. That's all."

I remembered what Joe Riddley said: Smitty might be threatening to hurt Tyrone's mother. I took that a lot more seriously now than I had an hour ago. "Can you meet me somewhere later?"

He squirmed, shuffling those huge feet in the high grass. "I don't know—"

"Tyrone, we've got to get you out of this mess. It's getting worse than you know. Tell me when and where you can meet me. I'll be there."

"I can't," he said desperately. "I just can't. I gotta go." He lumbered toward the back.

I walked on spaghetti legs to my car and managed to drive back to the office, but I kept a close eye out for Charlie Muggins's cruiser. I was shaking like somebody who'd been drinking steadily for a week.

❧ 23 ❧

I was real surprised around nine that night to answer the phone and hear a husky whisper. "Judge Yarbrough? It's Tyrone. Listen, I'll meet you, if you tell me where."

"Where are you now?" Lightning flickered outside while I waited for his answer.

"At the pay phone at the Bi-Lo. I came to see if Mama wanted me to walk her home, but she already left." A rumble of thunder followed the lightning. The storm was getting close.

"I'll come get you. Are you hungry?" He grunted, which I took for a yes. "Let's go out to Dad's BarBeQue." It was unlikely that Smitty or his friends would be there. Dad's was several miles out of town, primarily a family place, and so isolated, you'd think nobody would ever find it. However, it had been going strong since 1937, started by the current owner's granddaddy. In the winter, Dad's closed at eight, but during the summertime it was open until well after ten to satisfy whatever cravings for barbeque might strike Hope County.

Dad (who had been called that so long most folks had forgotten his name was Raymond) was a burly Primitive Baptist with biceps like ham butts. His chief cook, Eddie, was a Pentecostal preacher cut from the same mold. Between them, they set straight any troublemaker who was unwise enough to stop in.

"I'll be there in a minute," I told Tyrone. "If it starts raining, wait inside at the door and I'll pull up. Okay?"

"No. I'll start walking home. Pick me up on the road. Pretend you're just drivin' by."

"It may be pouring by then."

"That's okay. I don't mind getting wet."

Joe Riddley was watching *Patton* in the den. I grabbed my pocketbook and stuck my head in the room. "I'm going out for a little while. Will you be okay?"

He pushed the mute button. "You going down to the jail?"

"No. Meeting somebody."

"Not Martha. She's working tonight." He pulled the lever on his recliner and lowered his feet. "I'll come with you."

I stared in astonishment. "What about your program?" Joe Riddley thinks life isn't complete without one World War II movie a month, even if he can repeat the lines by heart.

He pushed the power button and the screen flashed and went dark. "I've got other nights to watch movies. I've only got one wife." I was so astonished, I stepped back without a word to let him pass. He took his cap from the hook and spoke over his shoulder. "I didn't major in math like you did, Little Bit, but I can add four ones and come up with the right answer." He held up fingers as he counted. "One, you went down to the jail this afternoon for a hearing and took twice as long as normal. Two, you came back shaking like Lulu when she knows she deserves a whipping. Three, a customer came in before you did and said somebody was shooting mighty close to the highway out on the Waynesboro Road. Four, Smitty Smith lives out on the Waynesboro Road." He felt in his pockets to be sure his keys were still there, then reached out and grabbed me in a bear hug. "I know you think Smitty had something to do with De-Wayne's death. If you think I'm going to let you meet him alone at this hour—"

"It's Tyrone, honey, not Smitty," I said against his chest.

"I hope I can get him to testify that Smitty helped paint the school. We're going out to Dad's."

He let me go. "One more reason to go along. That little bit of supper you fixed isn't going to hold me all night." He settled his cap on his head. Bo flew down, of course—he loved to ride on that cap. Joe Riddley took him to the barn and settled him for the night, then met me at his car. Rain was already pattering down, but by the time I thought about going back for my raincoat, he was already starting the engine. The rain was streaming by the time we got to the Bi-Lo.

When I told Joe Riddley we were to drive by Tyrone and offer him a ride, he grunted. "You forgot your cloak and dagger." But he drove slow until we saw the big dripping figure trudging down the road, then pulled to the side, rolled down his window and called real loud, "You need a ride, Tyrone? The judge and I are heading your way." Joe Riddley always got a kick out of calling me "the judge," since he'd been the judge for so many years.

Tyrone wasn't a real great actor—nobody would have been fooled by his pretending to be surprised—but I didn't see anybody standing around in the rain to watch our performance.

"Joe Riddley decided he'd like to come eat barbeque with us," I said as Tyrone got in.

"That's cool." He smelled like wet boy, a scent like no other in the world. When he'd slammed the door behind him, he peered in all directions, tense and anxious. When you're scared of somebody, you begin to think your enemies might have invisibility cloaks like Harry Potter's.

The rain fell harder, but we were cozy inside with the swish of the wipers. Nobody spoke until we pulled into Dad's parking lot, which was now a sea of red, sticky mud. Joe Riddley drove the Lincoln close to the door. "You all run for it. I'll park."

Tyrone and I climbed out into the fragrance of pork roasting in a pit out back, but we didn't stop to appreciate it. We got soaked dashing five feet to the door—which was little more than a screen held together by weathered boards.

Dad's had never wasted money on paint, polish, or air-conditioning. The floor was sawdust, dotted with heavy wooden picnic tables. Little plastic baskets lined with paper substituted for plates—red for beef, yellow for pork, blue for chicken. The eating area was more like a big screened porch, planked as high as my waist and screened to the bare rafters. As rain drummed on the tin roof, Dad was going around letting down big wooden flaps on the side where water was blowing in. I waved to a couple of people I knew and moseyed over to study the menu above the counter like I didn't know it by heart. Rain seemed to make everything smell stronger—the sawdust, the cooking meat, the sweat of Eddie, who leaned on his elbow, white paper hat askew. "What you folks want tonight?"

"The usual," I told him. "Small pork sandwich, cole slaw and corn on the cob with lots of butter." I added to Tyrone, "Get whatever you want."

Joe Riddley came in, shaking his wet cap at the door and pulling his shirt away from his body. "Always eat a lot when a woman's paying," he told Tyrone. "It happens so rarely. Anybody notice it's started to rain?" Rain fell so loud on the roof, we could hardly hear him.

Joe Riddley decided on a plate of ribs with Brunswick stew and found it necessary to tell Eddie we'd already eaten supper but I hadn't fed him enough to keep a man alive until morning.

I carried my plate to a table in the far corner and squirted Dad's good honey sauce over the meat, pretending I was squirting it all over Joe Riddley's head. If you haven't eaten southern barbeque, you may not know it isn't cooked in sauce. It's slow cooked in a pit and laid on the bread. You add whatever sauces you want to. Dad's offers honey, hot, spicy, or mustard.

The way Tyrone ordered, I might have to get a part-time job at the superstore to pay our Visa bill. When he spread his food out on the table, Joe Riddley and I barely had space for our own food. We all dug in and didn't talk until we'd made a dent in our orders. Finally, I wiped the sauce off my chin and tried to think about what I wanted to ask first.

Joe Riddley beat me to it. "When's your court date, son?"

"Next Monday at nine o'clock." Tyrone finished his second sandwich and reached for his third. Since he was busy squirting it with sauce, he could be forgiven for not looking our way.

Joe Riddley leaned across the table like they were discussing the high school's chances of winning a football game. "Did the judge tell you it would go easier for you if you told him who else was involved in painting the school?"

Tyrone nodded, his eyes still fixed on the sandwich clutched in his hand. His fingers were so dirty, I averted my eyes to his face, but it was so pink, plump, and miserable, I couldn't help thinking of a pig awaiting slaughter.

"Are you going to tell him?" I demanded.

Still Tyrone stared at that sandwich. Maybe he hoped it would turn into a crystal ball and give him a magic answer.

I opened my mouth to urge him to tell everything he knew, but Joe Riddley put a hand on my arm. "Son, somebody is scaring you. I can see that real clear. Is Smitty threatening your mother?"

Tyrone shook his head.

"Who then?" Joe Riddley's tone was so normal, you'd have thought people threatening each other was nothing unusual.

Tyrone swallowed a big bite. "Hollis." It was little more than a hoarse whisper. "He says he'll hurt her real bad. And he will, too." The eyes that met ours were full of more anguish than anybody ought to know at that age.

"And Hollis is your friend." I hoped my voice was as calm as Joe Riddley's.

Tyrone nodded and gulped. "We've been friends since—well, practically forever. She's not my girlfriend or anything"—he flushed beet red, so I knew he'd had a few thoughts in that direction—"but if something happened to her because of me—"

Maybe that was why she had been holed up in her house this past week. "Have you warned her?" I asked, testing that theory.

"Sorta. I told her to stay away from Smitty and watch out not to be by herself on the street or anything after last Saturday—when she made fun of him over at Myrtle's."

"If Smitty were in detention, he couldn't hurt Hollis," Joe Riddley pointed out, "but the only way he'll go to detention is if somebody talks. Did Smitty help paint the school?"

It took Tyrone a few seconds to get used to the idea of telling what he knew, but once he started, a torrent of words nearly swept us away. "It was his idea. He says black folks are taking over the country and need to be stopped. He says they'll get all the good jobs and elected to offices and even start marrying all the good women, if we don't do something to stop them. You saw the way Hollis and the others were carrying on. It like to made me sick to my stomach. We gotta do something." He looked up and met Joe Riddley's gaze, but he found no sympathy there. Quickly he lowered his eyes and changed direction. "Smitty said writing on the school was one way to warn folks," he muttered. "He did the words and stuff. I just painted the picture."

"Did you help paint up Mr. Evans's house Friday night?" I was too angry to even try to be subtle.

Tyrone shook his head. "No way. I'd just gotten out of juvey. If I'da done something like that, they'd send me away next Monday." He seemed earnest enough, but I pressed him.

"Did Smitty? Could he have painted the house that night after, say, one?"

"I don't know. Mama made me stay home that night. Smitty said he was over at Willie's playing video games, but I don't know for sure."

"Could they have surfed the net, looking up things about Mr. Evans?"

"Not unless they went somewhere else. Willie doesn't have an Internet connection. His mama stopped paying after we—well, she stopped it." He added in righteous indignation, "They don't even have cable. All we can do there now is play games and watch videos. And she's told the video store he can't rent R-rated ones, just PG-13." You'd have thought they were restricted to *Cinderella* and *Snow White*.

"Does Smitty have a computer at home?" Joe Riddley asked in the mild tone he used to use when our boys were getting a bit too het up about something.

Sure enough, Tyrone calmed down. "Not yet. He keeps saying he's going to pick one up—"

"I hope he pays for it after he picks it up," I snapped.

Joe Riddley gave me a warning pat under the table. Tyrone flushed and bent his head to suck his drink.

I thought of something else. "Was it you or Smitty who wrote notes to DeWayne and the newspaper?"

He shook his head without looking up. "I don't know anything about no notes."

"They were written on pages torn from the back of your notebook—the one with your drawings in it."

His brains nearly rattled, he shook his head so hard. "I told you already, over at juvey—I lost it. Left it at Myrtle's and it disappeared."

"You all came back and got it."

He gave a disgusted sigh. "We came back for it, yeah, and Smitty hit on Garnet so Willie and I could get it, but somebody else had already swiped it."

"You didn't toss it in a garbage can next to the school?"

The look he gave me convinced me even before he demanded, "Why would I toss it? It had all my drawings in it."

I didn't have an answer. That had been bothering me, too. But if he hadn't tossed it, who did?

"Tell us about painting the school," Joe Riddley suggested.

Tyrone shrugged his husky shoulders. "What's to tell? We met over there a little after twelve—they've taken off night patrols, so we waited until the last cop went by—then we started."

Great. Criminals already knew we had no night patrols—it was just decent folks who didn't know.

"Smitty brought the paint and I brought a ladder," Tyrone finished. He sucked up the last of his Coke and gave us a worried look. "But I'm not going to tell all this to any judge. Who'd believe me with Willie saying Smitty was over at his place? Others'll back Willie up, and all I'll do is make Smitty mad."

"Willie," I said thoughtfully. Hadn't I heard something recently . . .? I tried to remember while Joe Riddley asked Tyrone if he'd like another Coke and headed to the counter to fetch it. Like St. Augustine says, memory is a convoluted thing: You can remember you have forgotten something and can even remember what it was that you forgot, but you can't remember the thing. What was it I had heard about Willie Keller? Suddenly I knew what it was and reached for my cell phone. "Let me see if Dad's got a phone book."

Chancey Carter answered the phone after the first ring, her voice breathless. "Oh, Mac, I'm so glad it's you. I was scared it was the nursing home. Mama had another spell tonight, and I just ran home for a minute to get a few things so I can go over there to sleep."

"I won't keep you then, but I need to ask about something you told me yesterday. You said you were at the nursing home last Wednesday night?"

"Yes. That was when Mama had her last spell. She's been having a lot of them lately. I'm so worried about her, but the doctor says it's to be expected at her age."

"And you couldn't get the nurses' aide because she was talking to her son about money?"

"They weren't talking. They were fighting. We needed her because . . ." Off Chancey went into another description of her mother's intestinal activities. I finally steered her back to the aide. "Yes, I rang and rang, but Linda didn't come. Fi-nally, I went to look for her, thinking she must be with another patient or talking to one of the nurses. Instead, she was with a real scruffy-looking boy down the hall. They weren't talking loud, but the way they were waving their arms, I knew they were fighting. He looked so awful, he scared me to death, to tell the truth, so I went back and emptied the pan myself, which families are not supposed to have to do. That's clearly stated in the papers I signed, that all personal needs will be taken care of."

"How did you know he was her son?"

"She told me, when she finally came. Said her son had been there wanting money, as usual, and she wasn't made of money, that he needed to get a job."

"And you remember when this happened?"

"Sure. I wrote it on the pad I keep in my pocketbook, in case I ever have to report somebody. Mama's bowels moved exactly at midnight—remember, I told you—but it was 12:30 before I got the aide to come. They were fighting all that time. But listen, Mac, I can't go into all this. Mama's real bad tonight and they may be trying to call me."

"One more thing." I tried not to sound miffed that she accused me of keeping her on the phone when she'd been the one going into such graphic detail. "What was the aide's last name?"

"Keller. Linda Keller. It's on her badge." She sounded like I should have remembered from the few times I'd been to see her mother. "But I really do have to fly."

"Go on. And thanks." I hung up, picturing Chancey flying across the housetops toward her mother's room. When I got back to the table, I informed Tyrone, "I can prove that Willie wasn't home around twelve that night. He can't alibi Smitty. Is that enough to make you testify?"

Tyrone shook his head. "Even if you can prove Willie's lying, you can't guarantee the same thing won't happen to Smitty as happened to me—he'll go to his detention hearing and get released to his mom. He'd have time to hurt Hollis before his trial."

I appreciated that he seemed more worried about Hollis than about himself.

Joe Riddley sucked up the last of his own Coke and looked at the cup in disgust. "Dad puts too much ice in these things. Get me a refill, will you, Little Bit?" I knew he wanted me out of the way so he could talk man-to-man with Tyrone. As I headed to the counter, I heard him say, "Son, intimidation is an ancient art."

There was a line at the counter. By the time I got back, Joe Riddley had gotten Tyrone to agree to testify by promising we'd ask Hollis to move in with us until Smitty went to detention. I sent Tyrone to the counter for three pieces of lemon icebox pie, which Dad bought from Myrtle. I had something important to say to my husband. Alone.

"You don't know if Hollis will want to stay with us, and you don't know Smitty will get a sentence. It's a first offense, remember? And how are we going to explain why we've practically adopted Hollis for who knows how long without scaring Sara Meg to death? Besides, we aren't at home much of the time, and Clarinda leaves at two. How is Hollis going to be safer down at our place than at her own?"

He scratched his chin. "We could see if Ridd and his family might like a week at the beach, taking Hollis along."

I sighed. Joe Riddley is the kindest man in the world, but he doesn't always think things through. "A week wouldn't be anywhere near long enough. Besides, Ridd and the girls have ball practice, and you know they won't give that up."

"We'll have to think of something. Unless he knows Hollis is safe, Tyrone won't testify. He says Smitty is holding something like this over almost everybody in the gang—a sister, a girlfriend, somebody who will get hurt if they don't do things his way. That boy's got to be stopped, Little Bit."

"So I keep hearing. I just haven't been told why I'm the one who's supposed to entertain a teenager for an indefinite period of time so it can happen."

"Because these are lost children, honey. The other day when Cricket got lost, it scared me to death. Afterwards, I got to thinking. We got all het up about one little boy riding a mile on his bicycle—"

"He could have been killed!"

"He could have been, but he wasn't. And he's got folks who care about what happens to him. What about kids whose parents don't or can't take care of them? They're lost a lot of the time. Somebody needs to be as concerned about them as we were about Crick. If we aren't, who will be?"

I heaved a sigh and gave him a sour look. "You know what makes me mad? You're right, dang it. And I can't stand it when you're nicer than me."

He grinned. "Happens all the time."

Tyrone carefully set three pieces of pie on the table, and I tried to ignore the black thumbprint on my Styrofoam plate. He and Joe Riddley talked about football while we ate. Tyrone seemed a lot happier since he'd shared his burden with us.

When they'd settled the upcoming football season between them, I told Joe Riddley that Tyrone was a good artist who might get to go to art school if he got his grades up and got a job to help pay for it. Joe Riddley said he sure could use a strong back to help down at the nursery between then and the Fourth of July sale. Next thing we all knew, Tyrone was joining the payroll. We all got up from the table in lighter spirits.

"Don't worry, Little Bit," Joe Riddley told me as we were pulling back onto Oglethorpe after dropping Tyrone off. "Things are going to work out. Just wait and see."

I looked down that gloomy damp street, lit only by streetlights, and thought it looked a lot like life in Hopemore right then: long dark stretches illuminated by patches of caring. "Things don't work out, honey—people have to work them out. You know that."

He frowned in the dim light and slowed the car. "From some of the things you were saying to Tyrone, you've been working more out than you ought to. How'd you know about Tyrone's notebook, that there's anything on the Internet about DeWayne Evans, or that somebody sent notes to DeWayne and the newspaper?" When I didn't answer, he put a big, warm hand on my leg. "I've told you already, Little Bit, I don't want you messing around in this. I nearly lost you back in February. I can't go through that again. You hear me?"

I understood. I'd nearly lost him the previous summer. So I was glad to reassure him with a squeeze on his arm. "I won't do anything dangerous. I promise."

I really meant it, at the time.

❧ 24 ❧

Joe Riddley slammed on the brakes and I nearly lost half my bosom to the seat belt. "Sara Meg's lights are on," he said with satisfaction. "Let's talk to her about Hollis now, before we forget."

Hollis herself answered the door and said they were all in the den watching television. When we got back there, we found Buddy, too.

Joe Riddley told them what Tyrone had said—how Smitty was threatening Hollis and some other girls to keep his troops in line—and invited Hollis "or both girls" to move down to our place for a while. I tried not to let them see that his inviting Garnet was as much a surprise to me as the whole idea was to the rest of them.

Hollis shook her head vehemently. "No, thanks. I mean, it's real nice of you and everything"—her blue eyes looked as earnest as Tyrone's had a little while before—"but I'd feel safer here. Nobody can get in. We have good locks."

Sara Meg sat looking at us like she didn't believe anything dangerous could really be threatening her daughters.

Buddy offered to move into their place for the time being, and Garnet and Hollis said "No!" at the same time. Then they glared at each other as if they couldn't stand to agree on anything.

Sara Meg gazed at them in bewilderment. "If it's true, wouldn't you feel a lot safer with a man in the house?"

"It might be for only a short time," I told them. "We're hoping Smitty will get arrested in the next day or so, and we'll use any influence we have to get him kept in juvenile detention until his trial comes up."

"But you can't guarantee that he won't get probation, can you?" Buddy demanded. "He could be back on the streets in a couple of weeks."

Hollis was adamant. "I'm not scared of Smitty. I'll stay in the house except when I have to go to work or practice. I'll be fine. We don't need you here, Buddy."

"I can at least start driving Garnet again." Buddy spoke not to Hollis but to Sara Meg. "That way Hollis won't be driving all the way out to the school and coming back alone."

Sara Meg nodded. "That would be helpful. This seems so unreal."

I didn't look at Joe Riddley, because I knew he'd be sending me looks that said *She's not facing up to things again.*

That's how we left it: Hollis would be careful and drive their car to the pool, and Buddy would take Garnet to and from class. Even that didn't please Hollis. "I can drive Garnet."

"What does it matter who's driving?" Garnet swept scornfully up the stairs. I figured she was annoyed that her sister was getting so much attention.

Late afternoon the following Tuesday, Ike called to say Smitty had been arrested on charges of painting the school. It had taken that long for the gears of justice to work after Tyrone testified Monday morning at his own trial. They had to substantiate Chancey's report about Willie being with his mother while he claimed to be at his house with Smitty, and they had to get a warrant to search Smitty's mother's house, which yielded absolutely nothing. As Ike had said, Smitty was smart—too smart to leave incriminating evidence at home. It was Willie's evasiveness that finally steered them to the Kellers' garage, where they found partially used cans of blue, red and white spray paint hidden up in the rafters with Smitty's prints on the cans. Smitty's reaction was to hurl a stream of invective toward Willie for not throwing out the paint.

"Poor Willie," Ike said with a chuckle. "The whole time Smitty was yelling at him, he was cowering against the wall, sniffling and protesting over and over, 'But there's still good paint in there, and Mama won't give me money for no more.'"

"That's a relief," I told him. "Maybe our graffiti days are over."

"Fondly do we hope, fervently do we pray," Ike replied.

At Smitty's detention hearing the next morning, though, the out-of-town judge standing in for Judge Roland decided that the charges were not serious enough to warrant detention until trial, and released Smitty to his mother. I saw Smitty on the street that afternoon, and the venom in his eyes made me shiver. I immediately called Hollis and warned her to stay real close to home unless she traveled in a group.

"I will," she assured me. "Don't worry."

When the paper came out Wednesday afternoon, I grabbed it and hurried to my office, actually afraid to see what Slade had written about DeWayne's death. He'd remained true to his editorial roots in the news article—included every one of the gory facts: graffiti on the school and DeWayne's house, all that was in the clippings sent to the newspaper "and possibly to Evans himself," and the gruesome discovery of DeWayne's body in the locker room. He didn't mention that it was murder, so I figured the police were holding that information back for some reason. Slade did leave my name out of the article, as I had requested, and told the whole truth about DeWayne's college episode.

Bethany filled me in on the Stantons that week. I was glad to hear that Hollis was taking serious safety precautions. She stayed at the pool all day instead of popping out to meet friends for lunch. She drove straight to ball practice after work, and called to be sure Garnet or Sara Meg was at home before she left the other girls. Bethany followed her home.

I was surprised to learn Friday that Garnet had started driving again, too. Bethany said that when Laura MacDonald got wind that Hollis was in danger, she concluded Garnet might be, as well. So Laura offered Garnet a loaner company car and persuaded her to resume driving while she still lived in a small, familiar town. Garnet phoned the insurance company to see how much it would cost her to get insured again and discovered that although Buddy had said he'd canceled her policy after her little accident, he'd never actually gotten around to doing it. She was now driving Laura's car to school and work.

"We're being really careful," Hollis promised with her saucy grin at church on Sunday.

Buddy frowned. "I keep telling Sara Meg we ought to take the girls to the beach until Smitty's trial. I offered to rent a place, but she won't go."

"I can't leave the store right now," Sara Meg snapped. "I don't know if it can survive, but it certainly can't if I go gallivanting all over the world."

Buddy turned away. "Maybe I'll just take them myself." That was the first time I ever remembered hearing them quarrel.

Bethany reported there was a huge fight later that afternoon when Buddy suggested again that he and the girls go to the beach alone. Garnet refused to miss work. Hollis refused to give up ball practice. Buddy stormed out, furious. Bethany said he looked so funny that she and Hollis collapsed in giggles. I hoped Buddy hadn't heard them, after all the trouble he'd been willing to take to keep his nieces safe.

Monday afternoon I went down to Myrtle's for a little peace and quiet. Joe Riddley was ordering fall stock on his desk phone, and he tended to get noisy when folks said they couldn't deliver when he wanted things delivered. Myrtle's was cool and empty in the middle of the afternoon, and Art was sitting over in a corner scribbling in a notebook. "Writing poems?" I asked.

He flushed to the roots of his hair and shut his notebook abruptly. "Yeah," he muttered. "You want coffee?"

"Make it iced tea today, with lots of lemon. It's too hot for coffee." I stretched out in a booth and slipped my feet out of my shoes to rest them.

When he clumped back over a few minutes later, I asked, "Have you sent any more poems to the paper lately? Slade said he got an anonymous one about Othello last week—pretty good rhymes, I understand. Made me think of the poetry you write."

Art looked over his shoulder to be sure Myrtle was safely in the kitchen, then leaned down and said earnestly, "I was real sorry I sent it when I did. I hadn't heard Coach Evans was dead when I mailed it, so I was sorta glad Mr. Rutherford decided not to print it." He stopped to lick his lips. "But I felt like I had to write it. I know Coach Evans was a friend of yours and everything, and I'm real sorry he died, but I just couldn't stand to see him hugging and kissing those girls. And Garnet—well, she didn't hug or kiss him or anything, but she liked him more than she ought to. You want chocolate pie with that?"

"Yeah." While he was gone, I pictured a little meter we could all carry around to let us know exactly how much we ought to like each person we meet. Handy little things they could be, except when they told you what you didn't want to hear. I was wondering who would program them, and determine the "liking voltage," when Art came back with my pie. I sipped my tea, which was strong, sweet and cold, and asked casually, "You like Garnet a lot, don't you?"

He bobbed his head so hard his Adam's apple jiggled. "Yes, ma'am. She's real special, don't you think? I mean, she's so dedicated to her music and her studies, and so—pure, somehow. So untouched by the rest of the world. I don't know how to explain it, but—" He came to a dead stop.

"But she makes you want to write poems." I smiled to let him know I was on his side.

"She sure does." He practically lit up the room with his wide, wet smile. Then he returned to his poems and I tackled my pie, wondering if Smitty was the only reason Hollis was sticking so close to home and whether Garnet had ulterior motives for refusing to leave town.

If she and Art were the two people Hollis had wanted to discuss with DeWayne, Sara Meg might have to face some unfortunate facts, whether she liked it or not.

❧ 25 ❧

Before I'd settled in my mind whether to ask Hollis straight out whether she was worried about Garnet and Art, or whether to suggest to Sara Meg that she ask Garnet about him, Police Chief Charlie Muggins dropped by my office Tuesday morning with a bombshell.

"Well, Judge, I have some good news and some bad news for you. Which you want first?" He took off his hat and lowered himself warily into my visitors' chair. I listened to it creak beneath him and swivelled my own chair around so I could watch if it broke under his weight. I also checked to be sure my skirt was modest in that position. Chief Muggins tends to have wandering eyes.

"Oh, give me the bad news first and sweeten it with the good." I was racking my brain trying to figure out what bad news he could possibly be in a position to bring me. Had he persuaded the chief magistrate to fire me? Chief Muggins had never made any bones about the fact that he'd opposed my appointment.

He slowly laid his cap on one thigh, giving himself more time to build up the suspense. "That Evans fellow you found? He didn't kill himself like you thought he did. He was murdered. We found all sorts of evidence to back that up."

He sounded as if I'd personally insisted on suicide and was going to be real disappointed to learn a fine man hadn't decided to end his own existence. I considered pointing out that I was the one who had called Ike to first suggest it could be murder, but I bit my tongue and kept my face in the "Be Sweet" position Mama had drilled into me for years. "That's not bad news, Chief. It's real good news. I had a hard time believing DeWayne would kill himself. So what's your good news?"

"We know who did it."

"Smitty Smith?"

He threw back his head and laughed, showing more fillings than teeth. "I knew you were going to say that. But Smitty's got a real alibi this time."

"He always does," I pointed out, "but if you lean on his friends, maybe you can break it."

"No, this one's airtight." He sprawled in his chair with his legs stuck out, proud of himself. "He's been pretty evasive about where he was that night, which made me suspicious, so I started doing some checking. Turns out his mama got herself beat up earlier that night on a date and didn't want anybody to know. So Smitty drove her—without a license, mind you—to the emergency room in Augusta so none of her friends would see her looking like that." He beamed at me, expecting me to share the joke. I thought instead of his own wife and how often Martha had seen her in our emergency room before she got smart and left town. I almost missed hearing him add, "They clocked into the hospital at eleven Friday night and she was sent up to a room around four in the morning. The nurses say Smitty was with her until after lunch."

"Then who else could it be?" I scarcely breathed, waiting for his answer. I already knew what he was going to say: Tyrone Noland. Tyrone was certainly strong enough, and if he were fixated on Hollis and thought she had a crush on DeWayne . . .

The chief surprised me. "That Franklin boy. Art, he calls himself. Real airy-fairy kind of fellow."

"He calls himself Art because his name is Arthur."

Maybe I sounded a bit testy, but I don't like that kind of language in my office, especially when I'm sharing it with Chief Muggins. There never seems to be enough air in the room for the two of us.

Charlie picked his hat up by the brim and started patting it on his thigh. "He's a weirdo, whatever his name is. Writes poems, acts in plays, and wears black all the time, just like those kids who shoot up their schools."

"They don't all shoot up schools," I objected. "Besides, Art's scrawny. How on earth could he kill DeWayne, even if he wanted to? And what makes you think he did?"

"I shouldn't be telling you this, but since you asked, we found a piece of a note in Evans's wastebasket written in block letters. Slade Rutherford down at the paper got another note the next day—well, on Monday—written in the same block letters. I mentioned that to Myrtle, over at the restaurant, and last night she called and said she'd found a book of poems written in those same block letters. Franklin had written them to somebody with 'hair like russet leaves' and 'eyes of delicious brown.' From what we can ascertain, there isn't but one person in town who that's likely to be— little Garnet Stanton. Myrtle says they're real sweet on each other."

"He's made no secret of the fact that he likes Garnet," I admitted, the stuffing knocked out of me so bad, it was all I could do to sit erect. I asked the first thing that came to mind. "Why on earth would Art kill DeWayne?"

"We don't have to prove motive—you know that, Judge. It's enough for me that I got a witness who puts him on that side street by the school at the right time, around eight Saturday morning, and I got notes and poems all written in block letters. That's a pretty good start, wouldn't you say? Oh, and there's one more thing: Lab reports show that the two notes were written on paper from the notebook you found—and lost—at Myrtle's, the one Tyrone Noland admits was his. Now, Tyrone says he hasn't had the notebook since he left it in the booth at Myrtle's, and he also says there were blank pages in the back when he lost it. When my men fished it out of a wastebasket near the school a few hours later, there were no blank pages. Who was in a better position than Art to take that notebook and tear out the pages?"

I thought back to that day and shook my head. "I was watching the booth the whole time until Art and Smitty started a fight. Art was never near it. During the fight, while I wasn't watching it, he and Smitty were punching each other. He couldn't have taken it. I would swear to that in court."

Chief Muggins glared at me, breathing hard. "Don't make life more difficult than you have to, Judge. You asked about motive a while back. Maybe he thought the Evans fellow was making time with Garnet. I hear she liked him—Myrtle said she was actually smiling at Evans the afternoon after the championship game, and you know as well as I do, that girl doesn't smile."

"Have you asked Garnet about any of this?"

He stuck his thumbs in the pockets of his jacket. "I'm heading over to interview her now."

"You know she'll be at MacDonald Motors, not at home? She just got a job there."

He looked disconcerted, and I knew he'd looked forward to talking to Garnet alone at home, the old lech. Even the idea of him alone with her in one of Laura's offices was enough to make me reach for my pocketbook. "Maybe I ought to come with you. I know her pretty well, and—you know, a woman's touch." Although, at that moment, the only woman's touch I felt like giving was a smack to the side of his head.

To my surprise, he took me up on my offer. As we crossed the parking lot, he said—so casually I might have missed its importance—"I hope she'll have something for us, because we can't actually match the handwriting."

I stopped, astounded. "Why not?"

"The notes and poems are both written in the kind of

block letters they teach in drafting class, engineering school, art school, architectural drawing—lots of places. Hard to match. And there weren't any prints on the notes, either. Looks like whoever wrote them wore gloves. Let's hope little Garnet is willing to help us out."

She might be, if he called her Little Garnet to her face. Help him right out the door.

To my surprise, when we got to MacDonald's, Laura nodded toward her father's old office at the back. "Garnet and her mother are in there."

Sara Meg opened the door, her face flushed. I wondered if she'd come so she could be there for the interview to protect her daughter or to make sure Garnet didn't embarrass the family. I was even more surprised when Chief Muggins announced we were there to interview Garnet. If he hadn't called ahead of time, why was Sara Meg away from her store in the middle of the day?

Garnet sat in a chair across the room, white and shaking. Charlie took the big desk chair that used to hold Skye MacDonald's bulk, and my eyes misted with tears at that memory. Sara Meg took another chair, and I took the one that was left, over in a corner.

Garnet sat there pale and remote, her eyes straying to the door like she wanted to get back to work.

"Who's minding the store?" I asked Sara Meg.

Garnet glared. "*She* could be, if she wanted to. I certainly don't need her here."

Sara Meg gave a nervous little laugh. "So what can we do for you?" She turned to face Chief Muggins and crossed her hands in her lap.

Chief Muggins set his hat on the desk and leaned on his elbows. "I have a few questions for Garnet, here. You're good friends with Art Franklin, right?"

Garnet shrugged. "We have some classes together."

"But he writes poems about you, correct?"

She looked at her hands. "He writes poems. They aren't necessarily about me."

"This is really distressing for her," Sara Meg interjected. "People keep thinking there is something between them when there isn't. Isn't that right, honey?"

"We just have some classes together." She paused. "I rode home from school with him once."

Chief Muggins clasped his hands before him on the desk like a friendly uncle. "What if I told you Franklin may have murdered DeWayne Evans? Would you have something to say to that?" He watched her carefully.

Garnet's gaze flew to his face. "He was m-m-murdered?"

"Maybe so. Do you know anything about how Evans and Franklin felt about each other? Were they both sweet on you, maybe?" He leaned even nearer and gave her a wink.

Sara Meg answered for Garnet. "Of course not! Garnet wouldn't—she hasn't—she—"

Garnet shuddered and wrapped her arms around herself like a blast of Arctic air had swept through Georgia. Finding out somebody you knew and maybe liked has been murdered can do that to you. I still felt chilled by DeWayne's murder myself.

Chief Muggins's voice grew low and smarmy. "We already have evidence that Art may have killed Mr. Evans, so tell me, little lady, what was going on between you and the chemistry teacher?"

Garnet jumped to her feet and pressed her hands over her ears. "Mr. Evans was the kindest, smartest, dearest—" She dashed through the door and slammed it behind her.

Sara Meg stood, her face like ice. "Get out of here! You, too, Mac. I know the law has a job to do, but you all have gone too far." She strode to the door and held it open for us.

"I'm sorry," I whispered as we left. "If I'd known you were going to be here, I wouldn't have come."

Her eyes were dark and stormy. "As if I didn't have trouble enough without all this."

Chief Muggins talked on the way home about how Garnet would come around when she'd had time to think things over. You'd have thought he expected her to beat him to the police station with a statement to convict Art. I sat in miserable silence wishing Joe Riddley and I had gone with Walker and Cindy to Hawaii, the way they'd wanted us to. I could be lying on a sunny beach right then, not knowing a thing about what was going on in Hopemore.

I didn't realize we'd parked in our parking lot until a voice outside my window startled me. "If you are going to have a fling with the police chief, Little Bit, couldn't you find a more private place?" Joe Riddley opened the door and leaned across me. "If you want her, Charlie, you can have her, but I warn you, she can't cook."

I supposed Chief Muggins meant to leer, but he looked just like a polecat. "Then the deal's off, Judge. Sorry. You're gonna have to stay with this old coot, like it or not. But you think about what we been talking about, okay?"

I sighed. "As if I could help it."

⊰ 26 ⊱

Bethany told me the next afternoon why Sara Meg had gone to MacDonald Motors. Hollis had seen Garnet sneak a suitcase into the trunk of her car that morning and called her mother from the pool. Sara Meg had gone over to confront Garnet.

"Garnet wouldn't tell her where she was going, though, or who with," Bethany reported, sitting in my chair and twisting a long strand of hair around her finger. "She wouldn't even tell Hollis, and she was furious with her for telling their mama. Sara Meg told Buddy, of course, and he got mad at Garnet and Hollis both. Hollis says things are real tense over there now. Nobody's talking to anybody. She asked if she could spend the night with me, and Mama said she could. I'm so lucky, Me-mama. My folks never fuss like that."

Apparently she had not only forgiven Ridd for Saturday night, but forgotten, as well.

She stood to leave, then turned with a sigh. "But I wish Mama would let Hollis and me drive to California before school starts. Would you ask her? Please?"

"Not likely, honey. I have a feeling you're going to have to be a little older and wiser before your folks let you go that far alone."

"I wouldn't be alone. I'd be with Hollis."

I spoke before I thought. "Better Hollis than Todd."

She wrinkled her nose. "He is such a scumbag. Don't ever mention his name to me again." It might not be too long before she'd be mature enough to drive to California, after all.

We generally went to church supper on Wednesdays, but that night I decided to let Joe Riddley go alone. We'd have had to take two cars anyway, because he had a meeting and wanted to drop by Ridd's afterwards to discuss some business. Martha would later say my decision to stay home was me hearing and obeying the voice of God, but the truth was, I was too tuckered out to even listen. I just wanted an evening by myself.

This was the lightest week of the year, so the sun didn't go down until after eight. I wanted to putter around in the yard while the long evening lasted, but the gnats got bad, so after I'd had a little bite to eat, I sat in my rocker on our screened side porch and watched the moon come up, fat and full.

"I don't want DeWayne's killer to be poor Art," I told the Boss Upstairs, "but I can't think of who else it could be, except Smitty. You've told us to pray for our enemies, and Smitty's the closest thing I've got right now, so I'll ask you to bless him and stop him doing any more harm around here. That's the best I can do. If he's responsible for all this mess that's been happening, please let that be found out. If he's not, please help Ike"—I had to make myself say the next part—"or Charlie find the right person. If there's something I can do to help, I'm here."

If you think that's not a proper prayer, you do it your way and I'll do it mine.

I truly believe God holds the world in loving hands and that we can trust things to work out for good ultimately. But in tough times, I have to line myself up with that polestar called faith time and time again. Comforted, I took a good, deep breath and settled back to watch the fireflies and listen to the crickets. I couldn't hear a single sound of civilization except the soft whir of our refrigerator. I took another deep breath, sorting out the smells of Joe Riddley's new-mown grass, honeysuckle over by the barn, and my gardenias beside the back door. For a little while, I stopped thinking about the awful things that had happened and let my mind drift. I may have even dozed, because the next thing I knew, the dogs were barking and I heard a car coming down our road.

Since we're at the end of the road, except for Ridd's fields, our ears perk and our dogs bark at the sound of tires. My watch said nine-thirty, so I didn't think it was Joe Riddley already. It could be company coming, but there were several other alternatives. Folks with cars too old to fix or trade often decide to abandon them on other people's property. We've had a number of them over the years, and invariably we spend a lot of time tracing the owners or pay good money to have them towed away. Or it might be a courting couple, uninformed about Joe Riddley's reputation for sneaking up on parked kids with a big flashlight. It could even be somebody coming to look at Hubert's house, although I'd never known a Realtor to show a house in the dark.

When I heard the engine stop somewhere between Hubert's and our house (you get good at judging those things when you've lived down a gravel road as long as we had), I was truly puzzled, so I went upstairs and peered out across Hubert's watermelon patch. I saw headlights switch off up near the pasture and a flash of light as a car door opened, then something long and white got out.

We don't have many ghosts in Hopemore. If this was a real one, I didn't want to miss a chance to see it. If it wasn't, I didn't want anybody hunting in the little plantation of pines we had put in for pulpwood, or messing with Hubert's cow pond. Hubert had stocked it with fish a couple of years ago, and occasionally one of my sons or grandchildren got the urge to sit on the grass for an afternoon and catch my supper. Even a prankster with a gallon of liquid soap could make things real unpleasant.

The full moon bathed the whole world in soft white light, drawing me outside anyway, so I decided to go investigate. And in case you're thinking I am one of those disgusting women in books and shows who foolishly climb unlit steps into towers, tiptoe into dark cellars, or otherwise go stupidly into danger, let me assure you I was going armed with a flashlight and a cell phone, and was taking with me a three-legged beagle who was well able to protect me from anything on two.

Furthermore, I'd stay well back. I just wanted to see who it was and what they were up to. Remember, I knew almost everybody in Hope County at least by sight. More important, since Joe Riddley had been a magistrate for thirty years and I was one now, everybody knew who I was. If this was kids up to tricks, I'd send them home with a stern warning. If it were anything more dangerous, I'd hightail it back down the road and call the sheriff. I just didn't want to call out the troops for something silly.

I heard another car stop as I snapped on Lulu's leash. I tied a dish towel around her muzzle so she wouldn't bark in case I surprised a courting couple and wanted to make a quick, silent getaway. That didn't please her much, but she always enjoys a walk. I also stopped by the kitchen closet to put on my garden shoes. I had on my house slippers and didn't want sharp gravel bruising my feet.

It was a pleasant night for a walk—or fishing. It was entirely possible I would find Hubert and a couple of his cronies on the banks of the pond. The sky looked taller, somehow, in the bright moonlight, and shadows spread a lovely leafy carpet on the road. Night birds sounded downright friendly as we passed. Lulu whined when I wouldn't let her investigate rustles in the undergrowth, but I knew the rabbits and squirrels were grateful. It was too nice a night for anything to feel hunted.

I was surprised to reach the pasture and recognize Sara Meg's silver SUV. I wondered again where she had found money for that vehicle. Had Fred left her more than she'd let on? More important, what was Sara Meg doing in Hubert's pasture? Or had Hollis brought Bethany down to fish? Martha said Hollis drove that car more often than Sara Meg did.

Behind the SUV was the old jalopy I recognized as Art Franklin's. Were he and Garnet meeting by the pond in the moonlight? I didn't want to bother them, but if Art had murdered DeWayne, was Garnet safe?

I was still standing in the road trying to decide what to do when I heard a sharp cry.

Lulu strained at her leash, whining, so I bunched up my skirt and managed to get between two strands of the barbed-wire fence without doing permanent damage to my clothes or my skin. That dratted dog, of course, slid under the bottom strand, so we had to spend a minute disentangling her leash.

The pasture was awash in moonlight as I climbed a slight rise toward the pond. A lanky form weaved back and forth across the uneven grass, straight at me, flapping its hands and crying, "Help! Oh, help her!"

Lulu growled deep in her throat. I bent and released her dish towel, and she gave a short volley of barks, then jerked the leash from my hand and ran toward the pond in full bay. Down at our place, Joe Riddley's hunting dogs added three-part harmony from their pen.

"Help her! Oh, please, help her. I can't swim!" Art Franklin grabbed my arm and pulled me toward a little dock Hubert had built when he'd stocked the pond with fish. Just beyond it, I saw a widening set of gentle circles. Lulu danced on the edge of the water, urging me on.

Nobody swam in that pond. It wasn't but five-and-a-half feet deep in the middle and had been well manured for years by cows.

I clearly remembered that last fact as I dropped my skirt and kicked off my shoes. To my dying day, I will consider running into that filthy water one of the bravest things I've ever done.

Near the middle, right at the end of the dock, my feet landed on something soft. I was over my head by then and so startled that I opened my mouth. Gagging and coughing, I bobbed to the surface. Only willpower and terror enabled me to take a deep breath and dive back under. Of course, the bottom of the pond wasn't far. If I'd stood on tiptoes and raised my arms, my elbows would have been out of the water. Instead, I groped with both hands and found something soft and silky. Hair. I grabbed it and yanked, rose to the surface for air and hauled with all my might.

Garnet Stanton's pale face rose to meet the moonlight.

I let go of her hair and grabbed her shoulders awkwardly, wishing I'd taken that Red Cross lifesaving course with Joe Riddley back when we built our pool. At least I was smart enough to head straight to shore. "Come help me," I yelled to Art. "It's not deep." My feet were already touching bottom. He splashed in toward me and took her other side. Together, we walked up the shallow slope, letting the water take most of Garnet's weight.

Getting her up the muddy bank was harder. She might look like a ghost, but waterlogged and limp, she weighed more than marble. Art mostly got in the way, he was so hysterical.

"Do you know CPR?" I gasped when we reached the grass.

"No, ma'am. Is she going to die?" He looked like a specter himself, he was so pale.

"Grab my cell phone and call 911," I gasped, nodding toward it. I rolled Garnet over so she was facedown and hoped that was right. Lulu danced around, encouraging me with sharp little barks.

I straddled Garnet's slender back and started pushing hard on her shoulders like I'd seen folks do in movies, and all the time I was praying over and over, "Help, God. Don't let her die."

"Get up, Little Bit. She can't breathe with you sitting on her." Joe Riddley took five years off my life, coming up behind me like that. He put a hand on my shoulder and shoved me away. Then he knelt over her and began to pump her back with strong even strokes.

I'd never been so glad to see him, but I wasn't going to let him know it, not after that rude remark. "How did you know I was here?" I asked, squatting back on my heels.

"I was riding with my windows down and heard Lulu's serenade, and then I saw the cars." He kept pumping, but Garnet didn't move. Art hovered over us, wringing his hands.

I saw now why I'd thought Garnet was a ghost. She wore a long white gown with short puffy sleeves. She'd have looked like a Victorian princess if the gown hadn't been rusty red from the muddy water.

Across the fields I heard the ambulance start its wail over at the hospital. As it came nearer, I prayed while Joe Riddley pumped.

"Go . . . show them . . . the way." He sounded absolutely exhausted, and I saw in his eyes that he was afraid we were going to lose her.

I shoved damp feet into muddy shoes and ran, tugging my skirt over my head. I wasn't about to greet anybody in a muddy slip if I could help it.

Finally, as I brought the technicians over the little hill between the pond and the road, Garnet moaned and threw up like she'd swallowed half the pond. The technicians ran toward her and took over so efficiently, I was proud to know them.

Joe Riddley pulled Art away when they strapped her to a stretcher, or I think he'd have gotten on it with her. As the techs headed back across the pasture, I walked beside her, saying dumb things like, "You're going to be all right, honey. You're going to be all right." She gave no sign that she heard. Or maybe she didn't believe things were going to be all right.

Only once did she open her eyes. When she saw Art hovering over her, she moaned, closed her eyes and lay as still as a sodden Sleeping Beauty who'd rejected her prince. Joe Riddley gave the information the technicians required while Garnet lay like alabaster in the moonlight. As they lifted her stretcher and slid it into the truck, Art begged, "Will she be okay?"

"Can't tell yet," said one, heading for the driver's seat.

"She took in a lot of water," said the other, running for his seat.

Art ran to his car and followed them. As they all roared away into the night, I stood in that road and sobbed.

"You okay?" Joe Riddley draped an arm around my shoulders and held me close, sopping though I was. He was trembling, but he was warm. "She's going to be all right. Come on home for some dry clothes."

"I want to go with her."

"Get yourself dry first, and then we'll go. The breeze is picking up, and I don't want you catching your death of cold." His fingers gently rubbed my neck.

He peered into the SUV. "Keys are in the ignition. You drive it. I'll bring Lulu in my car." We both needed some private time to recover.

My hair hung wet and muddy on my cheeks. I'd have to call Phyllis first thing in the morning to see if she could work me in for a shampoo and set before I went to the store. As I started the ignition, my knees shook so hard I could hardly get my foot on the gas pedal. I drove slowly, peering through the windshield as though I were peering down the long, bleak tunnel of Garnet's life. What could have driven her to do such a thing? Did she not know how precious life is?

I glanced in my rearview mirror at Joe Riddley driving through the leaf-dappled brightness with Lulu beside him, her head hung out the window to sniff the breeze. Neither seemed to notice the spot where they'd both been shot last August, but I shivered to remember how long it had taken him to recover and how near we'd come to losing Lulu and not just her leg. As I pulled into our drive, I sent up a silent word of thanks that they were still around and asked the same blessing for Garnet.

❧ 27 ❧

Joe Riddley spent weeks in the hospital after he was shot, and I spent a week there in February, getting pills out of my system. Neither of us looked forward to yet another dash to the emergency room with hearts fluttering and prayers ascending that we'd make it in time.

"We'll have to go get Sara Meg and take her to the hospital," I pointed out as I sloshed across the yard to the kitchen door, "since we've got her car."

It was only that afternoon that Sara Meg had asked me to leave Skye MacDonald's office. I dreaded explaining to her about fishing Garnet out of the pond tonight, so I was real grateful when Joe Riddley said, "I'll go get her. You get dressed and come in your car."

"Take the cell phone and call her to say you're coming." I grabbed it from my pocketbook and thrust it at him.

She and Joe Riddley were already at the information desk when I arrived. "Where's Garnet Stanton?" Sara Meg was demanding in a tight voice.

The clerk checked her list. "Room five, but the doctors are with her now. You can't go in there yet."

"I'm her mother!" Sara Meg headed for the doors marked NO ADMITTANCE without noticing I was there.

Art crouched in the waiting room on an orange plastic chair. "Why were you down at the pond?" I asked as I sat down beside him.

"I was going to help her run away this evening after I got off work. I was going to drive her to Swainsboro, but she didn't come, so finally I went to her house. I saw her come out and drive off, and I followed."

Joe Riddley joined us and we all sat on those hard orange chairs and waited. We watched patients come in with runny noses and runny eyes, bullets to be removed, sprains to be braced, broken wrists to be set, and sore throats to be soothed. I kept my mind off Garnet by wondering which of the patients would appear before my magistrate's bench as soon as they were released and which of us would be the first to come down with something we'd caught in the emergency room.

Art sat hunched with his hands between his knees, seldom saying a word.

Joe Riddley stood all of a sudden. "I think we ought to invite the hospital board to hold their next meeting here, to see how long *they* can stand these chairs." He started prowling.

When he next orbited past me, I said, "We ought to call Hollis."

"She's okay. She's spending the night with Bethany."

"I know, but I think she ought to be here. You've got the phone. Call her."

He wandered over to a quiet corner to make the call, then came back and reported that Sara Meg had already called Buddy, and he was stopping for Hollis on his way to the hospital.

I hadn't realized Martha was on duty until she hurried over and sat down in the chair Joe Riddley had vacated. "Somebody told me you all were out here. Is it about Garnet?"

"How is she?" Art demanded.

"She's going to be all right. She's being processed for a room right now. The EMTs said it was you who called. What happened?"

"She jumped in before I could stop her," Art said. I thought he was going to burst into tears.

"And I went after her and got myself a new hairdo." I shoved back my hair, which was matted, filthy and straggled down my neck.

"She was suicidal?" Martha was on her feet as soon as I nodded. "That changes things. Excuse me." She hurried out. When she came back a few minutes later, she reported, "They've sent her to the psychiatric unit. We can't take the chance that she'll try something else. Can you tell me everything that happened?"

We didn't get a chance. Sara Meg dashed out and headed straight for Martha, shooting sparks ahead of her. "Why are they changing Garnet's room? I was filling out paperwork and heard them say she's being sent to Three-C. Is that still the psychiatric ward?" I remembered that Sara Meg's mother-in-law had been there for a few days after Fred's death.

"It's only for a night or two," Martha soothed her. "She tried to take her own life."

"Take her own life?" Sara Meg's voice rose. "Garnet? You have been trying to get her to see a psychiatrist for weeks. There is nothing the matter—"

"Mama?" None of us had noticed that Hollis and Buddy had arrived until Hollis spoke.

Sara Meg turned and gathered Hollis in her arms. "Oh, honey, Garnet's been hurt. She's real bad."

"What happened?" Buddy demanded.

Sara Meg shook her head. "I don't know. She fell in the Yarbroughs' pool or something and nearly drowned." Three pairs of eyes turned to me accusingly.

Joe Riddley circled by again right then and overheard. "Garnet was in Hubert's cattle pond," he corrected them. "MacLaren jumped in and pulled her out." I was annoyed they hadn't been able to figure out by looking at me that I hadn't been in my pool. I looked like I had been dragged through a mud puddle.

"Did she try to kill herself?" That was Hollis again, her

face so white that even her freckles were pale. When we hesitated, she demanded, "Did she?"

"Of course she didn't," Buddy answered.

"Yes, she did," Art said with a glower.

Sara Meg seemed to notice him for the first time, and she visibly cringed. I couldn't blame her, since the poor boy had been branded a murderer by Chief Muggins not many hours before. She moved a step closer to her brother, and Buddy said, "What are you doing here? Go on home. You have no place here."

Art bristled, but Joe Riddley put a hand on his shoulder. "You won't get to see her, son. We'll stick around and I'll call you if there's any change. Go on home now."

Art slunk out like the stray cats Mama used to evict from our backyard.

Hollis turned to me, her blue eyes blazing. "Did she try to kill herself, Miss Mac?"

I reluctantly nodded. "I'm not sure, but I think so. I saw her get out of the car and head toward the pond. By the time I got there, she'd already been under the water awhile." I shivered. The hospital was definitely too cold. Joe Riddley came over to put his arm around me, and I leaned close to him. For a second there, I'd been back in Hubert's pond.

Joe Riddley peered down at Martha. "How long before Garnet will be ready for her folks to see her? Is there time for us all to go get a cup of coffee?"

"Why don't you go on up to the waiting room just outside the unit?" she suggested. "There's a coffeepot there, and I doubt there are other families up there at this hour."

Hopemore doesn't have much call for a psychiatric unit at the hospital. It's really just four rooms at one end of a hall, with a little lobby outside a set of double doors. Martha personally escorted us up to the lobby, which had a big round table, and made a fresh pot of coffee. She also found a box of assorted cookies that still had a few good ones left. With the bright lights dimmed, it was a pleasant enough place to wait at that hour.

Martha indicated the double doors. "Usually you'd ring to be admitted, but right now they're getting her settled. I'll tell them to come get you when you can go back." The last was for Sara Meg, whose eyes were greedy on those doors.

Martha inserted a key and the doors opened with a swoosh. I saw a second set of locked doors beyond them. The unit might be small, but it was certainly secure.

We ranged ourselves around the table, with Hollis between Joe Riddley and me and Buddy and Sara Meg on the other side. Joe Riddley poured coffee and brought milk and sugar. As we munched on cookies, I wondered if like me, everybody else was wondering what to say.

Hollis knew. She said in a low, furious voice, "This has got to stop." Her fists were clenched on the table before her and her jaw jutted out as she glowered across the table at her mother and uncle.

Buddy put one arm around Sara Meg's chair. "Don't worry your mother now."

"Don't worry your mother." Hollis's parody made something terrible of those words. "Ever since Daddy died, that's all we hear from you. 'Don't worry your mother.' It's time she got worried. It's time she got real worried. It's time she found out exactly what's been going on."

"Hollis." His voice was stern.

I didn't know what he was warning her against, and neither did Sara Meg. She looked from one to the other, bewildered. "What are you talking about?"

"Nothing," Buddy told her.

Hollis glared at him. "Ask this—this uncle, this vermin, if he's sleeping with Garnet."

She might as well have poured ice water down our backs, she shocked us so. I stared at her. Joe Riddley froze with his coffee halfway to his mouth. Sara Meg wore the embarrassed expression most mothers get when a child tells a particularly shocking lie in public.

Hollis ignored us and went right on. "I can't believe I never suspected before, but you were so clever, Uncle

Buddy. Always dropping me off at places before you took Garnet to the club to play tennis or home to practice the piano or study." Her tone made the last word into something dark and nasty.

I dared to look at Buddy and was relieved to see he looked merely baffled. "What on earth are you talking about?"

She jutted out her chin. "The day of the big storm, I came home early. I saw your car leaving our drive as I came around the corner. Garnet was taking a shower—in the middle of the day. And washing her hair—when she'd washed it that morning—like she'd gotten filthy—" She stopped to swallow hard. "And her bed was messed up. I may be naive—I mean, it's not like we ever got any real sex education at home"—she ignored her mother's flinch—"but I'm not dumb. I know what messes up a bed like that. I know what she'd been doing. You don't need to deny it, Buddy. I saw your car."

Buddy drained the rest of his coffee and set his cup on the table before he bothered to answer. "Maybe it's you we ought to leave in the psychiatric ward. You're making up a whole poultry farm out of one chicken. I was over there that day, yes. I went to see if you'd gotten home from the pool or if you needed a ride. Garnet said you had your bike. She'd gotten up from a nap and said the radio predicted we were in for a big storm, so she wanted to wash her hair in case the power went out—as it did, if you remember. I must have left just as you got home, and you put two and two together and got five. That's all. You never were real good in math." He picked up his empty cup, peered at it in surprise, and set it down again.

Hollis looked from Buddy to the rest of us. Doubt crept into her eyes. "Then why did she plan to run away? Why did she try to kill herself?"

"We don't know that she tried to kill herself," Joe Riddley reminded her. "We'll have to wait for Garnet herself to tell us."

Buddy stood. "Don't make things worse by letting your imagination run wild." He went to get himself more coffee.

Hollis slumped back in her chair, flushed and sulking. Her breath came in quick, angry pants. Sara Meg leaned across the table and spoke sharply to her. "I can't believe you said those things. After all Buddy's done for us—for *you*—"

Maybe it was her saying his name that made me look over at him just then. I caught the quick breath he expelled as coffee filled his cup. I saw how he straightened his shoulders as he turned back to the table. He looked just like a kid who has been given a hard word in a spelling bee and spelled it right, to his own surprise and elation. I found sickening little doubts rising in me.

Sara Meg had no doubts. As Buddy came back to the table, she reached out to lightly touch his arm in support. Hollis glared. Joe Riddley looked as discombobulated as I felt. It was one of those moments when I wondered how on earth we could get from there to anywhere else.

Martha bustled through the doors like an angel of deliverance. "It will just be a few more minutes until she's settled in. They'll call you. Everything okay for now?"

I knew she wanted to get back downstairs, but I motioned her over. "Do you have a few minutes to sit down?"

"A few. My feet would enjoy a little vacation." She took the chair between Joe Riddley and Sara Meg.

"We're having a discussion here I think you could shed some light on. Would you give us a quick description of a girl who has been sexually abused? Just a thumbnail of your usual lecture. What does she look like? How does she act?" I wanted to demonstrate to us all—particularly Hollis and myself—that Garnet wasn't that girl. After all, Garnet had heard Martha's lecture, I told myself. She could have talked about herself when she was telling Martha about her pupil. But Hollis needed reassurance, and she'd listen to Martha, who was an expert.

Hollis leaned forward, dogged determination in the set of

her shoulders. She had crossed some sort of Rubicon tonight and was not going back without a fight.

Everybody else was finding the tabletop mighty interesting.

If Martha was startled by my request, her training kept her from showing it. She took a few seconds to gather her thoughts, then began. "Well, first, she has diametrically opposed feelings that flip back and forth. She's terribly ashamed and feels powerless, yet another side of her is very sexualized, so she can look at other girls and feel superior, or think, 'I know things about which you know nothing at all.' She might look very prudish and demure, but she may go home and watch the adult Spice Channel or look up porn sites on the computer."

Hollis caught a quick breath, but nobody else seemed to hear her. Sara Meg was more interested in watching the door. Buddy sneaked a peek at his watch under the table.

"She will be tinged with cynicism," Martha went on. "She knows how bad the world can be. She will try to avoid the perpetrator whenever possible, but if he is around, she will do all she can to be nice to him. She fears his violence, you see. So while she looks calm to other people, she is real tense inside. She may clench her fists, pull out her hair, or bite her lips so hard she draws blood. And she will be withdrawn, real secretive."

I was beginning to feel queasy, and I noticed that Martha was talking slower. Her eyes sought mine as she said, "Almost as soon as the abuse begins, people will remark on how quickly she has grown up."

It fit. She and I both knew it. If I felt terrible for not noticing, how much worse must Martha feel? I truly pitied her as she reached out to cover Sara Meg's hand with her own. "Do you suspect that Garnet—?"

"Of course not." Sara Meg pulled her hand away as if Martha's touch was as distasteful as what she was discussing. "It's a friend of Hollis's—and Bethany's," she added.

"It is *not*! It's Garnet!" Hollis pounded her fists on the table and stamped her feet on the floor. "It's Garnet, dammit, and you just won't see it! Why won't you see it?" Her voice rose in a desperate scream.

Sara Meg looked at Hollis with shocked, rebuking eyes. Buddy had his arm around his sister, protecting her. And I finally knew why the ancients used to kill a messenger who brought bad news. We were all so *distressed* with that furious child for the way she was shredding our comfortable world. Then we heard a distant voice beyond the two sets of doors. "That's my sister! I have to get out there. Please!"

Martha hurried toward the doors. She came back in a minute, supporting Garnet. I swear, that child was beautiful even in a shrunken white johnny gown with her hair tumbled on her shoulders. She stood looking at Hollis with large, unfocused eyes. "What's the matter? I heard you shouting." Then she looked from one of us to the other as if she couldn't see clearly—probably the result of something to make her sleep. She walked woozily toward the table, leaning heavily on Martha's arm, and stood there, obviously puzzled.

A nurse hovered at the door. "I'll be here," Martha assured her.

As the nurse left, Hollis turned to Garnet, calm and pale. "Tell them what Uncle Buddy's done to you. Tell them, Garnie. Don't let him do it anymore."

Garnet's eyes flicked around the table. When she saw Buddy, she gave him a hesitant smile.

"Go back to bed, honey," Sara Meg urged. "You need your rest."

"I'm okay. But you don't have to be here, you know. You have to work tomorrow." Garnet's emphasis on *work* made it a criticism.

Martha pulled out the chair she'd been sitting in beside Joe Riddley and gently steered Garnet into it. "Hollis has been saying some pretty serious things, honey. Is there something you need to tell us?"

"Of course there isn't." Sara Meg's voice was sharp.

Martha turned to Garnet and her eyes never left the girl's pale face as she said softly, "The most painful thing in an abused child's world is the knowledge that somehow her mother is to blame. Mothers are supposed to protect us, but her own mother hasn't done it. She won't be able to deal with that, so her relationship with her mother will be passive aggressive. She'll say things designed to hurt. She'll pick at her whole family like a sore."

Buddy barked a short laugh. "Come on, Martha. You're describing every teenager I know. Secretive, passive aggressive, picking at their parents—isn't that normal adolescent behavior?" He looked around the table, inviting us to laugh with him. Sara Meg tried to smile, but it was a pitiful attempt.

"Stop it!" Hollis shoved back her chair and jumped to her feet again. "Stop sitting there pretending this is just a discussion." She looked from Buddy to Garnet, her face bright red. "He did it and we three know it. He's been doing it for years, hasn't he? You've been weird almost since Daddy died. Is that when it started? Is it?"

Garnet made a high little sound, but she did not nod.

"My God, Hollis!" Buddy slammed his palms onto the table. "You've got sex on the brain! First you go talking to DeWayne about how somebody you know is having sex and what you should do. Now this! What are you trying to do to me?"

"DeWayne?" I asked before I thought.

Buddy heaved a disgusted sigh. "He came to me embarrassed to death, saying Hollis suspected somebody she knew was sleeping with somebody. He said he was telling me because if it were his niece or sister saying things like that, he'd want to know. Is this what you were trying to tell him, Hollis? Thank God you didn't."

"Yes, thank God I didn't," Hollis blazed back, "because then you *might* have killed him, like I was scared at first you did."

"You're crazy, girl." He flung himself back in his chair. "Stop this nonsense right now. You are worrying your mother."

Garnet froze.

Hollis breathed heavily through her nose, and as she began to speak, tears streamed down her cheeks. "She ought to get worried. Garnet cries all the time in her room, and she won't talk to people, and she avoids boys, and she's mean to Mama and me. I thought she'd gotten all weird because Daddy died, but that wasn't it. It wasn't it at all!" She whirled around, covered her face and sobbed. Through her fingers, her voice was muffled. "I hate you! I want my sister back!" She stood there, shaking and crying as if her heart had broken.

Joe Riddley—an old softie who can't stand to see a woman cry—scraped back his chair and went to her. "There, there," he said, patting her back. She turned and sobbed stormily against his shirt while he stroked her hair as he had stroked Bethany's that dreadful Saturday when DeWayne died.

Garnet moved her eyes from Hollis to her mother without saying a word, but I saw a small drop of blood begin to form where she had bitten through her lip. Sara Meg was as white as the Styrofoam cup before her, her eyes enormous and confused.

Buddy frowned at Hollis as if she were a toddler having a public tantrum, then he looked over at Garnet and shrugged, with a wry smile that said *Let her get it out of her system.*

"Wipe that smile off your face," Martha snapped. In that instant, I knew Hollis had one ally. I soon discovered she had another.

Joe Riddley spoke over Hollis's head. "What about the fellow? What kind of person is he? How does he keep that going on without the child telling somebody?"

Buddy again checked his watch, like he needed to get

home if he was going to work in the morning. I automatically checked mine, too. It was well after midnight.

Martha laughed, but there was no mirth in it. "Oh, the perpetrator is a clever fellow. He will always try to convince the child it's her own fault. At first he'll use mild threats: 'You seduced me. I was just trying to make you feel better, I would never have done this if you hadn't wanted it.'"

I looked at Garnet, but for all the expression on her face, she could have been anywhere except right there.

Martha kept talking. "Over the years, if she tries to break the relationship, he moves to harder threats, like 'Nobody will believe you—they will believe me' or 'Your mother would never understand. If you tell, it will break her heart.'"

Hollis sniffed against Joe Riddley's shirt. "Don't worry your mother," she said bitterly.

Still Garnet didn't move.

"If she tries to break it off at that point," Martha continued in a soft, calm voice, "the perpetrator will threaten violence against her, or he will threaten that maybe another, younger relative could take her place. To protect the other child, she will continue the relationship."

Hollis wrenched away from Joe Riddley to grab Garnet's nearest shoulder. "Is that what he told you? Is it? That if you didn't, I would?" She whirled on Buddy. "I never would. It's wrong, wrong, wrong. Do you hear me? It's wrong!" She had never seemed so gallant to me as when she stood there with her hair wild and tears streaming.

Finally Garnet spoke. "It's not really *wrong,* Hollie," she said in a sweet, reasoning voice. "It's even in the Bible. Genesis eleven?" She gave Buddy a quick look for confirmation, but he was checking his fingernails. "Abraham's niece Milcah married her uncle Nahor. It's in the Bible." Her large dark eyes circled the table, urging us to understand.

Understand? I couldn't even breathe. Garnet had jumped back in the filthy pond and taken us all underwater with her.

Martha got up and put a hand on Hollis's shoulder. "Go

wash your face. The rest room is just down the hall to the right."

"Do you believe me, Mrs. Yarbrough?" Hollis gave her a long, searching look. She seemed satisfied with what she saw, for she turned and stumbled out the door, sobbing.

Martha sat down again beside Garnet. "Honey, it is wrong. You know that as well as I do, but it's hard to admit it, isn't it?"

Garnet didn't move. I had the impression that when we hadn't believed what she'd said, she had departed for another planet and left only her beautiful shell behind.

"But why would anybody put up with that—not tell somebody?" I asked, confused.

Martha put a hand on Garnet's shoulder. "Because she is afraid of his threats. She will have seen his violence, which he will probably have hidden from anybody else. But you don't have to be afraid anymore, Garnet."

"I'm not afraid," Garnet said. She sounded like she was surprised anybody would think she was. Martha looked at me, and I read the word "denial" in her eyes. She reached for the silver chain around Garnet's neck and held up the silver tiger's eye necklace I had admired at Myrtle's. "There's another thing about the perpetrator. He almost always showers the girl and her family with gifts."

"Like a new kitchen?" I could name them without thinking twice. "A new car? Trips to the beach?" Sara Meg's eyes widened with each item I named. Now she seemed to be having trouble breathing, too.

Joe Riddley squeezed my shoulder. "That's enough, Little Bit."

Buddy shoved back his chair. He rested his fingertips on the table and leaned into them, looming over us all. "This is ridiculous. I am not on trial here. And I am not having sex with my niece. Look at her. Does she seem afraid of me? Disgusted by me? No, she doesn't. Do I mess with you, Garnet? Tell these nice people. Do I mess with you?"

Her eyes flew to his and his held hers. Slowly she shook her head.

He gave us a triumphant smile. "See? So maybe Garnet has been having sex with somebody—Art Franklin, for instance. I don't know and I don't plan to ask. I happen to think that sort of thing is real private. And yes, I have certainly helped my sister out through some rough times and tried to repay some of what she and her husband did for me over the years. But I'm being accused of some serious stuff here, and it's a lie. Do you hear me? It's a lie. I don't know what Hollis's game is, what everybody's game is, but if this continues, you can discuss it with my lawyer. This is my life you're playing with, and I've had enough." He turned on his heel, strode swiftly to the elevator and pressed the button.

The elevator was still there from when we came up. As the door opened, he turned as if he'd had a sudden thought. He came around the table and took Garnet by the arm.

"I don't want them saying these filthy things to you, either—these psychological geniuses." Before any of us knew what was happening, he'd drawn her into the open elevator and closed the door.

Sara Meg collapsed in a faint.

⇥ 28 ⇤

"Help her!" I cried to Joe Riddley as I ran after Martha to the stairs.

Breathless—for we are both too plump for that nonsense—we clattered down. My knees were jelly after two flights.

We burst into the emergency room and looked frantically toward the elevators. They were both open. Neither Buddy nor Garnet was in sight.

"I can't go after him," Martha gasped. "I have to stay here."

"I'll follow and call the police," I promised.

I reached the outside door in time to see Buddy in the shadows beyond the emergency room door, running down the sidewalk and pulling Garnet after him.

"Stop!" I shouted as he reached his car. He shoved her into his backseat, slammed the door, and jumped in the front.

"Help!" I called over one shoulder as I dashed out. "He's kidnapping her!"

That certainly got attention, but by the time a crowd filled the door and I reached my own car, Buddy's Toyota—the old car we'd been so proud of him for driving so he could help out Sara Meg—was pulling from the lot.

I followed, fumbling for my cell phone, not daring to take my eyes off the taillights ahead. I have the police on autodial. With one button I could summon help and keep them abreast of developments until they caught up with us. I felt brilliant and modern—until I remembered Joe Riddley had the cell phone.

"Oh, God," I moaned. "Help!"

Up ahead, Buddy turned and headed down Oglethorpe Street. Maybe he was taking Garnet home, as he'd implied.

Or maybe not. He passed their house without a change of speed and rolled through town—past the courthouse, past Yarbrough's, where the bunting was already up advertising our Fourth of July sale, out past the end of town. When he turned down our road, I cut my lights and turned behind him.

Joe Riddley taught me to drive on that road nearly fifty years ago, and I've always claimed I could drive it blind-folded. That night was the closest I've ever come to testing that theory, and I was real grateful for the full moon that made the road and woods all silvery, like in a fairy tale. If this were a fantasy, though, I hoped I'd soon get back to re-ality.

When Buddy's brake lights glowed, I slowed. When he stopped next to Hubert's pasture, near where Garnet had parked earlier, I turned into Hubert's drive and hoped his big hydrangea would hide the light while I opened my door. As I climbed out, Art Franklin's old car crunched past me on the road and slid to a stop behind Buddy's.

Our dogs started singing four-part harmony, and the air was so clear I could even hear Bo shrieking, "Hello, hello, hello!" from the barn. I'd never realized what a noisy wel-come we offered folks this far from the house.

I left my keys in the ignition, in case I had to get out quick, and gently pushed my door just barely closed. Then I hurried on tiptoes around Hubert's hydrangea. A light flashed in Buddy's car and I heard him say impatiently, "Come on. Get out." Garnet whimpered a protest.

Art shouted, "You let her go! You hear me?"

I tried to figure out what I ought to do. I wouldn't be of

any help to Art personally, but our dogs and telephone were only a few hundred yards down the road. Could I get past Buddy unseen, run home, call for help, and get back with the dogs while Art stalled him?

When you have only one choice, you take it. Bent low, I hurried across the road and crept into the shadow of the pines on the other side. That was a young plantation we'd put in to sell for paper, and the pines were small. Their nettles would mask my footsteps and their branches partly conceal me, if I didn't move abruptly and catch Buddy's eye.

I didn't need to worry at the moment. He was occupied in dragging Garnet from the car while Art tried to shove him away from her. Garnet seemed to be fighting them both, and I would never have believed she knew all the words she was using.

While I worked my way down the trees, Buddy shoved Art across the road with one fierce push. He sprawled in the dust and gravel while Buddy jerked Garnet out. Then he pulled one arm behind her back and stiff walked her toward the fence. "No! No! No!" she gasped all the way.

When Art climbed to his feet, Buddy shoved Garnet's arm farther up her back. She yelped in pain.

"Let her go!" Art screamed.

"Go home, or I'll hurt her bad," Buddy promised. "I mean it." He grabbed Garnet's mass of hair with his free hand and yanked. She shrieked.

Art flung himself on Buddy, pummeling him with his fists.

It was a brave, stupid act. Buddy played tennis every week and worked out regularly at a gym. Art waited tables and wrote poems. In two seconds Art was flat on his back on our gravel, his nose spurting blood. But his courage gave Garnet the seconds she needed to slip between two strands of barbed wire and dash up the hill, where she stood poised to run again. In the moonlight, she was as white as chalk.

Buddy turned to follow her. I stooped, picked up a length

of pine branch maybe three inches thick, held it behind me, and stepped into the dappled road.

"Give it up, Buddy." I sure sounded a lot more confident than I felt.

He huffed out a huge breath and shook his head, like he needed to clear it. "Go on home, Judge. You shouldn't be out here."

"Garnet and I will both go—back to the hospital." I moved toward him, holding the log behind my back. Art moaned and rolled over to sit up, but Buddy and I ignored him.

Buddy pressed down the top strand of wire and swung one leg over. "Go on back, then, but by yourself. We don't need you here."

"I can't let you hurt her, Buddy."

He laughed and stood with one leg over the wire, holding it with both hands like a very skinny horse. "I'm not going to hurt her. It was your family's meddling that started all this mess. Ridd getting DeWayne to coach the team, convincing Garnet and Hollis he was some sort of hero. Martha teaching that stuff to Garnet's class that made her think what we were doing was wrong. It's not wrong, Judge. You heard her. It's in the Bible. There's nothing dirty about it. The only thing dirty around here is you. You stink to high heaven of cow manure from that pond."

If he thought I was dumb enough to care about that right then, he could think again.

He kept right on talking. "Go home and take a bath. Garnet and I need to have a little talk." He looked over his shoulder. "Garnet, come here."

Like someone in a dream, she started toward him.

I ran across the road, pine log aloft, and brought my puny weapon down on his head.

"Ooof!" He staggered and fell forward on the wire, yelled as a barb found its mark. But my log had shattered, leaving just a stub. Daddy always said pine's too brittle to trust. He would never have pines near his house.

Still, I lifted it again, ready to club him until I had nothing left but sawdust.

That's when I heard an incredulous voice. "Miss Mac?"

Ronnie and Yasheika stood in the moonlit road. Lulu squirmed in Ronnie's arms, fighting the fingers that muzzled her. "Lulu!" I yelled. "Take him!"

She gave a ferocious wiggle and Ronnie dropped her. She hit the ground already flinging herself at the leg on our side of the fence. She caught Buddy's pants in her teeth and held on while he bounced on that wire, swearing and trying to kick her off. She held firm, growling like she'd eat him bite by bite as soon as I gave permission. Lulu might have lost a leg, but she hadn't lost an ounce of courage.

I figured I might as well add my voice to the din. I looked around for Yasheika. "My car's in the next driveway," I panted for breath. "Keys are in it. Take Garnet to the hospital and call 911. Run!"

Like I've said before, Yasheika is smart. With a quick nod, she hared toward the car, calling up the hill, "Come on, Garnet! Come with me."

Garnet hesitated, then turned and stumbled toward my car, bare legged and barefoot.

When they were nearly there, I said, "Okay, Lulu. That's enough. Good dog."

She backed off and sat down. Buddy put the rest of the fence between them, eyeing her warily. She rumbled deep in her throat and showed her teeth to prove she still had fight left in her.

"What's going on?" Ronnie looked from me to Buddy and back.

"More than you want to know." I didn't feel free to tell him much. It wasn't my secret.

Buddy had no such inhibitions. "A big misunderstanding," he told Ronnie man-to-man. "Garnet fell in that cattle pond tonight and the judge rescued her. Hollis got real upset about what happened to Garnet and made some accusations about her. Between them, she, Mac, and Martha got Garnet locked up in the psycho ward. I rescued her and thought I'd bring her back here to look at the pond and see it's just a little-bitty thing, nothing to be scared of. But Art showed up trying to fight me. Then the judge misunderstood my motives and attacked me with a pine tree." He gave Ronnie a rueful grin, and Ronnie's face creased in a sympathetic smile.

I waited until Yasheika had driven away, then I said, "You're looking at a child molester, Ronnie, pure and simple—if anything is pure and simple anymore."

"No!" Art moaned from the dirt at my feet. "No!" He dropped his face to his hands. Poor thing, I was sorry he'd heard that. I had plumb forgotten he was there.

Buddy shook his head. "That hasn't been proven, Mac. You're skating real close to slander here." Ronnie looked from one of us to the other, clearly baffled.

Seeing Buddy there, so handsome in the silver light, I couldn't blame Ronnie for doubting what I was saying. I almost disbelieved myself. But then a shadow passed over the moon and Buddy's face dissolved into darkness. I'm not much on signs and portents, but when the moon came back out, I saw him in a whole new light. He wasn't really handsome. He was evil incarnate, held together by a fancy skin.

"I suspect he's a murderer, too," I said, feeling sad and very old and tired. "He's cleverer than Tyrone or even Smitty. Clever enough to copy their badness and use it to his own advantage. The purple ink on the notes was a nice touch, Buddy."

Ronnie stared like I had gone plumb crazy. Buddy lifted both hands and backed farther up the slope with a little laugh. "Whoa! First a molester and now a murderer? Come on, Mac, who am I supposed to have murdered?"

"DeWayne, of course. You said you talked to him on the phone that Saturday before he died. You were making sure where he was, weren't you? So you could drop by the school with clippings that would scare him nearly to death, just thinking they might be spread all over Hopemore. Then, when he was trembling so bad he had to sit down, you left the room—for what? Did you tell him you'd get him a glass of water? Instead, you went to the gym and cut off a piece of rope with that pocketknife you're so proud of, put it around his neck, and pulled. Then you dragged him down the hall and strung him up in the locker room to make it look like suicide. You even wrote a short note for Yasheika, using purple ink and block letters you learned in architecture classes. I guess it was you who burned the clippings in his wastebasket, wasn't it, so the police would think DeWayne had done it? Then you wiped your prints off the doorknobs and scrubbed the seat of the chair DeWayne was sitting in when he died."

I had Ronnie's attention, but Buddy shook his head and leaned his wrists on the fence like we were neighboring farmers. "'I guess'?" he mocked me. "You better give up being a judge and start writing fiction. I worked Saturday, in my office. I was nowhere near the school."

"I saw you at the school early that morning." Art climbed stiffly to his feet and limped toward Buddy. His voice was hoarse, his face streaked with blood. "I had to sleep in my car that night, because—" He stopped. "Well, I just did." I figured his mama had a man at home and he preferred not to be in the house. Or maybe they'd had a fight, or he was drunk or writing a poem. While I was having those interesting speculations, Art had gone on talking.

". . . down the side street that goes by the school, about the time I was waking up, I heard a car park up the street. I checked my watch to be sure I wasn't going to be late for work. It was five after eight and Myrtle wanted me there by ten-thirty, so I had time to go home and change. Then I saw you in my rearview mirror. You got out of your car and dropped something in the wastebasket over across the street. Then you went up the path behind the science rooms—"

"You never saw jack," Buddy told him fiercely, "because I wasn't there."

"He was, Miss Mac." Art turned to me, his eyes huge in

the dimness. "I saw him. I even went over to see what he'd thrown away, but it was just empty cans of paint."

"You even painted his house?" I was so disgusted I could hardly stand.

Art didn't give me time to say more. He looked at Buddy and his big gray eyes swam with tears. "Were you really— you know, sleeping with Garnet? She always seemed so pure. " He stumbled toward his car and fell across the hood, sobbing.

Buddy called after him, "It was somebody else you saw, Franklin. I wasn't there." He turned back to me. "Why would I kill DeWayne? We were friends years ago. I was looking forward to getting to know him again." But I noticed him eyeing his car, as if measuring the distance, so I moved toward it. Lulu growled.

"You took the notebook, too," I said, talking more to myself than to him. "You showed up behind me, so you had circled around and beat Tyrone and Willie to it. You could easily pick it up and stick it in your pocket. You had heard me tell Ike it was important." I thought of something else, too. "You are one person DeWayne would have let in the back door of his classroom."

"But that's because he and DeWayne liked each other," Ronnie argued. I didn't blame him for still sitting on the fence about how much of this was true. The man was his boss and his friend. He hadn't seen Buddy sling Garnet in the car and yank her hair or heard what she'd called him.

"Maybe so," I said. "But I think Buddy killed him in spite of that. Garnet and Hollis were both too fond of DeWayne for your liking, weren't they, Buddy?"

"Hollis . . . " Ronnie said her name as though it were a new idea. He turned to me. "DeWayne told Buddy that Hollis had come to see him with a story about somebody she knew who was sleeping with somebody she shouldn't be sleeping with. He didn't mention any names or anything—"

"You didn't tell me that," I rebuked him.

He ducked his head. "I didn't like to mention it. Seemed

kind of private. But you think DeWayne was talking about Buddy and Garnet?"

"I don't think he knew who he was talking about, because Hollis couldn't quite bring herself to name names. But it was all coming apart, wasn't it, Buddy? Hollis suspected, and now she was talking to DeWayne. Next time she might tell him exactly who she meant, and you couldn't afford that. Hollis didn't know what to do except tell a grown-up, but DeWayne knew. He'd have had to report you if he suspected anything was going on."

Buddy climbed back over the fence. "Folks, this has been a most interesting evening, but I'm going home now. There is not one shred of proof for any of these wild stories you all are concocting at my expense, but first thing tomorrow, I am calling my lawyer. You'd better be calling yours, too, if any of this gets beyond this stretch of road."

As he moved toward his car, Lulu growled again, but I shushed her. Garnet was safe. As for the rest, it was a matter for the police. And I was afraid Buddy was right: Nobody would find a shred of evidence to prove it.

Deep down, I do believe that evil is eventually punished and good wins out, but this was one of the times I might have to chalk up to "not in this lifetime."

Ronnie, however, had a question. "Man, tell me straight. Did you kill DeWayne?"

Buddy lifted both hands in mock surrender. "The way things are getting twisted tonight, I'm not saying another word without my lawyer, Ron."

Ronnie grabbed his shirt. "I'm just asking for one word, Buddy. All I need is a simple 'no.' Can you give me that much?"

When Buddy hesitated, Ronnie drew back and planted a lovely punch on Buddy's face. I wished Yasheika could have been there to see it.

‍❧ 29 ❧

A police cruiser wailed down our road and skidded to a stop on the gravel just as Buddy bloodied Ronnie's nose.

Joe Riddley, Sara Meg, and Hollis arrived in Sara Meg's SUV in time to see Ronnie send Buddy crashing to the ground. He still lay there winded when Yasheika and Garnet pulled in behind the SUV.

Sara Meg ran at once to kneel by Buddy while Isaac James and a deputy strolled over from the cruiser.

"What happened here?" Isaac addressed Ronnie and me, but Buddy hauled himself to a sitting position, cradled his head in his hands, and answered.

"You aren't going to believe this, Isaac, but I brought Garnet, there, down here to see if she could remember why she jumped in the cattle pond earlier this evening. Then Judge Yarbrough showed up and starting hitting me with pine logs, and Ronnie showed up right after that and tore into me like a wild man." He gave Ronnie a grin. "Of course, I gave as good as I got."

"That the way you saw it, Ronnie?"

Ronnie felt his jaw gingerly. "Partly. My grandmama heard Joe Riddley had gone to the hospital with Garnet's mother, so she told me and Yasheika to come down and see if Miss Mac was all right. Grandmama's been pretty nervous about the way Miss Mac's been riling Smitty Smith, you know?"

"I know," Isaac told him.

"But Miss Mac wasn't home, so we waited for her on the porch."

I didn't know Joe Riddley had come up behind me until I heard a little snort at the word "waited." He and I had done some serious "waiting" on that same porch in our day.

Ronnie was still explaining. "Then we heard cars, and her dogs set up a ferocious noise. Lulu, there, was about to tear the kitchen door down to get out, so we brought her with us and came to investigate. We found Miss Mac here pounding away at Mr. Tanner with a rotten pine log."

Buddy was the first to laugh, and the rest joined in. In the midst of that general hilarity, Isaac peered around. "Where is the log?"

"Sawdust," I said. "It was rotten, all right, through and through. I certainly didn't hit him that hard." Folks laughed again.

Isaac looked at the crowd. "We got a report that Garnet Stanton was abducted from Hopemore Hospital by her uncle Buddy Tanner. Miss Stanton, are you here?"

"Yes." Garnet, who'd been standing with Yasheika beside my car, edged out of the shadows and winced as her bare feet met sharp stones.

"What are you doing here?" I demanded. "Yasheika, I told you to take her back to the hospital."

"I did," she assured me, "but we saw your husband, Hollis, and her mama just leaving the hospital parking lot, so I blew the horn to make them stop and told him you and Mr. Tanner were having a fight out on your road. They tore off in his direction, and Garnet had a fit until I followed him."

Ike called to Garnet, "Would you come over here, please, where I can see you?" When she edged a bit closer and he saw that all she had on was a johnny gown, he said hastily, "That's fine. Now tell me in your own words what happened tonight."

Garnet looked around at the faces bathed in soft light. People weren't laughing any longer. Art stood down by his car, so brokenhearted I wanted to cry just looking at him. Hollis stood alone by the silver SUV, her freckled face crumpled like she'd cry again in a minute if we gave her cause. Sara Meg knelt by Buddy, strained and anxious. Buddy frowned at Garnet from where he still sat on the ground. Ronnie nursed his jaw and dabbed his face with a tissue from a box Yasheika held ready in case he needed more. I didn't know how I looked, but it certainly wasn't my best, after all I'd been through. The only one of us who looked halfway normal was Joe Riddley, who Mama used to say would keep his looks through a tornado.

Lulu, sensing that something was wrong, whined. Garnet looked down at her, and it was to Lulu that she spoke. "I tried to kill myself tonight. It wasn't right, I know that now. I'm sorry. But Buddy—Buddy—" Her voice dwindled to a whisper and disappeared.

"What about your uncle?" Isaac's voice was gentle.

Garnet took a long time answering. I saw Hollis open her mouth, but Joe Riddley held up his hand and she closed it again.

Garnet looked from Hollis to Buddy, then back at Isaac. She took a deep breath and spoke like one having a final say before going bravely to the executioner. "Uncle Buddy seduced me when I was twelve. Ever since then, he's"—she swallowed and seemed to have a hard time framing a word— "used me like a wife." Her head bent in shame.

I heard Yasheika moan and saw Ronnie steal an arm around her waist. She seemed glad of his comfort.

"Wait a minute here!" Buddy shouted, holding up a hand to ward her off.

"You'll get your turn," Isaac assured him. "Go on, Miss Stanton."

"At first I didn't like it, but I didn't know it was wrong. But then Uncle Buddy kept saying we mustn't tell Mama or Hollis"—her eyes flicked toward Hollis, then back to the ground—"and finally, Hollis started suspecting this summer and staying at the house all the time. I was scared Buddy would get mad, so I knew I had to do something."

I knew exactly what she had decided to do, and when. "I need a job!" she had cried after she'd heard about her piano pupil.

"I tried avoiding him, but he kept pestering me, wanting—wanting—" She stopped and left that unfinished. "I asked Art to take me to my daddy's relatives down in Swainsboro. I don't know them, but I thought they'd let me stay there awhile, maybe. But Mama found out . . ." She looked at Ike, and her eyes swam with tears in the moonlight. "I didn't want to live all dirty like this. . . ."

Sara Meg rose to her feet and shouted, "Not one word of this is true, and you know it! Why are you saying such things about somebody who's been so good to us? We couldn't have made it without Buddy. So why are you spreading this pack of lies?" Her voice had grown shrill. When she came to an abrupt stop, the crickets trilled louder, taking up the slack.

"Okay, Mr. Tanner. What do you have to say to this little lady's statement?"

Buddy hauled himself to his feet, as well, and straightened his shirt and pants. Ruefully he looked at a rip in his sleeve. "I think my whole dadgum family has gone crazy with this full moon. I hear it takes some people that way. Sara Meg getting herself all hot and bothered here. Hollis, Garnet, even Mac there—of course, she's not in the family, but we've seen so much of her lately she might as well be. Poking her nose into everything, meddling—well, that's neither here nor there. But all I can say is exactly what Sara Meg just said. It's a pack of lies." He raised both hands and shrugged. "There's just not a dadblamed thing I can do to prove it."

"Talk to Martha, Isaac," Joe Riddley said behind me. "She's an expert on child abuse. She can tell you some of the symptoms, and you can ask around and see if they fit Garnet. Martha and I both think they do," he added. I suspected he wanted to get that in the notes the deputy was writing in his notebook over beside the cruiser.

Isaac gave a short nod. "I happen to be an expert, too. My uncle abused one of my cousins for several years before anybody found out what was going on." He spoke gently to Garnet. "I don't know if it makes any difference to you or not, but I believe your story, and I'm proud of you for finally having the courage to tell it. Come on, Buddy. Let's you and me take a drive." He rolled out the familiar words of the Miranda warning.

"No!" Sara Meg cried. She clutched Buddy's arm. "You can't arrest him! He hasn't hurt anybody."

Isaac gave her a long, level look. "Ma'am, the hurt he has inflicted is only beginning to be known. This child will live with it the rest of her life."

"Buddy?" Her plea came out a whimper.

He looked down at her in contempt and tugged his arm away. "This is all your fault. Do you know that? You never paid me a speck of attention, once you met Fred."

"Fred?" She sounded as confused as I felt.

"You married him and off you went to Gatlinburg, leaving me home with Fred's fat old mama. If Anne hadn't died, I don't know when you might have come home."

"Anne?" She seemed to have reached that stage of numbness where all she could do was parrot his last word.

"Anne Colder. Surely you remember her? Or were you too much in love to notice she died? Gerrick Lawton killed her, you know."

"Playing house." I didn't know I was going to speak until I did, but so long as I had the floor, I might as well get it all off my chest. "DeWayne was remembering how you all used to play house in the cemetery. Anne was the mama, you the daddy, and he the little boy. Did you try to play house for real that Saturday when DeWayne didn't come? Was Anne the first, before Garnet? And when she objected, did you hit her with a rock until she died? Then you'd have gone home to wash, because you have always liked things neat and tidy, but Fred's mother was old and hard of hearing. She wouldn't have known you were in the house until you came in the back door wheedling for a picnic lunch. That gave you a real good reason to go back and discover the body. Poor Gerrick was just icing on your cake, wasn't he?"

Yasheika shrieked and would have flung herself on him, but Ronnie held her back. She sobbed loudly in the shadows.

I didn't pay them much attention. I was remembering Buddy's tears in the courtroom, those nights when he woke screaming in his bed. Was it all an act? Why hadn't anybody checked his story more carefully at the time? Looked for bloody clothes? Seen if one of DeWayne's tramps had been around that day?

Because Gerrick had panicked. He knew, God help us all, that our fathers and mothers, like theirs before them, had taught us to trust the word of a white child over that of a black man. In that bright, truth-filled moonlight, those sins rose up to haunt me, and there was no place short of heaven to make that story come out right.

Buddy ignored everything I had said. He was still talking to Sara Meg. "Whatever happens to me, remember it is all your fault. You never loved me the way you loved the others."

"What others?" Sara Meg's voice was a hoarse whisper. She reached out and clutched his shirt again, every line of her body pleading with him to say none of this was true.

"Fred, Garnet, and Hollis."

"You love Garnet and Hollis," she protested.

His lips widened in a smile. "Oh, yes. I have loved Garnet."

I considered getting sick all over the road. Hollis gagged noisily.

He turned and pointed to her. "You even got my name. My name!"

Sara Meg stepped back, puzzled. "It was our mother's name."

"It was *my* name. Mama was dead. What did she care?

But I cared. I didn't want anybody else called Hollis. But what did you care? You never cared about me. Never! You went to college and left me with Daddy. Daddy! Nobody would believe the things he did to me after you left. You think what I did to Garnet was nasty? When you get to hell, ask our daddy what he did to his own little boy!" He turned away, shaking and white.

I felt as if I'd stepped out my front door and discovered the porch was no longer there. How had we failed to notice what was going on?

Phrases flitted through my head, phrases I'd heard on television or read in newspapers: "He was a quiet person. A real sweet man. Nobody would have guessed he'd do such a thing."

But *we* wouldn't have guessed because we'd never looked. We were all too busy. We consoled Walter, took him casseroles, then left him alone. We thought it was admirable the way he took care of Buddy when Sara Meg went to college. We never asked how the child was dealing with his mother's death, why he became so quiet and mature after his sister left. Later, we never wondered why as a young man he was content to spend all his time with Sara Meg and her girls, never wondered what was going on all those hours Sara Meg was at the store. We stayed busy while a warped child grew to manhood, and we never *saw*.

Isaac James stepped forward and put out his hand. "Come on, Buddy. Time to go. Judge Yarbrough, since you were present here, I'll need to request another magistrate for the preliminary hearing."

There are no words to express how glad I was about that.

I went to the hearing with Joe Riddley, Ridd, Martha, and Bethany, to support Hollis and Garnet. Isaac had persuaded Chief Muggins to reserve the murder charge while they lined up more evidence, which eventually would include Buddy's pocketknife and the two last pages from Tyrone's notebook, found hidden under the blotter on Buddy's desk.

The initial charges, therefore, were child molestation, enticing a child for indecent purposes, and incest.

We all agreed that was enough.

I never attended a sadder hearing. When Garnet started to testify, and began, "Soon after Daddy died . . . ," there wasn't a dry eye in the place.

Well, except two.

The judge was sad, Isaac was sad, the defense attorney was sad, the witnesses were sad, Sara Meg was devastated, and even the newspaper editor wore an unusually mournful face.

The only person who wasn't sad was the defendant. He sat there the whole time as if he'd dropped in for a little while because he had some time on his hands.

❧ 30 ❧

The last Saturday in June was a gosh-awful, muggy day.

That afternoon, the Hope County senior girls' fast-pitch softball team played their district championship game. Our mayor had declared it DeWayne Evans Day in Hopemore, and over three hundred people drove ninety miles each way to cheer the team.

We were a miserable bunch of fans, though. As we waited for the game to begin, gnats swarmed like one of Moses' plagues, biting us in places we'd forgotten we had. The sun beat down on our heads, burning any places where we'd forgotten to apply sunscreen. Under a red Yarbrough's cap that I'd brought from the store to match Joe Riddley's, I could feel my new hairdo, which Phyllis had fixed just that morning, getting as limp and dry as Spanish moss.

As much as we were sweating in the bleachers, the girls had it worse on the field. "I hope Ridd and Ronnie brought enough water and Gatorade," I told Martha, beside me. Clarinda sat on my other side, with Cricket between her and Joe Riddley. The way Clarinda was handing Cricket juice boxes, he'd spend the game running up and down the bleachers to the bathroom.

Martha shaded her eyes under the straw brim of what Ridd called her "mule's hat" and peered down at our team's bench. "They did. Yasheika insisted on it. I sure was glad she flew back here after DeWayne's funeral up north, to help coach. Ridd's not real confident about the team, to tell the truth. They haven't had a lot of time to practice."

I tried not to notice how much better the other team was catching and hitting in their pregame warm-up.

"That girl is still determined to go to law school," Clarinda said in disgust, "even if the governor pardons her daddy. Says she wants to major in sports law."

I hadn't thought Joe Riddley was listening until he chimed in. "Good for her! With the money professional athletes make, she can support us all in our old age."

Martha waved back to Bethany, who had looked up to see where we were sitting. "You think those letters you all wrote the governor will get Gerrick pardoned?"

"I hope so." I waved, too. "It wasn't just us. Isaac James wrote, and several county commissioners."

Joe Riddley reached for his third juice box. He'd be the one taking Cricket up and down. "Gusta told me she called the governor." He thrust the straw through that little-bitty hole without having to wiggle it like I always did. "She says they used to play hide-and-seek together in the mansion, back when her granddaddy was governor and his was Speaker of the House."

Martha chuckled. "We can all relax, then. If Augusta Wainwright was on the case, Gerrick will be out of prison by Labor Day. Anybody want a Coke while they're still cold?"

Augusta Wainwright is past eighty, one of my oldest friends, and the closest thing we have to aristocracy in Hopemore. As I took a Coke, popped the top, and took a long swallow, I remembered a Sunday when she'd been the one to lead our Sunday school class in prayer. She was praying for the safety of missionaries in a war-torn region and ended with, "And, Lord, you know I am not accustomed to being denied in these matters." Ever since, that had summed up Gusta for me.

"What's Ronnie gonna do now that Buddy's office is closed?" Martha leaned across me to hand a Coke to Clarinda. "You think he's going to stick around here?"

Clarinda huffed. "Says he's going up to New Haven to get a job there." You'd have thought he planned to go to the top of a Himalayan peak and become a hermit.

"Clarinda doesn't want him to leave," I said, "but he could do worse. DeWayne once said that Ronnie and Yasheika were like magnets with the same pole, always repelling, but DeWayne's death has changed them. I'm betting they'll get married."

Now it was Joe Riddley huffing. "Woman, let them decide that for themselves, in their own good time. We don't want Ronnie rushing into things and winding up like I did, shackled for life."

"Don't want nobody rushing into things," Clarinda seconded the motion.

"I wish the game would rush," Cricket complained. "How many more minutes, Pop?"

He was distracted by a woman with a tin of oatmeal cookies, who was handing them up and down our row. I smiled my appreciation, and told Martha softly, "Seems like half the women of Hopemore brought cookies to share today. We'll all go home five pounds heavier."

"Don't you think folks are looking for ways to make up for not noticing what was going on over at the Stantons' and stopping it sooner? I've seen lots of positive changes in town since Buddy got arrested."

I sighed. "I just wish people would stop talking about it. From the number of 'eyewitness' accounts going around about that night down on our road, you'd have thought we'd had a circus out there and sold tickets."

"At least people have been kinder, even about Buddy, than I'd have expected them to be," Martha pointed out.

"I think everybody feels like we share a little bit of blame for not noticing what was happening to him when he was little." I would have said more, but Clarinda shouted.

"Look! There's the banner!"

Four Hope County team members carried out a long white banner with a red heart in each corner and WE LOVE

YOU, DEWAYNE printed in big blue letters. They tied the banner to the fence where they could see it both from the field and while batting. Then, without worrying or caring whether he'd be hauled before the Supreme Court, Ridd gathered his team together and they bowed their heads.

Those Hope County girls played their hearts out. Every time one of our girls came to bat, she looked at the banner. I saw a lot of them wipe away tears before they swung. Every time Bethany wound up for a pitch, she looked at it, too. She pitched three no-hit innings.

Cookies kept passing up and down the rows, and I saw several old codgers Joe Riddley's age give theirs to children. Of course, they made sure the kids' parents agreed. During one time-out, Shana Wethers made a point of coming over to tell Martha and me, "I sure was sorry to hear about Hollis's sister. She's so lovely."

You may be thinking that with so much goodwill flowing, we easily won the game. We didn't. This time we were the families trickling down the bleachers in a stream of disappointment while another bunch of girls jumped and squealed over by home plate.

Hollis and Bethany had ridden with Ridd, and Ronnie and Yasheika had come together, so Clarinda, Martha and Cricket had come with us. Cricket elected to stay and ride back with his daddy, so the four of us got in the car and headed home, hoping we wouldn't collapse from heat exhaustion before the air conditioner kicked in.

"It seems like a lot longer than a month since the last game," Martha said from the backseat as Joe Riddley started the engine.

"Seems like a year, at least," I agreed. "It's no wonder that other team beat us, with everything that's been going on. I'll bet their catcher hasn't had a family crisis and their coach hasn't buried her brother in the past two weeks."

"Face it, Little Bit"—Joe Riddley pulled into the stream of traffic with the caution I use separating eggs— "Washington County has a better team. They're more experienced.

And don't poke your lip out like that. It makes you look just like Cricket."

I gave him a little swat. "What you mean is, our winning before was a fluke."

"Bethany and Hollis aren't ever going to be good hitters," Martha admitted.

"Oh, *they* played real good," Clarinda insisted stoutly. "It was the rest of the team that wasn't up to snuff. If it had just been the Honeybees . . ."

"They all played fine," Joe Riddley said firmly. "We sponsor summer sports to give kids something fun to do, and the way those girls played today, you could tell they were having fun."

"I hope that Franklin boy gives them a good write-up," Clarinda worried. "Looks like, for such an important game, Mr. Rutherford would have come himself."

"Art will do okay," Martha promised. "He used to write for his high-school paper."

I added my bit. "Slade told me this week he's decided to work with Art. He thinks he could go on to journalism school if he wants to, so he said he wanted to give Art a chance today to show what he can do. He said Art has been reading up on fast-pitch softball all week to get the terms right, and he has the makings of a good writer, but he needs some grounding before he can fly—whatever that means."

"Whatever it means, a lot of grown-ups in this town are taking more interest in our young people," Martha said with satisfaction. "Speaking of which, Hollis has asked if she can live with us next year. Garnet's going out of state to college, and Hollis thinks Sara Meg will probably leave, too. We don't have space for Hollis, but I was wondering if you all might."

Joe Riddley and I exchanged a look. I nodded, and he cleared his throat. "We hadn't meant to say anything to you and Ridd until this ball game was over, but Little Bit here and I did some talking and decided we need a smaller place." He ignored Clarinda's gasp in the backseat. "We want you all to move down into our place so Cricket can swim, Ridd can farm, and you can take in all the children you want."

"But—" Martha started to protest.

I interrupted her. "Don't object, honey. We've known for nearly a year that this was coming sooner or later. It's finally time. We looked at several houses, and just yesterday, we signed a contract to buy one over on Honeysuckle Way. It's got only two steps up, for the days when we are older and infirm, and there's two bedrooms, a living room, a dining room, a kitchen, and a nice screened porch to one side. Just our size."

"And it's brick, with no eaves, so it won't need much painting," Joe Riddley added. "And it's got a yard I can mow in half an hour."

"And we can walk to work and church. It's even a nice walk over to Walker's," I finished up. Joe Riddley and I had listed all the things we wanted to brag about as soon as we'd decided to get the house, so Martha and Ridd wouldn't know how hard this change was going to be.

"Do you think your parents hated leaving as much as I do?" I had asked Joe Riddley wistfully.

He had thought, then nodded. "I saw Mama cry for the only time in my life when they shut the door on the moving van," he admitted. "But she told me she just had an allergy to all the dust that got stirred up moving stuff out."

"If you're sure . . ." Martha said doubtfully.

"We'd better be sure. We gave them our earnest money," Joe Riddley told her.

"I bet it's got a little-bitty kitchen you can't even turn around in," Clarinda grumbled. I hadn't realized that this might be as hard on her as it was on us—or that she'd need reassurance we'd still want her in the new house.

"You'll be able to turn around just fine," I told her, "if you lose a couple of pounds. And you can organize it any way you like." That satisfied her. Next thing we heard, she was gently snoring. That sounded like such a good idea, I propped my pocketbook against the window and dozed the rest of the way home, too.

Three weeks later, Ridd, Martha, Joe Riddley, and I sat through Buddy's trial to give Sara Meg and her girls some support. After heart-wrenching testimony, though, when Buddy was convicted of molesting Garnet, Sara Meg told us coldly, "I don't care what they say. I won't believe it."

She never has.

She left that courtroom, looked at the shambles of her family and the superstore rising on her economic horizon, and had herself a nervous breakdown. Hollis tells us she's in a place with good food and a lovely garden. At first, Sara Meg alternated between wanting to kill Buddy for "dragging our family through the dirt" and wanting to kill herself. Then she got involved with art therapy and started to paint again.

Her pictures all look like they're crying. Daisies in the rain. Gladioli with huge tears dripping from gigantic cups. I have one of a small white snowdrop with a bent head and one drop of dew in its cup. Hollis says that since her mother started painting again, she doesn't want to kill anybody. That's a definite improvement.

Another improvement is that Sara Meg has another man who loves her, a salesman who used to call on her selling toys. Harvey Wiseman is his name, and he lives in Macon. He came through town the day Buddy's trial began, and when he heard what was going on, he stayed and sat with Sara Meg through the whole thing. Now he goes to see her every weekend. He came to town recently, took Hollis to lunch, and asked permission to marry her mother as soon as Sara Meg gets well. I think Hollis described him best when she said, "He's not pretty, but he's patient, and he loves my mama to death. He'll be good to her."

Garnet left Hopemore as soon as the trial ended. She went first to stay with my brother, Jake, and his wife, Glenna, over in Montgomery. Glenna helped her apply to the University of

Washington in Seattle—about as far from Hopemore as she could get. She's planning to get a doctorate in counseling so she can help other girls like herself. Martha thinks she'll make it. She says Garnet is strong enough to be a thriver, not merely a survivor.

When they accepted we really were going to move, Ridd and Martha asked for all the bedroom furniture we didn't need. They're already taking classes to become foster parents, so they can take in more kids. Tyrone spends so much time over at their place, he might as well live there.

When I culled out the stuff we wanted, what Martha and Ridd wanted, and a few things Walker and Cindy wanted, there was still a lot left. In forty years, you carry in a lot of stuff you never carry back out. Hubert's son, Maynard, who's been clearing out their place, took a lot of stuff I considered junk for the Hope County Historical Museum. Then Maynard suggested that we go in together and hold what he advertised as Hopemore's Biggest Garage Sale Ever. It was so successful, I've convinced Joe Riddley we can afford to go to Europe next spring.

Meanwhile, Joe Riddley and I are making adjustments in the way we spend our time. We're volunteering more, now that we know we're responsible for all the children in the world, not just those in our family. As Joe Riddley puts it, "I used to be concerned for the kids in my wallet. Now I'm concerned for those in God's wallet."

I thought he took that a bit far, though, when he brought home Smitty.

Smitty had been in detention for a nice long vacation. After Tyrone decided to testify, some of the other boys got braver, too. I even told the judge how he shot at me that day.

When Smitty got out, Joe Riddley asked the probation officer to let him come work for us. He told me, "Little Bit, this is a test of our faith. If we really believe all things are possible for God, we'll believe God can make something of Smitty, and we'll work to help that happen. And relax, honey. After all we've been through together, we can survive this."

Ridd has started taking Smitty out to the fields with him, and Joe Riddley has him working with him around the nursery. They claim he's turning into a right good little horticulturist. I confess that some days—like the one when Smitty mowed down the little forsythias I'd just planted in our new yard—I'm not sure if we aren't expecting too much of both God and Smitty. But there was also a day when Smitty came toward me brandishing hedge clippers and asked politely, "Judge, would you show me how to prune a rose?"

According to Tyrone, Smitty's talking about joining the Future Farmers of America next year, and he plans to raise prizewinning vegetables in their yard. So, as Ridd says, "Who knows? If Isaac is right, and Smitty has the intelligence to become a CEO, maybe someday we'll buy a tomato with a little sticker on it: *Smitty Smith Fine Produce.*"

A Personal Word

Nothing would be more rewarding for me as the author of this story than for readers to put it down with a stronger commitment to make a difference for children.

While writing this book, I was also being trained as a court-appointed special advocate (CASA), a volunteer assigned to one child or family of children who have entered the court system for neglect, deprivation, or abuse. While caseworkers and foster homes come and go, the CASA remains a constant in that child's life, providing the child with a "voice in court." Lawyers, parents, even the system designed to protect children may have various agendas. A CASA has one only: to advocate for the best interests of the child in order to quickly move that child into a safe and permanent home. In years of volunteer service, I have found no program with more potential to make a lasting, positive difference in a child's life.

This is a federal program that operates at the local level. You can learn about the CASA program in your county juvenile court system by contacting the National CASA Association, 100 W. Harrison St., North Tower, Suite 500, Seattle, WA 98119. 1-800-628-3233. Or check their Web site: www.nationalcasa.org.

SIGNET

COMING IN NOVEMBER 2003
FROM SIGNET MYSTERY

THE DEVIL'S HIGHWAY
A Mystery of Georgian England
by Hannah March   0-451-21071-9

Traveling to his new employer's country home, private
tutor Robert Fairfax discovers a tipped stagecoach—and
the dead bodies within it. But this is more than a
robbery. And the victims are not who they appear to be.

MURDER OF A BARBIE AND KEN
A Scumble River Mystery
by Denise Swanson   0-451-21072-7

Skye joins Scumble River's social club and ends up
at a party at the home of socialites Barbie and Ken
Addison. But not long after, Skye gets caught up in a
murder mystery when she finds the perfect couple,
perfectly dead.

**Available wherever books are sold, or
to order call: 1-800-788-6262**